Toothaches and Wedding Cakes

The Tooth Fairy Chronicles

Book Two

Victoria Rocus

For my children, mine by blood as well as gifted to me through marriage. You are truly the wax that seals the knot and loved beyond measure.

ALSO BY VICTORIA ROCUS

The Tooth Fairy Chronicles

Tooth Decay With A Side Of Fae

Toothaches And Wedding Cakes

Baby Tooth And Tangled Roots

Wisdom Tooth And The Awful Truth

GLOSSARY AND PRONUNCIATION OF ANCIENT OTHERWORLD GAELIC

A Mhuirnin - (Ā Mor-nin) - "My Darling"

Athair - (ă-hair) - "father" - when capitalized, used as a formal title

Aine - (Ŏn-yă) - "radiance" - A Celtic female name (Rosie's mother's Fae name and Rosie's Fae middle name)

Bairns - (băr-ns) - infants/babies

Bean cheile ag goid - (băn Kālă egg gute) "wife stealing" - refers to the traditional Fae prank in which the mate of a newly handfasted male is "kidnapped" on the couple's handfast night

Bogie - (bō -gē) - a Fae, gender neutral, shape-shifting race

Buime - (Bwĕ-mă) - a wet nurse or nanny

Cac - (cŏck) - "shit" – slang word

Cealgaire - (căl-a-gooda) - "seducer"

Chiorcal cairde - (chĕrkle car-ja) "circle of friends"

Cinneadh - (kĭn-ya) decision

Col ceathrar - (caul carer) - cousin

Comharthai Gra - (kore-hē Grăh) - "Love Token" - a small

cake given as a gift to guests attending a Fae handfast as a sign of fertility

Crann Bethadh (Krŏn Bĕ-hĕ) - "Tree of Life" - the royal seat of The Morrigan, Queen Maeve, built out of a giant, ancient oak; sometimes referred to as "The Raven's Nest"

Cu Chulainn - (Koo Koo-lane) - an Irish demi-god of legendary warrior fame; Royal Consort to The Morrigan, Queen Maeve

Dagada - (*Dág-da*) - an ancient Celtic male earth god

Danu - (Dŏ-new) - the Celtic mother goddess

Deaglan - (Dĕk-lĕn) - "full of goodness" - the Otherworld spelling of Declan

Deirfiur - (jă-fer) - sister

Diabhal Bas - (dowl bŏs) - "Death Devil" - an Otherworld insect with a highly toxic and dangerous venom

Dubnos - (dŏv-nus) - the Fae version of the Underworld

Dun Siorai - (Dune Shear-ē) "Eternal Fortress" - House *Nuada's* ancestral home

Fear na bainnse - (firh na bŏn-yas) - bridegroom

Fiacail - (Fē-ăh-kel) - "tooth" - the House to which all tooth fairies belong

Fianain - (fē-anon) - cookies

Finne (fin-yeah) - witness at a handfast

Gancanagh - (ghan-kan-ah) - "love talker" - Celtic incubus

Gille gaolach - (gilya gear-lak) - "beloved boy"

Giumar - (goo-mer) - mood

Iarmhairti (ear-wot-ot) - consequences of one's actions

I Idir - (ē ēdar) "In Between" - the Fae kingdom in the Otherworld ruled by The Morrigan, Queen Maeve, as its monarch.

Lugh - (Loo) - ancient warrior and king of Otherworld history; skilled in the arts

Mac- (mc)- "son of"- a title given to an eldest son and heir of a Ruling House

Macushla - (ma-cush-la) - "Love of my Life"/ "My Pulse"

Mathair - (mă-hair) - "mother" - when capitalized, used as a formal title

Magairli - (ma-gar-lee) - "balls" - vulgar slang for testicles

Milsean - (mil-shawn) - "Sweetie"

Mo Anam Cara - (mō aun-im-KAHR-ah) - "My Soulmate"

Mo Shiorghra - (mō hear-gra) - "My Eternal Love"

Mo Stor - (mō store) - "My Treasure"

Na Glaschnoic - (nŏ glasknik) - "The Green Hills"

Nuada - (new-a-da) - the name of an ancient Celtic king who possessed a silver arm; a major House from that bloodline within *I Idir's* Ruling Council

Nuada Airgeadlamh - (new-a-da ar-gus-luv) - "King Silver-hand" - first King of the *Tuatha de Danann*

Ridre Dubh - (rid-ada dōv) - "Black Knight" - the "Hand of Justice in *I Idir*" and The Morrigan's right-hand counsel; a position currently held by the 27th Merlin, Theodore H. Beckett (Myrdynn)

Rois Gaoithe - (rō-sha gwē-da) - "Rush of Wind" - The name of Declan's racing horse

Sidhe - (Shē) - the term used for the Fae race in Celtic mythology, as well as the forts and mounds they once lived in during ancient times.

Siobhan - (Shiv-awn) - a Celtic female name meaning "gracious gift"- Declan's mother's name

Spideog - (Spē- doj) - "robin" - Dr. Brannigan's Fae first name

Tachran - (tŏ-rŏn) - child

Tuatha de Danann - (two-ha de dan-an) "The Shining Ones"- a race of ancient, magically gifted Fae with royal bloodlines. They currently compose *I Idir's* ruling council under the Monarchy of The Morrigan, Queen Maeve

Uisce na Beatha (ISH-ca ba-ha) - "Water of Life" - alcoholic Fae beverage similar to scotch whiskey

TOOTHACHE 1

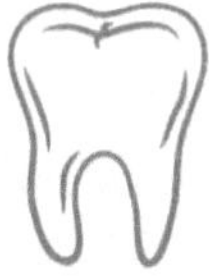

DEAR DIARY

As promised, I, Rosalinda Parker, have started this journal to record my innermost, personal thoughts regarding this new path upon which the Universe has set me. Had anyone told me a mere month ago that I would find the love of my life and be in the process of planning our handfasting in the Fae Otherworld, I would have told them to seek immediate help for obvious mental illness. Hell, before I scalded my Tax Man's family jewels (accidentally, of course), I adamantly was convinced that I would never, ever become involved with a male of Fae origin, even if he were the last man in either the Mundane world, the Otherworld, or any other dimensions yet to be discovered.

These past two weeks have turned my life and my thinking totally upside down. Despite my mother's dire warnings about the true nature of Fae men, I find myself loco-loony over Declan Phineas Fitzpatrick, aka Lord

Mac Nuada. He is not only Fae, but a beat-the-band, top-of-the-mountain, big-league, card-carrying *Tuatha de Danann* kind of *Sidhe.* This irony doesn't escape me. I have been carrying around my own self-loathing about being both Fae and a tooth fairy for as long as I can remember, even to the point of pea-green envy toward my older sister, Claire, whose Fae-free DNA made her normal.

If finding and falling in love with Declan is a lesson the Universe set out to teach me, then I am now its star pupil. Though I admit I still prefer the lifestyle I enjoy in the Mundane World to that of the Otherworld, I am of late embarrassed regarding the unfair prejudices I have placed on the shoulders of my Fae brothers and sisters. With everything that's happened during the past week, I have come to know some very fine Fae men, all of whom I've found to be courageous, honorable, and beyond sweet. Not just my adorable Tax Man, but also his cousin and the rest of the guys on his team. Mac O'Kelly, a traditionally grumpy leprechaun, recently moved me to tears with his gift of a beautiful book of Irish love poetry, a surprisingly thoughtful gesture from a *Sidhe* type not known to be overly generous. Even the Black Knight, who mostly scares me to death, has come by to check on my healing process and to congratulate Declan and me on our upcoming handfast.

In truth, I never really understood my mother's fiercely negative view of Fae men, nor her overwhelming disdain regarding the cultural differences between the Mundane World and the Otherworld. While I was growing up, mom always held a *live and let live* attitude involving the various religious and ethnic differences of the Mundane World; unfortunately, she felt quite differ-ently about the Otherworld Community. A lot of her Fae prejudices found their way into my thinking, making me feel a tad guilty about what she must be feeling in the Hereafter over my relationship with Declan.

Since my experiences with the Tax Man, I have vowed not to judge anyone on the basis of their origins or beliefs, be they Fae, human or anything else. From this day forward, I promise I will take people as they are and view them in light of their words and actions and not by the components of their DNA. To prove this, I will begin my Anti-Prejudice of the Fae journey with Declan's *mathair,* whom I whole-heartedly would DETEST in any dimen-sion from which she hailed. I consider *Siobhan* Donnelly Fitzpatrick, aka Lady *Nuada,* a royal bitch no matter which side of the DNA fence she sits on.

Because my Tax Man always believes in doing the "rrrright and rrrresponsible thing," (*keep rolling those r's, Babe! It makes me go weak in the knees...*) he has formally contacted his parents, in the traditional manner, with the news that the two of us were in the process of setting a date for our joining. Frankly, it would have been much easier for Declan to just pop over there and tell them in person, but proper protocol required him to send a formally worded Raven-gram. Each House in the Other-world has their own collection of specially trained birds to deliver messages between the two dimensions. House *Nuada's* ravens wear tiny braided collars in the House colors of burgundy and gold to set them apart from birds of another source. In my opinion, there is a sound reason that a group of ravens is sometimes called a treachery or a conspiracy. As Otherworld birds go, message ravens are the ickiest.

I've never been a fan of these dimension-crossing, magical birds. They always seem to be spying, their beady, little eyes gauging a person's personal reaction to the news they bear only so they can then spread their gossip back in the Otherworld. I am sure the bird that arrived this morning will have a beak-full to share with his buddies over my ripostes regarding Declan's *Mathair's* response. I am including the words of her Raven-gram in this journal so that I can offer up her spite-filled, mean-spirited tirade to the Universe in preparation for...umm... forgiveness:

Your father and I received your Raven-gram. It is little wonder that the bird did not drop dead in flight carrying such dreadful and heart-breaking news. I am distraught to learn that you have chosen to disregard my sound and practical advice to abandon this ridiculous notion of joining yourself to a common tooth fairy. You disrespect your sacred heritage by risking the chance of muddying your ancient bloodline with offspring from this sort. Surely, this is yet another sign by the Universe that you have been cursed from birth and now intend to drag your entire family into the dirt with you.
I will not be a party to this gross injustice. Do not expect me to participate in such a joining of dubious and shameful quality.
Your Devoted Mathair

It wasn't like we both didn't expect such a response.

His mother made her feelings perfectly known during her early morning visit a few days ago. But it pains me to the core to see her hurt my Tax Man this way, and I did not remain politely silent on the topic. I spit out every curse word I knew, including a few in Gaelic that I've recently learned from the guys on D.P.'s spy team. Declan pretends it doesn't bother him, but I've begun to take careful notice of my Sweetie's aura since becoming his *Mo Shiorghra,* and it always darkens when his Lady *Mathair* is involved.

Strangely enough, his mother's awful letter was followed by yet another Raven-gram, this one from his father, the Lord *Nuada.* I also am including it here as a counter-balance to the earlier one:

Greetings, My Son
Please disregard the previous missive from your mathair.
She and I will expect you at the ancestral home in I Idir at
your earliest convenience to discuss the preparations for
your handfasting day.
Blessings to you and your Lady.
Your Devoted Aithar
P.S. I hope you are taking my advice about an heir seriously.

Oh boy! Isn't this just peachy? All I can say is that the Fitzpatricks, both Lord and Lady *Nuada,* surely put the fun in family dysfunction.

TOOTHACHE 2

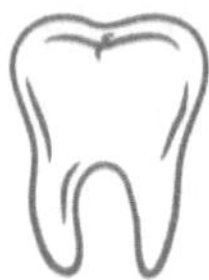

SNOOP SNAFU

ON DAYS that we mentally mark as special, why is it we pay extra attention to the weather? Does it cement these special moments more solidly in our memories, or are our senses made more acute in response to our anticipation of things to come? Is it perhaps that we just naturally like to set descriptive scenes for the stories of our lives? You don't believe me? Then think about a particularly memorable event…a wedding…a holiday…a funeral, and ponder whether you don't also remember that the bride wore a plastic bag over her head to keep the torrential rains from ruining her just-done hair, that it was the coldest, windiest Christmas ever, or that Aunt Gladys passed out at Grannie's funeral because it was 107 degrees in the shade that day. It's simply a fact that people notice the weather on important days.

This is why it's so utterly disappointing to me that today is just a normal, routine, June weather day for

Salem, MA. The sun is out, the blue sky is littered with cumulus clouds, the wind is coming in from its usual easterly direction, and the temperature is a normal 82 degrees. Same ole', same ole' anyway you look at it. On a day as monumental as this, the weather should be a little less ordinary.

I finish packing my little travel bag, unsure what activities the next few days will bring. I'm still on the mend from the harrowing events of a few days ago, so I doubt my Tax Man will be planning marathons of physical activity. If this were the trip I'm dreading to his ancestral home in *I Idir*, I would be far less excited and much more panicked. But Declan and I have decided to wait for that rollercoaster ride until I'm feeling more like myself and my cheek looks less like an eggplant. Today, I'm just packing for a weekend stay at Declan's townhome on the other side of Salem.

One might be wondering why I'm so pumped about going a mere five miles southeast of where I currently stand. After all, it's not like I'm jetting to Paris with my new lover. But the fact is, I've never been to said lover's home; in all honesty, I don't even know his address, what type of building it is, or what to even expect regarding its style or furnishings. This is one of the big drawbacks to agreeing to marry someone I've met a mere two weeks ago. Our entire history together, short as it is, has centered around the Tax Man being in my personal space, so I am whole-heartedly looking forward to spending a little bit of time in his.

Declan comes into the bedroom and grabs my travel bag to carry it out for me. He makes an exaggerated face as he tests its weight. "I dunno know why ya packed so much, Lass. It's not like yar gonna need that many clothes." If that innocent comment is supposed to get my pulse racing, it succeeds, and I wish again that the day had brought with it more interesting weather conditions. I'll admit it; I'm more than a little excited to see my Tax Man's bedroom.

As of yet, we haven't made any decisions regarding… well… anything: not about the handfasting itself, where we'll live afterwards, or how we'll handle our finances, though I am sure that once he handles the IRS mess I'm currently in, my future accounting work will be handled exclusively by Declan P. Fitzpatrick, C.P.A., E.A. We also haven't yet broached the subject of children, though I know his father has reminded D.P. of the need for an heir twice since we've been a couple. Maybe in this new setting we'll be able to talk a few things out.

Declan lives on Derby Street in the Waterfront District, which is one of Salem's most expensive areas, a mix of historical and modern buildings. This doesn't surprise me. I could tell by his car, his office, and his choice of apparel that my Tax Man isn't hurting for money. Truthfully, this doesn't intimidate me. I'm not exactly a pauper myself, though I spend far less on my automobiles and my clothes than he does. My practice is doing extremely well, I've made some profitable investments over the past few years, and even if it's not in the Waterfront District, my home in Mill Hill is quite lovely and suits me perfectly. I wonder which of these places we will make our permanent home as a couple.

D.P. pulls his car directly into the attached garage of

his townhouse. He grabs my bag from the trunk and comes around to open my door for me, something he's done from day one of our relationship. This garage is my first view of the Tax Man's life before I became a part of it. The initial word that comes to mind is neat. There are no tools or gardening implements in residence but there is an abundance of sports equipment for tennis, pickleball, squash, badminton, and racquetball. There are basketballs, soccer balls, rugby, and traditional American footballs. On the other side of the garage, I notice ice skates and rollerblades and a large barrel full of hockey sticks next to a set of premium golf clubs. Taking up the other car space is a large motorcycle, a Harley of some sort, polished to a mirror finish.

If the Tax Man's wealth doesn't intimidate me, all of this sports shit makes me queasy. I knew Declan must be very physically active. One doesn't get the kind of physique he has sitting on one's ass in front of the TV. But if he regularly uses all this stuff, I'm in deep doo-doo. I am not an athlete of any kind, in any dimension. My favorite sports position is left out. I fervently hope that being Declan's *Mo Shiorghra* won't require me to participate in any of these activities including the motorcycle because I'm pretty sure my ass will not fit on that seat behind his.

We reach the door that leads into the house and the Tax Man puts down my overnight bag, opens the door, scoops me up under the knees and carries me inside like I don't weigh nearly what I know I do, kissing me before setting me down. "For good luck, Love," he says. This is so wonderfully romantic and so crazy hot that I'm one hundred percent ready to shed my clothes and do the nasty right there in the kitchen. But that's before I get a good look at said kitchen. It's so shiny, spanking clean, that I don't think anyone does anything in this kitchen. Ever. Even the faucets are free of water spots, and I can see my reflection in the stainless steel of the fridge. I'm itching to open the cabinets and the refrigerator to see whether there's actually anything inside, but the Tax Man already is leading me into the rest of the house.

We pass a small powder room and move into the living and dining rooms. These areas shock me as well. There is no furniture here; instead, this large, open space is home to an assortment of musical instruments. There is a baby grand piano, an electric organ, a drum set, both a bass and electric guitar, an acoustic guitar, and what I believe to be a lyre and a fiddle of Otherworld origin. The rest of the room is filled with various types of speakers and sound mixing equipment, a few chairs and stools, a vintage turntable and an entire wall filled with old vinyl records.

"You're a musician?" I ask, dumbfounded by the scene in front of me.

"Aye," Declan answers shyly, "though I am no professional. 'Tis just a hobby."

"And you play…all of these instruments?" I question.

The Tax Man shrugs. "Yes, though I am better with some than others."

The fact that I had no clue as to this side of Declan shocks me. Here I am, merrily going along like this is all a game, making plans to join my life with his, and the truth is, I know nothing about this man. Zippo. Zero. Nadda. For the first time since that dreadful abduction, a tiny seed of doubt regarding my decision is forcing its way into my subconscious. I push it down and tell myself that getting to know each other is a gift we'll share for a lifetime, but the immensity of what we're doing still creeps into my thoughts.

"Wow. This is amazing. You have a lot of instruments." I sound dumb even to my own ears, but it's the best I can do in this moment when I feel so out of my comfort zone. D.P. takes my hand and leads me up some narrow stairs to the second floor which contains a guest room, a guest bath, and his home office, all as immaculate as the rest of the house. The decor is modern, streamlined, and to my taste, much too sterile, but I keep my opinions to myself, double checking that I'm properly shielding my thoughts.

Finally, we reach the third floor which contains Declan's bedroom. The room and its bath as well as the laundry room take up the entire floor, and there's enough square footage to host a square dance. This room makes the bedroom we share at my house look like a closet. The east facing wall is all windows with a sliding glass door leading to a balcony that overlooks the waterfront of Massachusetts Bay. It's a spectacular view, and all I can do is stare and try not to drool with my mouth hanging open.

"Do you like it, Lass?" he asks, and the hopefulness in his voice makes me feel all melty and emotional. I realize my Tax Man is just as lost as I am when it comes to knowing each other. I choke up when I speak. "It's unbelievably beautiful, Declan. This is an amazing view."

"It is," he says. "I often like to sit and think on the balcony in the mornings. 'Tis very peaceful with only the sea birds for company." The emotion of the moment is interrupted by his cell phone ringer. Declan pulls it out and checks the number. "It's an important client. I will need to take this call, Rosie, Lass. I will try not to be long. Make yourself at home."

The Tax Man takes the call and wanders down the stairs to his office. I use the time to do a little exploring. I'm not looking to snoop, but I am starting to get slightly overwhelmed by the newness of everything. I hang the one and only summer dress I brought with me in the closet next to D.P.'s collection of Brooks Brothers, Armani, and Burberry. He's got a lot of clothes with an equal amount of shoes and ties, none of which I'm sure came from Target. I leave my toiletries in the bathroom, and, just for fun, I tuck my toothbrush into the slot next to the Tax Man's while I try to suppress a giggle.

I'm one of those girls who follows the old-fashioned advice to brush my hair one hundred times a night before going to bed. Of course, there is no lady's vanity in this male dominated room, so I put my hairbrush on top of the nightstand like I do at home. Then, because I decide it looks too messy in a room where absolutely nothing is out of place, I open the nightstand drawer to put it inside.

That's when I see it. An open box of condoms. A very large, open box of condoms. With more than half of its contents missing. I instantly slam the drawer shut then sit on the edge of the bed and consider what a giant, half empty box of condoms in his nightstand says about my new *Mo Shiorghra*.

TOOTHACHE 3

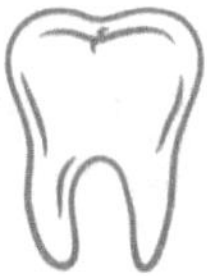

RAINCOAT REASONS

WHEN THE TAX Man returns from his business call, he finds me on the balcony watching the boats come and go in the harbor. I don't say a word about the large, economy-sized box of condoms or the fact so many of them obviously have been used. I tell myself it doesn't necessarily mean that D.P. was Salem's man about town, even if he's crazy good looking and is obviously very financially secure. Who knows how long that box has been there? In fact, it wouldn't surprise me if the C.P.A. in him might have found the Costco sized box to be a better long term investment. And now I worry that no matter how I try to explain how I came to find the box, I will end up looking like a busy-body snoop. The last thing I want to do is start this weekend off with a cringey, accusatory discussion about either of our pasts.

"Sorry to keep you sittin' here alone, Lass. It could not

be helped. This particular client is vera demandin'. She calls all the time with concerns that are just plain silly. Unfortunately, har' nonsense will alter our plans slightly for the day, but I still think we'll find time for lots of fun together."

I hear him talking and see his lips moving, but all I can focus on is that the client is a demanding woman who is comfortable enough to call him on his cellphone and ignore Eleanor the Office Gatekeeper. I can't help but wonder whether she was also the beneficiary of some of the missing raincoats in the nightstand. *What the hell Rosie? Did you think he waited in long- suffering celibacy for you? Get a grip girl.*

"So does that sound alright with ya Love? We can do something entirely different if yar' not up to doin' so much running around," the Tax Man asks.

I blink twice, because I haven't paid the slightest attention to anything he's proposed. "I'm sorry, Sweetie. Can you repeat that? My brain seems to be running slow this afternoon."

A look of immediate concern passes over his face. "Are you not feelin' well, Rosie, Lass? Shall I get in touch with Robyn?"

Now I feel guilty as well as embarrassed by my self-imposed jealousy. I double up the hold on my mental shield. This is so not the time to be leaking my thoughts all over the place. "I'm feeling fine, Hon." I wave my hand in front of the waterfront. "I just got lost in the view, I guess."

My answer seems to placate him. "Aye. I have often

found myself meditating on the vastness of the sea as well," he admits. "I find my magic is quite drawn to the energy of the waves."

Shit. My Tax Man is sharing his metaphysical reflections with me, and all I can focus on is the burning need to know just how many women he's boinked on his spectacular bed. *You better not lose hold of your mental shield, Girlfriend.* I lie through my teeth. "How ironic. I was thinking the same thing."

"Ya see, my Love," he says, "we are perfectly in tune with one another. Bless the Universe and its wisdom for this match." Declan looks so fervently and earnestly happy, that it makes me feel even more like a colossal poser-bitch.

"So, what's the plan for today?" I ask. Anything to move on from my big lie. Magic has never been a priority for me. It's something I just happen to have, like my cowlick or my allergy to bee stings. It's there, I live with it, and I don't spend a lot of time thinking about it.

"I have a few errands to run, but then I thought we could go over to Salem Willows and spend some time there. The promenade is worth the trip on its own. Have ya' been there befar', Lass?"

"Not since I was a kid," I admit. "That sounds perfect!"

"I also made reservations for an early dinner at Ledger on Washington Street. Then I thought we'd come back here, have a glass of wine and watch the day turn into night."

My Tax Man obviously has put a lot of thought into making the day special, which makes me want to slap myself for letting my imagination run away with me. Why do I always make drama where there possibly is none? I try not to wonder just how likely it is that this man has banged half of Salem's female population. Perhaps he'd just bought the box a very long, long time ago; that's my story and I'm gonna make my mind stick to it.

Since we're going out to dinner without returning here to change, I put on the one nice dress I've brought along with me before we start our afternoon excursion. I worry about the appearance of my bruised face, but with a wave of his hand my Fae *Mo Shiorghra* informs me that he has veiled that cheek with some fairy glamour magic and no human will notice any discoloration. This makes me feel a little more at ease until I learn that our first stop will be his office to pick up some paperwork for the client that's just called. He insists I go inside with him so he can introduce me to his personal assistant, Eleanor. I tell him I think this is a bad idea, but The Tax Man thinks I'm being silly and takes me by the hand inside. It turns out I am correct.

Upon hearing that I am her boss's new fiance, Ms. Pitch turns a bright shade of fuchsia and starts coughing profusely. She then asks to speak with him privately; I take this as my cue to wait in the car. When D.P. returns, he's got a sour look on his face and tells me that Ms. Pitch has given her notice. I wait for him to tell me that they have been "involved," but when he doesn't, I don't ask either because, well, I really don't want to hear the dirty details. *No, Rosie. You'd rather sit here for the next several hours imagining the worst. What a coward you are!*

We pick up Declan's dry cleaning, and I try to ignore that the lady behind the counter is behaving awfully flirty with a seemingly normal customer; we go through the drive through at the bank, and I dismiss the thought the female cashier is being suggestive when she winks at him and calls him Mr. Declan; and when we stop at the convenience mart for a few groceries (*I was right-the fridge is completely empty, and D.P. knows how I feel about magic 'shet'*), I have to work at not being pissed that the cashier hugs him like a long lost friend despite me standing right next to him with a ginormous engagement-type ring on my left hand.

It's a good thing that Salem Willows is our next destination. We walk along the promenade unnoticed, holding hands. The Tax Man insists on buying me anything I pick up to look at, so I try not to be too interested in any of the merchandise. Instead, I focus on the two of us being together. This is, for all intents and purposes, our very first Mundane date. Things happened between us so quickly and in such a strange and intense manner that we missed out on similar explorations of spending time doing simple things together. Declan is perfect...sweet, funny, and attentive...and I find myself forgetting about my earlier misgivings in the joy I'm feeling from the pleasant afternoon.

As planned, we arrive for an early dinner at Ledger, a hoity-toity, popular spot in the tourist area of the city. Apparently, my Tax Man is a regular here. The hostess greets him by name with a kiss on his cheek, and the Maitre de and the head chef stop at our table to say hello, as do three waitresses, the female bartender, and the lady sommelier. All my insecurities from this morning's inadvertent discovery overwhelm me, and when the wine lady, who has the balls to put her hands all over my *Mo Shiorghra's* shoulders, finally walks away, I lean over and tersely whisper, "Damn it to hell, Declan Fitzpatrick, have ya banged every eligible female in Salem?"

He blinks twice, his normal poker face registering absolute shock. He reaches out and takes my hand. "What in the Good Universe are ya talkin' about, Lass? Ya've been acting odd all day, with yar thoughts all locked up like feckin' Fort Knox! I have no idea what's stickn' in your craw this evening."

I pull my hand away. It's now or never. "I saw them, Fitzpatrick. Those condoms in your nightstand drawer. I wasn't trying to snoop. I was looking for a spot for my hairbrush, and wham-o...there they were. Staring me right in the face!"

"I know for a fact, Rosie, that ya have seen those very same condoms up close and personal," he argues. "Whatever are ya gettin' at?"

"Normal people don't have an industrial sized box of rubbers next to their bed, Tax Man, unless they need a never-ending supply of them. Your box was half empty. Did I somehow miss the revolving door to your bedroom?"

He doesn't answer me, instead waving the waitress over for the check and handing her his credit card. I can tell he's upset, but when I try to speak, he asks me to wait until we leave the restaurant. Outside, Declan takes me by the hand across the street to where there's a small park, a hideous statue of a witch on a broom in the center, and leads me toward several empty park benches. Finding the one furthest away, we both sit down. D.P. leans over and takes both of my hands in his, careful not to squeeze my sore ring finger. "I think it's high time we talk things over, Rosie Parker. Don't you?"

TOOTHACHE 4

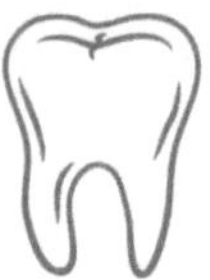

RITUAL

I KNOW what the Tax Man is going to say before he says it; the answer to my question is written plainly on his face, and the Mushroom La Campanelle that was so yummy thirty minutes ago is now dancing a rumba in my stomach. The old me wants to pull my hands away from his, but the new me can't seem to do it.

"There's no doubt yar not gonna like what I have to tell you, Love," Declan says. When someone starts a conversation in this way, there's little doubt that the rest of it will suck big time. "But I hope that ya'll at least try to keep an open mind until I explain it all." Yup. Suck. Suck. Suck.

"There's no point in fuzzy words," he says with the saddest face I've ever seen him wear. "You're one hundred percent correct about my past. I've been with a lot of women. I'm not proud of this fact, but I did what I had to do to keep my sanity, and I take full responsibility for my actions."

I can't help but pull my hands out from his. Pride and insecurities belonging to the old me won't allow me to do anything else. I sit on my hands so as not to be tempted to touch him. That's how strong the pull is between us. I can tell this action has hurt his feelings, but he continues. "Are you familiar with Otherworld history? The ancient texts?"

"A little," I respond tersely. "But I don't know how the hell that would have anything to do with us now or with the fact that you undoubtedly have screwed every pretty face in Salem and well beyond." D.P. cringes at the vulgarity of my comment, so I'm at least glad I had the sense not to use the f-word as I originally intended.

"Well, Lass, as a matter of fact they do," he says, and I can hear the tiniest bit of defensiveness in his voice. "Do you know the story surrounding the 'Dark Times?' How they came to be?"

I snort in derision. This is like asking a citizen of the United States if they've heard about the American Revolution. The Dark Times were a period in Otherworld history in which the entire dimension was awash in chaos, hatred, and violence. It was the impetus for a complete restructuring of the Otherworld's framework regarding morality, law, and government. Since this happened eight hundred years ago, I cannot imagine how it provides Declan Fitzpatrick the freedom to be a player. "Of course I know the background story," I say. "Some *Sidhe* Lord was hot for another *Sidhe* Lord's wife, so he stole her away from her intended mate with whom she'd already had a son. Then she had another son with the evil

Lord, and the two sons eventually went to war and caused the Dark Times. It's basic Fae History 101."

Now it's the Tax Man's turn to snort. "That is a very condensed version, but you are not incorrect. Do you also happen to know the names of the two Lords involved?"

I search my brain a bit, but it finally comes to me where D.P. is going with all of this. "The evil Lord was *Torin Nuada*, your ancestor, I presume?"

"Aye, Lass. The dark seed of my blood line. After the war's end, it was decided that something must be done to ensure that nothing like that would ever happen again. All of the ruling houses agreed that their eldest males, their heirs, would undergo 'The Ritual' and that their *Mo Shiogrhas* would be chosen by the magic of the Universe alone." Declan pushed up his sleeve revealing his ink work. The missing wolf part of his inkwork, now at home on my left shoulder, tingles underneath my dress, and I feel a deep, powerful sense of magic run down my spine. It's more than a little disconcerting.

"I've told you a little about the ritual, Lass, but not all of it. When I turned 14 and began to actively seek the company of females, my father called me to his chambers and explained to me in detail that it was time for me to become a man and to undergo the ritual that all heirs of the ruling houses must undergo. Like any boy that age I was a mite afraid but proud and excited that I would be considered an adult among the men of *I Idir*. A few days after my 14th birthday, the mage was called upon to begin the application of the ink and magic you and I wear today. It took several days and was far more painful than I had anticipated, but the after-effects were far worse than I could ever, at the time, have imagined. The spell worked into the tattoo does two things: it prevents the heir from conceiving a child with anyone but his chosen *Mo Shiorghra* and it completely closes off his ability to have normal emotional connections with anyone until his forever mate is revealed."

It takes me a few moments to completely digest what my Tax Man is telling me. It seems a bit incomprehensible. "Wait…you weren't able to feel any attachment or connection to…anyone? Not even your parents? Your friends? Like Duncan? Or the guys on your team?"

The words are too difficult for my *Mo Shiorghra* to speak. He shakes his head in the negative, which, of course, sends me into a self-righteous tirade. "That's totally ass-backwards and barbaric!" I swear. "Hell! What about your free will? I can't believe people actually went along with this bullshit! That your parents even put you through this! I can see your mother doing this, but your father seemed like a decent guy. Why would he do this to his own child after experiencing it himself? Did you know exactly what you were getting into when you agreed to have it done?"

Declan smiles sadly and touches his forehead to my heated one. "I appreciate your outrage on my behalf, my Love. But it is the path the Universe has set before me. I could not have deviated from it even if I had wanted to without perhaps disturbing the delicate balance of things. In my parents' defense, they could not have known that I would be made to wait twenty years to have the Universe reveal my *Mo Shiorghra*. No one in my family line ever waited more than eight or nine years, with most being handfasted, like my father, well before their twenty-first birthday. To be almost thirty-six is well…shocking."

I am angry beyond reason at the burden that was laid upon my Tax Man's boyhood self. I get up and begin pacing back and forth. "I knew the Ruling Houses all have sets of tenets to keep them in line, but good gracious, this is utterly ridiculous. It's almost like they locked up your damn soul! How does one even go about living like this? Surely you can't be the only heir that's been in this position. There are…what… fifteen Ruling Houses in *I Idir's* High Council? Someone else must have waited a really long time! I also can't believe The Morrigan even would agree to this archaic nonsense. She seems to be so modern thinking for a goddess."

Declan follows my pacing with his eyes. "I am told there was an heir of House Lugh about three hundred years ago who had gone sixteen years without finding his *Mo Shiorghra.* It is said that he went completely mad and jumped off a cliff, breaking his neck. Other than that, I am in my own category regarding bad luck." He grabs my arm to stop me from pacing. "Can ya please come sit back down, Lass. You're makin' me dizzy with your walking back and forth. I need to explain the rest of the story so you will understand fully." I sit next to him on the bench and take his hands again, feeling guilty for not having given him the benefit of the doubt, though I'm still a bit foggy as to why he needed to sleep with all of those different women.

The Tax Man looks both sad and serious. He begins by saying, "I am not saying this to make excuses for my behavior, Rosie, Lass, but I was so lonely. So vera, vera lonely. Like most males, Fae or otherwise, despite the magic of the Ritual, I react to sex in the same biological and physical way, and even though I felt nothing in my head or heart towards my many generous partners, the act itself made me feel not so alone in the world, if even for a little while. I did not want to become like the heir of House Lugh and resort to taking my own life. This does not mean that I did not feel guilty for using these women. For whatever reason, it seems women find me attractive. It was my saving grace, and the reason I was so adamant about the use of condoms. As I said, thanks to the workings of the spell, there was no chance that I might accidentally conceive a child with anyone who was not my *Mo Shiorghra*, and we Fae do not typically suffer from human diseases; but my use of condoms made it all feel more modernly casual and was more for my partners' piece of mind than for my own. Still, it does not change the fact that I have been with more women than will ever be acceptable to you. I am sorry for any hurt that this causes you. I'd truly given up hope of ever finding my soulmate, and I cannot begin to describe my joy the day you walked into your office and I saw you for the first time. It was like this chain broke inside of me, and I could finally feel things for the first time in so many, many years. It was vera…overwhelming. It is why I was in such a hurry to leave yar' office. Every time I heard ya giggle over my wet pants, I wanted to fall to my knees."

His admission now overwhelms me. "I thought you were just mad at me for spilling hot coffee in your lap," I admit.

D.P. laughs at my statement, and my heart leaps in my

chest. "I admit that the hot coffee did not feel particularly good, but I was too lost in ya, and too unsure of what to do next, ta even notice. You saved my life, Rosie Parker, and I will love ya all of my days if ya just will give me the chance."

I fall into my Tax Man's arms, sobbing like a baby. "Oh Declan, I am so sorry you had to go through all of those years feeling so damn alone! If I had only known you were looking for me, I would have worked harder to find you! I love you too, Declan Fitzpatrick! Now and always!" We are laughing and crying and kissing, and people are starting to stop and stare at us. I hold up my left hand with the ring and announce to the crowd, "We're getting married!" People smile and clap, and several point their cell phones at us. I am sure my ugly, red, crying face will be all over Instagram and TikTok later tonight.

We get ready to head back to the car when an ugly thought wiggles into my head, and I put my arm on the Tax Man to stop him from moving. "I want you to know, Lord *Mac Nuada*, that when we have a son, there's no frickin' way in hell I'm ever letting him go through this ridiculous ritual."

The Lord himself looks at me with this dumb smile on his face and his brogue is out in full force. "Why don' we wait, Lady *Mac Nuada,* to cross that bridge when we get to it. 'Tis vera bad luck to wish for things out loud, lest the Universe be listenin'. Up ta now, I have not been much favored."

It never crossed my mind that we might not be able to have children when we decide we want them; I wipe that negative thought from my mind and replace it with a new plan of action. We drive home, kissing at red lights, and when we arrive at his house the Tax Man and I don't give a rat's ass about wine or sunsets or boats in the harbor. I leave my dress somewhere on the second- floor landing, and when I hear my *Mo Shiorghra* open that nightstand drawer and reach inside, I say, "Why don't we just do away with those from now on…"

The man goes still on his side of the bed and turns to look at me. "Are ya sure this is what ya want, Lass? You are my *Mo Shiorghra*…you and I can…possibly…"

I smile and say, "Sure as sure can be, Tax Man. I'm not taking any rainchecks…or raincoats…on this decision."

TOOTHACHE 5

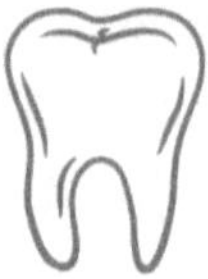

SATURDAY WITH THE TAX MAN

IT SEEMS my Tax Man and I have very different views on the purpose of Saturdays. Despite a previous evening of vigorous physical exercise, he is up at the crack of dawn with plans for a 2.3 mile run through Salem Woods. Being the generous soul he is, Declan invites me along, but I beg off with the excuse that I didn't bring along the proper running shoes, plus I have a generally held philosophy that I don't run anywhere unless I'm being chased. D.P. wickedly offers to chase me if "his Lassie is inta that sort of thing." I assure him his Lassie is not and roll over to catch another hour of sleep.

I am awoken from a crazy dream about Declan's *Mathair* raising baby hamsters with ginger colored hair by the very real sounds of grinding, chopping, and whirring. My trained ear recognizes the noise as a juicer/blender duo. I take this to mean that the Tax Man is home from his run and is, unfortunately, not coming back to bed.

Since this is my first visit to his home, I don't want to appear as the poster child for slothfulness, so I drag myself from bed, throw on a robe, and head downstairs to the kitchen.

My *Mo Shiogrha* is stripped down to his running shorts. He slides a green frothy concoction in a tall glass across the island towards me. "A power breakfast like no other," he explains. "I made ya one as well."

I am by no means a picky eater, and my culinary tastes are adventurous and eclectic, but the stuff in the glass looks like grass clippings straight from the bottom of a lawn mower and smells like a moldy dish rag. I smile as honestly as I can. "Oh, wow, thanks. Nothing better than a 'power breakfast,' right?" I take a sip. It can best be described as drinking a glass of fresh compost, and I have to work to keep from gagging. I watch as Declan sucks up a half glass of the shit in a single gulp. Maybe the super Faes have iron clad stomachs and non-discerning palates. He notices that I'm not drinking. "Don't ya like it, Love?"

I'm not going to even attempt to lie on the off chance he'll actually expect me to drink more of it. "Truthfully, Sweetie…I'm afraid I don't care for it. I'm sure it's as healthy as all get out, but umm…I don't think I can drink it. Sorry."

He shrugs. "No worries, Lass. I suppose it does take some gettin' used to. Besides, it's not like ya'll be playing today." He reaches over to the counter behind him and picks up a Starbucks cup and a small, white bag and pushes them toward me. "I picked up an alternative for ya just in case."

I'm stopped from attacking that steaming Venti Latte

and the goodies in the bag by his comment about me not playing. "What is it that I'm not playing today, Declan?"

"Rugby, Love. Big match today at North Shore. I was hopin' ya'd come watch me play."

Somehow, this wasn't what I figured we'd do on our first normal Saturday together, but at least it allows for a look into my Tax Man's unknown world. "Of course I'll come watch you play!" I jokingly add, "I'll be your number one cheerleader… as long as you don't expect me to wear one of those cute little costumes."

I expect a sexy, little comeback. Instead, the Tax Man replies with all seriousness, "Oh no, Rosie Lass! You wearin' a tight sweater and short skirt would be far too distractin'. The lads and I need to keep our minds on the game. 'Tis an important match." Then he slyly smiles and says, "But it is a fine idea for ya to wear such a thing when we return home." He finishes off his glass of weed and feed and spills mine down the drain before carefully washing and drying the two glasses and putting them back in the cabinet. I'm starting to see a neatnik pattern here. "Do ya know much about Rugby, Rosie?" Declan asks.

"Oh, just a little. Enough to follow the game," I lie. "But it's always fascinated me. I'm looking forward to learning more about it." Also a lie. I absolutely don't have any interest in any type of athletic endeavors, but if the equipment in his garage is any indication, my *Mo Shiorghra* is a super fan, and I will at least need to feign a reasonable amount of enthusiasm.

His face lights up, and I decide this little white lie was

definitely the right way to go. "What time is your match?" I innocently ask.

"Noon," he says. "But I will need the time before we leave to prep for the game, so I hope ya'll be patient with my lack of attention to ya, Rosie. I promise to make up for it later."

That comment elicits all kinds of butterflies. I'd sit naked in a frozen meat locker if it meant more one-on-one, personal time with my Tax Man. "You do what you have to do, Sweetie," I say. "I'll find things to keep myself busy until we have to leave for your match."

Declan gives me a knee wobbling kiss before heading to the garage to do heaven knows what before he can play rugby, and I head upstairs to shower, anxious to scour Google and learn everything I can about the game.

TOOTHACHE 6

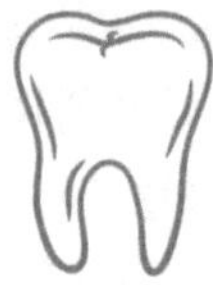

RAVISHING RUBY RED

NOT ONLY AM I unfamiliar with the game of Rugby, I'm also lost as to what I should wear to an event like this. I am by no means a fashionista, and the last thing I want is to look weird in front of Declan's friends. My Tax Man has suggested sweetly that I invite Mel to join us at the match so that I will be able to sit with someone I know. I figure my BFF will jump at the opportunity to watch a field full of half-dressed men run around in a testosterone-induced frenzy, and I am not wrong. She and I spend nearly an hour contemplating what I should wear from among the limited pieces I've brought along for the weekend. Declan's comment about not being a distraction weighs heavily, and I try to select something that is not too clingy or low cut, although when you're my size, the girls are hard to hide.

We settle on a cotton skirt in a red, black and white

print with a simple black t-shirt on top and a pair of flat strappy sandals. Mel insists that I wear red lipstick with this ensemble which is something I never wear and don't even own. She promises to bring along her favorite shade, and after we hang up I secretly hope she forgets all about it. Ever since I read an article in one of those check-out line magazines suggesting that the reason women wear bright lipstick is because it reminds men of their lady parts further south, I've been unable to dress my lips in anything but a neutral shade. I can't get over the fact that the lipstick I'm wearing might be a walking advertisement for my feminine plumbing down below.

My limited research of Rugby has given me only the barest of details, but when my Tax Man strides out of the garage with his thighs, ears and forehead covered in masking tape, I have some idea as to why. He's also wearing the number 10 on the back of his jersey, so I'm pretty proud of myself for realizing that Declan holds the position of Fly Half, the primary decision maker for his team. If all the gentlemen on the team look half as yummy in shorts and knee socks as my own, Mel is in for a very pleasant afternoon.

The Rugby field is located in Lynn, MA, which is about 20 mins south of Salem, just past Swampscott. This being a Saturday when traffic in the summer season is more congested, we leave Declan's house at 11:00 AM to allow plenty of time to get there. The Tax Man tells me I look "vera lovely," to which I respond that I hope I would not be a distraction.

He laughs and says, "Lass, ya'd be a distraction to me

even if ya'd be wearin' a shapeless burlap bag. I should probably be addin' blinders to me head like an old harse, though I dona expect it would do my game much good. I shall have to do my best to not look inta the stands during play."

This makes my heart melt, but I am still more nervous than I ought to be. I am a medical professional. I deal with people every day. Unfortunately, meeting Declan's teammates is doing a number on my self-confidence, not to mention the women who may be there who possibly may have had…uhmmm…a former relationship with my Tax Man. I fully understand what my *Mo Shiorghra* has explained about his past, and I have an enormous amount of sympathy for what he went through. However, I don't have to like the idea that he's had a huge sampling of Salem's female population.

We arrive at the field with plenty of time to spare. Several of the other players are there, including D.P.'s cousin, Duncan, whom I haven't seen since he carried my stinky self to the waiting ambulance on Wednesday. He waves and immediately comes over to us, looking first to Declan for an 'okay' before taking my hands and kissing my cheek. I feel that little tingle that comes from Duncan's *gancanagh* heritage. "Dr. Rosie, 'tis so good to see ya lookin' all gorgeous and healthy! I am thrilled to hear that we'll be witnessin' yar handfasting in just a few weeks. All of *I Idir* can talk of little else."

I try not to worry about exactly what the people of *I Idir* are saying about the *Nuada* heir joining himself to a lowly tooth fairy. Many of the Fae are no better than humans when it comes to judging people on things that shouldn't matter. Duncan doesn't strike me as one of those types, though I'm sure his dark Fae looks have earned him plenty of whispers as well. The Tax Man's cousin calls a group of his teammates over and introduces me to them before launching into a long, overly graphic story of how I took the brass bullet out of his groin and thus saved his life. This embarrasses the hell out of me, but my young Lord *Mac Nuada*'s got his chest puffed out over the story and he's smiling so widely I think his cheeks must hurt. I blush over his pride in me, and when I catch his eye, he gives me a wink that makes me dizzy.

Other players begin to arrive, and now because Fae men are front and center in my mind, I realize none of them are human. When Declan walks over to me, I ask him, "Are all the players Fae?"

"Aye," he explains, "'twould not be a fair match otherwise. We Fae are faster, stronger and heal quicker than human men. Rugby, especially the way we play it, is a vera physical game. Those of the Mundane World would just end up injured before the game came to a conclusion."

This makes me think of how much this will please Mel when at that exact moment, I see her coming towards me. I can tell that she is peering over her sunglasses at the assortment of male anatomy warming up on the field, and it is blatantly obvious many of them are staring back at her. Melanie Sparks is one of those comfortable-in-her-own-hot-girl-skin females. She's been this way since puberty. Her hair is more strawberry blonde than red, and the lashes over her light green eyes are long and lush without the slightest touch of mascara. Her eyes always have a twinkle of mischief in them, as if she's just waiting for you to suggest something fun and exciting. It also doesn't hurt that she has a lithe, petite body and always looks so casually perfect in anything she wears.

Mel sees me and waves, heading toward me through the ever-growing crowd of people. She sizes me up and nods in satisfaction, then sits down, pulls out a tube of lipstick and hands it to me. "This one is perfect for you, Rosie."

I slide the cap off of Ravishing Ruby Red and twist the stick up. It's definitely a red red. Not a pink red. Not a raspberry red. This is a bright, dark, blood-matching color. I make a face. "I don't think this is the right shade for me, Mel. Especially not at a rugby game. It's something one wears to a club or an evening soiree."

"Nonsense, Rosie," counters Mel. "With all that black you're wearing the red lipstick brings out your beautiful eyes and skin tone. Trust me…you'll thank me later when your *Mo Shiorghra* can't keep his hands off you."

I want to tell her that Declan keeping his hands on me hasn't been one bit of a problem, but to my ear it sounds like I'm bragging, so I pull my compact out of my purse and carefully apply the lipstick, pressing my lips together to set it. The reflection in the mirror looks like someone else. Not Dr. Rosie Parker, D.S.S., but some man's hot lover. Part of me is weirded out by that, but the other part likes it. "What do you think?" I ask Mel.

"Damn, girl," she says with a huge smile, "you look so hot. Like you're ready for a quick tumble here and now."

This makes me blush, but if I had any doubts, I see my

Tax Man look up, and when he notices me in the stands, he smiles widely and puts both hands next to his eyes in pantomime of a horse wearing blinders. Then he gives me a salacious wink and a thumbs up signal, and it's all I can do to remember just how long these damn games last.

TOOTHACHE 7

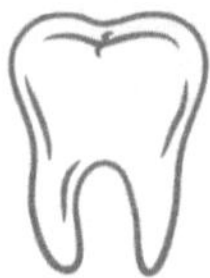

... AND WHAT THOSE GIRLS SAID

IN CASE YOU WERE CURIOUS, rugby union matches are usually eighty minutes long, equating to two forty-minute halves. But if one adds a fifteen-minute half-time, and all the stoppages for injuries and carry-offs, it's more like two hours. Two frickin' hours of biting my nails and watching in absolute terror as my Tax Man gets tossed, lifted, tackled, and pummeled. At one point, I see that he's sustained a bloody nose after an especially vicious tackle, and it's all I can do to force myself to stay in my seat and not run down to the field and check on his injury. In my head I hear him laugh. *'Tis naught but a little wallop, Love. I'm fine, though I do appreciate ya not coming out of the stands to my rescue. I donna think I could live that down."*

Sometime in the first half, Mel and I are joined by a young woman who introduces herself as Orla Dell, whose husband, Connor, is a member of Declan's spy shet group and also is the rugby team's Hooker. She has both a pixie-like appearance and a matching personality, and she makes the time go more quickly with amusing anecdotes about her job as a Kindergarten teacher. The rest of the spectators give us a wide berth. Or maybe this is just my imagination. I'm not really sure. I feel very self-conscious among so many Fae, most of whom probably know who I am while I don't know any of them.

The exceptions are two young *Sidhe* women sitting three rows below us who keep turning around to stare, then whisper between themselves. I'm pretty sure it's me that they're talking about, and I can't help but to imagine that they're former acquaintances of my *Mo Shiorghra*. Don't judge me. My rational self understands that at some point I need to move beyond Declan's past life before I was a part of it, but today I'm still a little…sensitive.

During halftime, I expect my Tax Man to come over and check on me, but he's busy going over plays with the #9 Scrum-Half and pays me no mind. Truth be told, I'm a little put out that he sends his cousin instead, with the excuse that the game is far too close for Declan's liking and that should they lose, my intended will be in a partic-ularly foul mood. I don't understand getting so worked up over a silly game, but I have no one to share this opinion with, as Duncan has switched his attention to Mel, the two of them doing that flirty little dance that seems to come easily to everyone except me.

For the entire second half, I hold my breath every time Declan's team falls behind. I don't enjoy a cranky Declan any more than Duncan does, and no one is more excited when his team finally scores seconds before the game ends, thus winning the match and allowing them to advance to the next round, which I secretly hope happens while we are away on our honeymoon. I'm tired of sitting on the hard bleachers and am looking forward to going back to the Tax Man's home for a more relaxed afternoon alone together. Unfortunately, that's not to be. Both teams are headed over to a local Salem pub to celebrate the thrill of victory and the agony of defeat with a couple of pints in the long-honored tradition of rugby.

I'm certainly not going to be a spoilsport, but frankly, I can't say I'm overly excited about these plans. I hope the pub has food as well, as I've had nothing to eat all day except a latte and a croissant, and I don't relish a couple of pints of Guinness on a near empty stomach. I keep all these thoughts safely locked up in my head. My beloved is on a winner's high, and I certainly don't want to be Debbie Downer to his genuine exuberance.

The pub is dark and crowded and smells like a urinal. I scope out the ladies' room and make my way there alone, as my BFF is busy batting those extra-long eyelashes at Declan's *gancanagh* cousin. I feel like I should warn her, but not here where someone might overhear us. It will have to wait until we are alone. I sit and think about these things while I am squirreled away in the bathroom stall until I hear other voices enter the restroom. They are giggling and laughing, and I recognize the voices as the two women that were sitting in front of me at the game.

"Poor Fitzie," one of them says. I freeze. At first, I'm not sure if they are referring to Declan or Duncan, but then the other one responds, "Yeah. His bad luck seems to go on and on. Imagine…being forced to handfast a tooth fairy."

Inside the stall, my face goes hot. There's no doubt now about whom they're referring to. I want to be anywhere but here right now, but I don't know how to escape without being seen. It's way before sunset, and here in the middle of the afternoon I have no magic to help me disappear.

"Not only a tooth fairy, but one on the thick side as well. She doesn't look anything like Fitzie's usual type. I can't imagine what the Universe has against House *Nuada*."

The second girl chimes in. "Maybe when the year and a day is up, that tooth fairy will do the right thing and set Fitz free. He'll have done away with his responsibility and be free to go back to what he really likes."

"Hell, I can wait the year out," the first one says.

"I as well," says the second. "I hope he doesn't knock her up. That would just complicate things."

The first one laughs, and it's like a knife through me. "Seriously, you saw her. Do you think he's gonna want a daily dose of that? Plus, with the kind of luck Declan has, a baby is a real improbability. They say he's 'cursed,' you know. Killed his own twin."

My hurt now turns to absolute rage. How dare they spread shit about my *Mo Shiorghra*! Or our possible future children! They can make all the fat jokes they want. I'm used to that. But I'll be damned if I'm gonna let them spread evil, malicious rumors about Declan. His mother's done enough of that to last a lifetime.

I flush, then step out of the stall, and I see the women's

faces go white in the mirror. "Don't let me interrupt your pile of garbage, girls," I snidely remark. "Yes…how 'bout that…it's me… 'Fitzie's' tooth fairy… his extremely pissed tooth fairy. How ironic, huh? How dare you spread venomous shit about him like that? It's mean…it's rude… it's untrue…and it's completely against Otherworld protocol."

The first girl spins around. "Please don't tell Lord *Mac Nuada* we said that. We were only…joking."

"Yeah," begs the second. "We didn't really mean it. We like Declan. He's a friend of ours. He'd be really upset with us if you told him. Plus, we'd be in all kinds of trouble with our parents. Honest. We truly apologize for saying those things about you, and I know it's your right to complain to him as his *Mo Shiorghra*, but please don't do it. It would go really bad for us."

I move through the two of them towards the sink and mirror without saying a word. I wash my hands, then take out the lipstick Mel gave me and give my lips a fresh coat of red, cheering on their look-alike-baby-making-lady-parts below. I can tell the women are nervous as hell waiting for what I'll say next. I drop the lipstick in my handbag and snap it shut. Then I turn to them and say, "I don't need to hide behind my *Mo Shiorghra* to handle the two of you. I've had plenty of experience dealing with self-absorbed bitches in both worlds, so when I leave this restroom, I won't give either of you another thought. In addition, I love Declan enough not to ruin my beloved's joyful mood with your sour, jealous nonsense. And…as to our sex life that you seem so voyeuristically interested in…you can rest assured that between Fated Mates, it's beyond your wildest dreams."

And then I walk out, leaving the two of them with their mouths hanging open like a couple of fish out of water.

TOOTHACHE 8

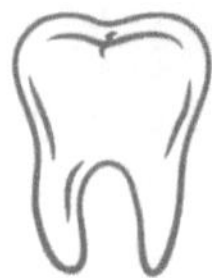

SHARING THE NEWS

IT ALSO APPEARS no one has ever explained to Declan
Phineas Fitzpatrick that Sunday in the Mundane World is
traditionally a day of rest. I am able to delay his morning
run for about forty minutes, but somewhere in the after-
glow I hear him get up and leave. At least this morning he
doesn't make the mistake of asking me to join him. By the
time he returns and jumps in the shower, I am awake.
Now it's his turn to tempt me, coaxing me to get out of
bed with the promise of a fabulous breakfast at his
favorite local spot.

I would have been just as happy to stay in and fix
something for the two of us, but I get the distinct feeling
my Tax Man would prefer his kitchen not be disturbed by
my cooking. To say that Declan is neat would be an
understatement. When I go into the bathroom to shower,
I find a squeegee on top of the stack of fresh towels he's
left me, a not-so-subtle hint that my *Mo Shiorghra* would

prefer that I didn't leave water spots on his shower doors. The sink is polished clean, the toothpaste is put away, and there are no wet towels hanging anywhere from his earlier use of the facilities.

My beloved's proclivity towards organization and cleanliness is going to take some getting used to on my end. I am, for the most part, oblivious to clutter and mess. It's not that I don't enjoy a sparkling clean environment, it's that I don't spend a lot of time thinking about it. If I'm in the middle of a craft project, or puttering in my garden, or cooking a fabulous recipe, I don't stop to think whether I've wiped a spill off the counter or put all the garden tools back in the shed. My mind is focused specifically on the task at hand; and when I've completed my labors, I always intend to pick up the aftermath of my activities. I just don't always get to it right away.

I make sure to squeegee the hell out of the glass and even run the damn thing over the condensation that's built up on the mirror. I wipe down the sink and then bundle up the wet towels and stack them on top of the washing machine in the tiny laundry room across from the bedroom. Doing this every morning when I'm most likely already running late for work seems like it will get old real quick, but for today, in the newness of our relationship, I don't rock the boat.

I'm not sure how to dress for the day since Declan hasn't given any indication of what he's planned for Sunday Funday. I think back to last Sunday, our first trip outside the house to the market. I smile and wonder whether we shouldn't go back and let Tony the butcher know we're getting married and that I'm off the market

...just for fun. Slipping on a robe, I go in search of him to make this suggestion and find him on the phone in his office. He holds up a finger to let me know to wait until he's finished. It takes me a minute of listening to figure out he's speaking Dutch, and for the life of me, I can't understand why. Worse yet, I realize that I didn't know he could speak any other languages besides Otherworld Gaelic and English. *Why are you so surprised at this, Rosie? There's a lifetime of things you don't know about him outside that bedroom. Let's face it...you've been a bit preoccupied with the smutty stuff. Hell, you don't even know his birthday, girlfriend!*

Declan ends his call and smiles sweetly at me. "Sorry, Love. I needed to handle some business in Belgium that couldn't wait. What da you need?"

"When's your birthday?" I blurt out.

He looks confused. "It's August 4th. Why do you ask?"

"No specific reason," I explain. "I just realized I didn't know when your birthday was."

He nods. "Aye. There is much left to learn about one another. It will be a joyous journey for us to take together." He pauses, and it's like we both can see the gigantic elephant of common sense sitting between us. "Yours?" he asks.

I assume he means my birthday. "December 15th," I say. "A child of the Frost Moon."

He grins. "Aye. I should have guessed that you would be the brightest thing in the Winter sky. Ya are certainly the brightest light in ma life, Love."

It is the sweetest, most romantic thing he's said today, and the common sense elephant shrinks to a more manageable size. "And you, Declan Fitzpatrick, are a man gifted with a silver tongue." Dirty thoughts cross my mind about the Tax Man's tongue, but I save them for later. I obviously am not shielding my thoughts very well, because I get a wicked grin in response. This whole mind communication thing does have its sexy perks. "Actually," I say, "I was hoping you could give me a heads up on our plans for today, so I can dress…or undress…accordingly."

D.P. leans back in his office chair and folds his hands behind his head. "There are a few things of importance we need to take care of before we head to *I Idir* to meet with my parents. I'd hoped we could take care of those after breakfast."

Thoughts of having to meet up with Lord and Lady *Nuada* act like a bucket of cold water to any amorous daydreams I might have had. "What kind of important things?" I ask.

"I must meet with your father, Rosie, and formally ask him for your hand. 'Tis the way things are done. Then, I thought it best we give your sister the news together. I am sure she will have her questions and doubts, and I am hoping it will be easier for you to explain if I am with you. Of course, if you would prefer to be alone with your sibling, I understand."

This is the very last thing I expected to do today, and I am caught off guard. It's not like I didn't plan on sharing the news with my tiny family, it's just that I thought I had more time to figure out what I would say to them. Frankly, most people would find our story unbelievable, and my sister Claire's life is rooted entirely in the Mundane World. I'm not even sure her husband fully understands our strange family history, and I have no clue as to how she'll react to the news that I'm running off to marry the first Fae guy I've never even dated.

My father is a completely different challenge. He was always extremely accepting of his family's connection to the Otherworld, but dementia has robbed him of his memories; most days I'm lucky if he remembers who I am. If Declan expects my father to understand truly what he's asking, I'm afraid my *Mo Shiorghra* is going to be very disappointed.

"Declan…Sweetie…I would love for you to come with me to visit my sister and her family, though I do expect Claire to tell me that I'm being crazy and moving too fast. My dad, on the other hand, is in a care facility due to memory issues. He doesn't recognize me most of the times I visit, and I don't think he'll be able to understand what it is you're trying to ask him."

My *Mo Shiorghra* folds his arms across his chest and sticks out his chin slightly, which even in the short period of time I've known him I recognize as a sign that he has no intention of giving up on his plans. "I understand what you're trying to tell me, Lass, but I will not take a man's daughter from him without at least attemptin' ta ask far' his blessing. T'would not be right. I must be allowed to try. To do otherwise would be dishonorable."

It's not a hill of contention I want to die on. My Tax Man will see that I am right with his own two eyes, though observing my dad's obvious confusion is always difficult for me. Still, I can be as brave and honorable as Declan. "If that's what you want, then so be it. Try not to get your hopes up too high," I warn.

His body language relaxes, relieved, I'm sure, that I have not put up a big fight over his plans for today. Declan gives me a sad sort of smile, "Yar lookin' at a man who has spent most of his life hopin', Rosie, and from my own personal experience, I've learned that without hope…ya got nothin'.'"

TOOTHACHE 9

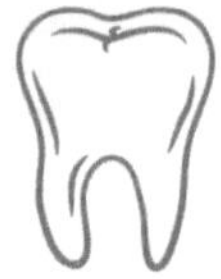

SEA COAST

DECLAN and I enjoy our breakfast at a charming little diner called Easy Overboard within walking distance of his townhouse. The restaurant is cute in an overly nautical way, the food is hearty and delicious, and the waitresses are all senior ladies who treat my *Mo Shiorghra* like a long-lost grandson and not an ex-lover. Again… don't judge me. I'm really trying. Over seafood omelets and homemade muffins we come to the hallmark decision regarding a date for our Otherworld handfasting.

Although both of us want it over and done with as quickly as possible, Declan is a member of one of *I Idir's* premiere Ruling Houses, so realistically the handfasting can't and won't be a simple, private affair. There is a shit load of traditions and protocols that must be met, and stuff like that takes time to arrange. Keeping in mind that I am planning to return to my practice on August 4th and that we'd like two weeks of honeymoon for ourselves, we decide on the date of July 18th. Of course, our chosen date needs to be checked by House *Nuada's* mages as suitable and magically sound and also will need to meet the approval of both of his parents. I don't say it, but I'm sure Lady *Nuada* would suggest that the perfect date for me to tie the knot with her son would be when Hell freezes over.

We leave the diner giddy that we've set a date. My Tax Man's joy is obvious when he insists on stopping at a flower cart that sells bouquets and floral pieces to Salem's thriving tourist crowd. He explains that we've just set a date to be married and asks the florist to create an arrangement his fiance can wear in her hair using mainly white gardenias. Truthfully, I feel rather silly at the thought of wearing flowers in my hair all day like a kid on vacation, but I don't share my opinion. I'm especially glad I've kept my thoughts to myself when my beloved explains that the Mundane World gardenia has a look-alike, smell-alike cousin in the Otherworld called *Siorai,* which translates as eternal for its ability to stay fresh far longer than most cut flowers. The *Siorai* is considered a Fae symbol for couples magically mated by the Universe. "I'll wager you'll have some of these in yar handfast bouquet, Lass," the Tax Man explains as he tucks the sweet-smelling flowers into the side of my messy bun. It's a very good thing I've parked myself on a nearby bench, because I'm pretty sure I'm turning into a giant, melty puddle thinking about our upcoming handfasting day.

From there, we decide to visit my dad first, as he's usually at his most alert in the mornings. Sea Coast Memory Care is located four miles away in Swampscott, so I use the downtime in the car to ask Declan about his family. He avoids talking about his parents but tells me about his five younger sisters whom he describes mostly as copies of his *Mathair,* with the exception of Meghan, the 15-year-old baby of the family. He smiles when he talks about her, so I get the impression he's genuinely fond of his little sister. "Meggie can start trouble where none should exist," Declans says. "She's been quite the handful for my parents from the cradle onward, and my Lady *Mathair* often threatens to send her ta live with her 'no-good brother in the Mundane World.' I don' doubt that just causes her to act up more. She once spent a week with me when she was about 12 years old. 'Twas the most exhausting week of ma life."

My Tax Man goes on about his ancestral home, *Dun Siorai* (Eternal Fortress) in *I Idir,* about the natural beauty of the land surrounding it and about his many family pets, including a dog named Abbot, an old cat called Galahad, and his favorite racing horse, a spirited thoroughbred-like creature he's named *Rois Gaoithe,* which translates to blast of wind. He takes his right hand off the steering wheel and takes my left one in his. "There is one person I canna wait to have you meet, Rosie. Magda was my *Buime*…my Otherworld nanny. If it was not for that woman, I dunno what I would have done growin' up. She was the buffer between my *Mathair* and me, and after the Ritual she kept on fussing over me even when I'd lost the ability to feel anything far her in return. Old Magda was the first and only parson I told after we met that day in yar office that I believed I'd finally found my *Mo Shiorghra.*"

It makes me feel a little better knowing that D.P. had at

least one person who cared for him growing up. It also means that there will be at least one person in *I Idir* who will be happy to see me tie the knot with my beloved. I pledge that when I meet this woman, she's going to get a special gift from me.

When we arrive at the nursing facility, Declan takes his suit jacket from the back seat and slips it on. I tried as hard as I could to talk him out of wearing a suit today, but there was no changing his mind. "I am meeting your family for the first time, Lass. 'Tis a monumental occasion and I should dress appropriately." He looks vastly over-dressed next to my cotton skirt and blouse, but it's not worth the argument. I won't be the one sweating my ass off in a wool suit.

It becomes very obvious when we walk through the corridors of Sea Coast that my *Mo Shiorghra* is unfamiliar with the concept of memory care or of the horrible diseases that robs some humans of their minds. Although the older Fae population may suffer minor cognitive impairments as they age, they aren't victims of Alzheimer's or other diseases that cause rapidly declining dementia. I can see the horror and pity in his eyes. When a few patients call out to him, Declan stops at each one to acknowledge them and pats their hands like he knows them. It makes me love him even more…if that's remotely possible.

My Dad is awake and staring blankly at the television when we walk into his room. He doesn't acknowledge our presence, and my heart sinks. D.P. and I take a chair on each side of his bed. I take my dad's hand and attempt to talk to him. "Hey, Daddy…it's me Rosie. How are you feeling today? I brought someone special I want you to meet. His name is Declan."

Dad doesn't respond at first, then he says, "The Indians always lose. It's not fair."

"What do you mean, Dad? What Indians?" I ask. He doesn't supply any more information, and it takes me at least three or four minutes before I realize that my father is talking about the old black and white Western film he's watching on the T.V. I feel the ache in the back of my throat and the tears biting at the corners of my eyes. Coming here was a mistake. My daddy is clearly never going to understand what Declan wants to ask him.

On the other side of the bed, my Tax Man tries a different approach. "Mr. Parker, you look uncomfortable sitting that way. Would you like me to fix your pillow so you can rest easier?" There's not a trace of brogue in D.P.'s speech, and he speaks slowly and clearly. My father seems to understand and nods his approval. Declan gets up and straightens the stack of pillows. I also see him lay his hand flat on the very top of my father's skull before he sits back down.

A few minutes later my dad blinks a few times at the television and then turns his head to look at me. "Rosie! It's you! You're looking so beautiful today...so grown-up. It seems like just yesterday you were a little girl playing with dolls and look at you now! The spitting image of your mother." He turns to my *Mo Shiorghra*. "Isn't my baby girl a knock-out?"

The Tax Man smiles broadly. "That she is, Sir. Rosie is the most beautiful woman I've ever met. Takes after her mother, of course."

My father laughs out loud. "Where did you find this guy, Rosie Posie? He's a hoot! You better not let this one get away."

I'm neither naive nor stupid. I realize that Lord *Mac Nuada* has done a little hocus-pocus on my father, but it appears as if it's really my Dad speaking and not some crazy ventriloquist's trick born of magic. Declan couldn't possibly know that Rosie Posie was my Daddy's pet name for me when I was a child. "Dad…I'd like you to meet my…boyfriend, Declan Fitzpatrick. Declan is a CPA. We met while he was helping me with my taxes."

My father turns to my *Mo Shiorghra*. "A CPA, huh? That's a fine occupation, young man. I worked with numbers myself. I was an actuary. Thirty years with Salem Five Bank." The two of them talk about insurance, lending, and other branches of finance while I sit there in stunned silence. After a few minutes, D.P. changes the topic. "Mr. Parker, I'm in love with your daughter. I want to marry her. I promise to forever treat her as the treasure she is if I were to receive your blessing, Sir."

My Dad looks at me with the biggest grin on his face, then takes my hand. "So that's why you're glowing, Rosie Posie! I've never seen you this radiant before. Do you love this young man, baby girl? Do you want to marry this Declan fellow?"

I feel this huge aching warmth in my throat, and I can barely get the words out. "Yes, Daddy. I love him very much. I want to spend the rest of my life with him."

My Dad takes my hand and then reaches over to my *Mo Shiorghra* and pulls Declan's hand toward mine, joining them across the bed. "You both have my blessing.

I'm just so happy that I'm here to see my little Rosie find her special someone, just like me and her mother."

The ache in my throat triples in size, and I know I'm about to lose my shit any second now. When those flood gates open, I'm not sure how or when I'll ever be able to stop crying. My father drops our hands, then looks blankly up at the television and says, "The Indians always lose. It's not fair." He takes the remote off the nightstand and clicks off the television. "Go away now," my dad growls. "I'm very tired."

And that's when the emotional dam breaks, and I can no longer hold back the deluge.

TOOTHACHE 10

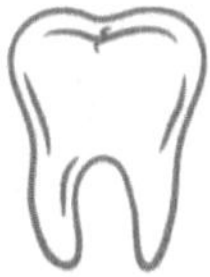

MY BIG SIS

THE NURSES and staff at Sea Coast Memory Care are no strangers to dealing with distraught family members. The diseases that affect the patients that call Sea Coast home cause them to suffer cruelly from the loss of who and what they once were. It is painful and heartbreaking for the loved ones who visit them, and my deep sobbing causes little disturbance other than a sympathetic expression or nod.

When I finally feel up to speaking, I ask the Tax Man, "That was your doing, wasn't it?"

"Aye," he says with a shrug. "I am sorry it couldn't have lasted longer. I canna' change what already is, but a little blast of magical energy can sometimes bring about a flash of mental clarity. I wanted yar' sire to know that you had found a mate, and I wanted for him to have the chance to bless our joining. He deserves at least that for his child.

What ya witnessed was truly your father as you knew him. 'Twas no trick."

This sets off my tears again, and I realize I need to pull myself together before I see my sister. I wasn't totally upfront with her about why I needed to visit. I had mentioned that I was bringing along a male friend, but I hadn't warned her that the news I would share would be life changing. Or that she wouldn't be part of it.

Crossing between the two dimensions is impossible for most life forms. People who are 100% human and Otherworld citizens who are 100% Fae have enormous issues going back and forth. Even if they can make the difficult jump, after just a short time in the alternative space, they suffer terrible physical effects which eventually leads to irreversible physiological damage, and, in some cases, even death. Those of us with mixed DNA, human and Fae, traditionally are able to survive physically and thrive in either space, though high rates of blood cancers are found in a small number of mixed blood Fae who spend an excessive amount of time going back and forth. My mom was an example of that, and I'm not sure whether the same thing might not also happen to me. No one really knows why some people are susceptible to this illness while others are not, but thanks to research scientists like Dr. Robyn Brannigan, progress is being made in figuring it all out. What's most strange is that a good percentage of Fae with pure ancient bloodlines going back to the beginning of time, those like Declan's father, seem able to live safely in both worlds as well. The widespread theory is that we all started as the same people in the same space, but that at some point the two groups split and became completely separate beings living in two different worlds. Aside from the existence of several myths and spiritual legends, no one truly knows the Universe's hidden secrets.

Still, the ability to cross over is highly desired among both groups of people. Mixed blood offspring are much coveted among the Fae and is one of the major reasons most of the Mundane world's countries seek samples of Fae DNA in the race to research and discover how to breach the walls between the two worlds successfully.

The bottom line is that when my *Mo Shiorghra* and I tie the knot in a few weeks, none of my blood family nor any of my close Mundane friends will be there. Declan already has suggested we have a Mundane civil ceremony and small celebration in Salem when I feel I am ready to do so. I know he means well and wants me to be happy, but it's not the same as having them attend our handfasting, which according to the beliefs the two of us hold, is the union of our souls. Of course, in some ways, my beloved is in the same boat as me. Though he has family, friends and acquaintances in *I Idir*, it's unclear how many of them will be truly happy for us.

My sister and her husband and their twin sons live in Swampscott, only a short drive from my dad's nursing facility. D.P. and I don't have much time to discuss how we're going to handle the impending meeting, but we cobble together a quick plan. I don't know how much Claire's husband, Scott, knows about my family's history, so we err on the side of caution: I will meet with Claire alone, while Declan makes idle chit-chat with her husband. It's not a great plan, but it is the best we can muster in the time we have.

I haven't seen my sister in several weeks, and I realize how much I've missed her when she greets us at the door. I introduce Declan as my boyfriend, which sounds ridiculous coming from a thirty plus year old woman. Obviously, I don't want to use the word fiance right out of the gate without first talking to her about it. Plus, I absolutely cannot make myself use the term significant other or partner, nor would I even be willing to say, "Claire, I'd like you to meet my hot, new lover..."

The Tax Man looks way more relaxed than I feel, and I start to think that when placed in unfamiliar situations, Declan easily assumes one of his spy 'shet' alter egos. When we are alone or with Otherworld residents, I've noticed his brogue is very prominent and his word choices far more colorful. However, around everyone else, he sounds very American, unless, of course, he's speaking in one of his many other known foreign languages.

We all fuss over the babies, but I feel my *Mo Shiorghra* tense up when he looks at her twin boys. I suppose his reaction isn't shocking. He's shielding his thoughts very tightly, but if I had to guess, I'd say he's not wishing for a pair of his own based on his personal history and the years of nasty abuse from his demon-tongued *Mathair*. I squeeze his hand and I feel him relax, though there's no way I can miss the change in his personal aura. He's not quite as relaxed as he appears.

I leave Declan with Scott in the parlor, the two of them discussing craft beers with one eye glued to the Boston Red Sox game on the family's enormous television. Claire and I each grab a cup of coffee and head to the deck to talk in private.

As soon as she slides the patio door closed, Claire is all over me. "OMG, Rosie! He's gorgeous!" She touches her hip and makes a silly sizzling sound, "That ass is near perfection."

I laugh and pretend to be shocked. "Gosh Claire, you're a respectable wife and mother. Looking at strange men's asses? What would Mama think?"

We both laugh because our mom was known to remark often on male perfection when she saw it. "Well, there is no denying it," I admit with a big smile. "Declan does have…nice parts." This gets us to giggling again like a couple of teenagers, and after the week I've had and my very recent experience with our dad, I need the love and camaraderie that only my older sister can provide.

"Spill it, Rosie Posie! Where did you meet him? How long have you been going out? Is this a 'serious' relationship or just a fling? Not that I would blame you for grabbing hold of some of that!" Claire shoots her barrage of questions machine gun style.

I take a deep breath and gather my thoughts, praying that my big sister doesn't shut me down before I can finish. "So, I'm gonna give you the whole scoop, Sis, but you have to promise to let me finish before you offer any commentary."

Claire frowns. "Now you're scaring me, Rose. Just go

ahead and tell me already. I promise to hold off until you finish."

And so I tell Claire the story. All of it, including the Chechens, how my Tax Man was my security detail, how we finally gave in to what we both felt, and finally, I slip my blouse off my shoulder and show her the ink work that marks me as *Lord Mac Nuada's Mo Shiorghra*.

Claire keeps her promise and doesn't speak until I finish, but her face reveals all her different emotions as my tale progresses. Then she reacts in a totally unexpected way. She gets up and hugs me, and I hear genuine emotion in her voice. "Oh Rosie...I'm so happy for you! It's like a Cinderella story come true." My big sister takes my hands in hers. "I knew you were in love with this man and he with you the moment you both walked in the door! You're both positively glowing!"

"That's the same thing Daddy said to me," I reveal.

Claire looks at me oddly. "Daddy was lucid?"

I explain what happened at Sea Coast, and by the time I finish the story, we both are crying. I think that my eyes will be swollen for the entire rest of the day. "This is so ironic, Rose," Claire says. "All those years you've avoided Fae men with a ten-foot pole. Now, you end up being the Fated Mate of one...just like that. Out of the blue. It doesn't surprise me, you know. I always knew my baby sister was someone special. I was so jealous of your magic, and all you wanted to do was hide it. You got to share Mama's world...one I wasn't part of. It's like this was destiny all along."

Destiny is exactly what it is, but Claire's Judeo- Christian beliefs have never before meshed with mine. "I can't believe you were jealous of me. I was super envious because you were normal…and I wasn't. It's funny how this all ended up. The Universe definitely has a sense of humor." I pause for a moment and add a concern to the mix. "I wonder how Mama really would feel about my handfasting Declan as he's not only Fae but from a Ruling Council family to boot. You know what she thought of all *Sidhe* males, especially the ones with hoity-toity pedigrees."

"Oh Rosalinda…I had hoped that you'd taken Mama's prejudice against Fae men with a grain of salt. She only felt that way because some Fae boy broke her heart when she was a teenager. Frankly, I'd hoped she would move on from those feelings someday, but, unfortunately, she never did. It makes me sad that she passed those negative feelings on to you. She was always so easygoing about everything else, but I guess she never let go of that heart-break from her youth."

"How do you know about this Fae boy and I don't?" I ask.

"I heard Mama and her cousin Rema talking about it one night after too many glasses of wine. Rema was sharing some gossip from *I Idir* and Mama cut her off. They argued about it, and Rema and Mama never spoke after that. Seeing how Mom reacted, I never had the guts to ask her about it. I suppose I didn't realize how much her opinions had shaped your beliefs."

"Still, it would be nice to know that I had Mama's blessing as well as Daddy's," I admit.

Claire takes my hands again and looks me square in the eye. "I know we don't share the same spiritual beliefs,

Rose. But I do believe that we're all destined to walk the path that's in front of us. Your path is yours, and Mama's path was hers; the two of you don't share the same path. Mama's disappointments have nothing to do with you and Declan."

TOOTHACHE 11

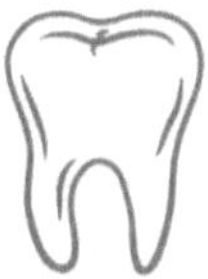

THE POETRY OF LOVE

IT'S a secret relief for me finally to be back home in my own space. Don't get me wrong. Declan's townhouse is gorgeous, and the view from his bedroom balcony is beyond compare. It's just that it felt so… sterile, like I was living in a great, big, empty, void. Although my *Mo Shiorghra's* personal belongings were all there, I didn't get a feeling that he, himself, was rooted in that space. Maybe I'm just overthinking it and being far too metaphysical about it. Or maybe my feelings have something to do with the intense emotions that encompassed the last three days. Whatever the cause, I heartily agree with the sentiment that there's no place like home. Frankly, even my Tax Man seems more relaxed here than he did at his own place, and I hope I'm reading this right when the time comes to decide where we'll live permanently.

We quickly fall into an easy, comfortable routine. Declan hasn't taken an official leave of absence from his firm, but he's cut back on his hours in the office and generally works out of my loft, which he's pretty much claimed as his own. This significantly limits access to my dollhouse and craft materials, and the few times I dared try to share the space I received the annoyed Declan look for singing out loud with my earbuds in. Instead, I take small projects downstairs to the kitchen island, but I easily can tell when he's working on my personal finances because I can hear a running barrage of Gaelic swear words. When he comes down for lunch, he looks at me, shakes his head, and says, "This mess ya made of yar finances will not be happenin' again, Rosie Lass." This doesn't offend me in the least. I'm more than happy to turn that part of my life over to someone much better at that kind of stuff. In return, the Tax Man is happy to call my place home.

Life is good. Very good, and I can't remember ever being this happy. Unfortunately, Wednesday morning, I forget to take my beloved's sage advice and make the most grievous mistake of wishing that days like these could go on forever. In magical philosophy, wishing is paramount to questioning the Universe's intended path, which is never a good idea. And, right on cue, D.P. waltzes downstairs to tell me that we really can't put off going home to *Dun Soirai* if we hope to solidify our July 18th handfasting date. He suggests we leave Salem in the early hours of Thursday morning, which is actually Friday afternoon in I Idir. As he grabs an apple from the fridge, Lord *Mac Nuada* mentions just a mite too casually that there are some Otherworld legal aspects we need to handle before we go and that he's asked a friend to come over this evening to help us with everything.

Of course, I'm all over that comment in two seconds flat. What legal aspects is he talking about, and who is this so-called friend? I get a song and dance routine in reply, with the excuse that my Tax Man has an important Zoom meeting with a client in Luxemburg in a half hour and that he needs to get everything in order before it begins so he doesn't have time right now to explain it all but will be happy to put me in the know later in the day.

When later rolls around and Declan is finished with his business meeting, he begins a really bang-up seduction routine which starts with his reading love poems from the book Mac O'Kelly gave us as an engagement gift, in full Gaelic brogue with tons of rolling r's, and I forget all about whatever it is that my *Mo Shiorghra* is supposed to explain. I'm not stupid. I understand fully that this is a ploy to distract me from whatever upcoming events I'm certain not to like, but how many times in a girl's life does she get the opportunity to spend the whole afternoon being seduced by an unbelievably hot man reading her love poetry? I'd have to be a full-on, cold-hearted saint to be able to resist this temptation. As you probably already have deduced, when it comes to the Tax Man, I'm no saint. I give in way too easily, figuring I always can worry about that other shit later.

And it's a good thing I decided to go that route. Letting myself be distracted gave me an afternoon of incredible memories to tuck away, while no amount of warning or explanation Declan could have given me would have made the ensuing events any easier for me to deal with.

TOOTHACHE 12

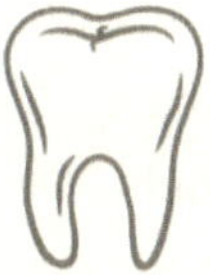

THE LEGAL EAGLE HAS LANDED

NOTHING COULD HAVE PREPARED me properly to learn that the friend Declan invited to help sort our handfast legal issues would be none other than the Black Knight himself, Sheriff Ted Beckett. Tonight, he's not here in Sheriff or Knight mode; in fact, he's dressed casually in slacks and a polo shirt, flashing his dimpled smiles freely and offering friendly handshakes. These gestures do absolutely nothing to diminish my rising apprehension. The last time this man was in my home was to inform me I was part of an insanely crazy Mundane world terrorist plot to steal DNA from Fae baby teeth. Of course, this became the driving factor between my *Mo Shiorghra* and me meeting our destiny. Still, I'm in no hurry to get involved in any more damn spy shet in which the Black Knight is involved.

In hindsight, the spy shet would have been easier to swallow. I look at my Tax Man, my eyes shooting daggers at him while at the same time blasting an all-out mental SOS: *"Declan...why in the hell is the Black Knight here? What in the Universe is going on?"*

"Trust me, Lass. He's only here to help you."

In no way is this an acceptable answer to me. Plus, I'm starting to hate when D.P. says, "trust me, Lass." I want facts, not pacification. I gather up my courage and directly ask the man in charge. "I'm afraid you have me at a disadvantage, Lord Knight. Declan says you're here for my benefit, but I don't have a clue as to what that means."

Beckett gives my Tax Man a knowing look and then explains. "Fitz asked me to represent you in regards to your Handfast Contract. There are no official positions in the Otherworld regarding legal representation, but I've passed the bar here in Massachusetts. I deal with contracts all the time and am very familiar with Other-world law in my capacity as Black Knight, so your *Mo Shiorghra* felt I might be of help to you. Usually, this position would go to your father or elder brother, but Fitz informed me that you don't have the benefit of either, so I'm hoping to fill those shoes."

I look at D.P. with a face that I hope screams "what the hell is happening?" Apparently, that's my beloved's cue to escape the room. "I will leave you both alone to conduct your business," he says.

I quickly interject. "I'd rather you stay, Declan."

He turns back around, and I note the same guilty, sheepish look I've seen before when he's trying to avoid something unpleasant. "I'm afraid I can't stay, Love. This discussion between you and your representation must stay private." Then he turns around and heads upstairs to the loft, leaving me entirely alone with the Black Knight and a million unanswered questions.

There's no way I'm not leaking all kinds of negative thoughts right now. The Black Knight, who also happens to be the Merlin's heir, is, I'm sure, sensing every one of them. "It's all fine, Dr. Parker. Really it is," he says. "This is just a formality, not unlike a Prenup here in the Mundane world. There's nothing to be worried about."

When I hear the word Prenup I think my heart must have stopped, because I feel like it's not pumping enough oxygen to my lungs. When I finally can speak, the words come out as a squeak. "I don't understand. If Declan wanted a Prenup why didn't he just tell me? Why go through all this subterfuge of having you come over to give me the news?" I hope D.P.'s ears are burning upstairs. Shit…I hope his whole head is on fire. This is not the kind of news one just drops on a person they intend to marry in less than a month.

I remind myself to make a conscientious effort to reign in my thoughts. Across from me, my legal representation suddenly looks uncomfortable. "I'm sorry, Dr. Parker, I believe I may have given you the wrong impression. The Handfast Contract is solely for your benefit. According to Otherworld tradition and law, you 'hold all the cards,' so to speak." My face must register utter confusion, so the Black Knight asks, "How much do you actually know about the legal terms of Otherworld handfasting, Doctor?"

I shrug. "The basics, I guess. It's a binding ceremony in which a couple forsakes all others and joins their lives together in a symbolic tying of hands. Not so different from the various matrimony ceremonies here in the Mundane world."

"That's not entirely correct," the Black Knight explains. "Handfasting has a set termination date of one year and a day. During that 366-day period, it is a conventional union, with all rights and boundaries that one would expect. Any children conceived during that time legally take their sire's name, any property purchased or income earned during this time is shared, death benefits stand as a spouse, and so forth. It's all pretty straight forward. After day 366, it becomes the female partner's decision whether she wants to stay in the union or dissolve it. If she makes the decision to stay, the Handfasting Contract is burned and replaced with a Union Statement, and this joining is forever unbreakable. There is no concept of legal divorce in the Otherworld, the philosophy being that when you make a decision after a year of living together you adhere to it permanently."

I nod as he speaks. "I actually knew all of that, but as Declan and I are Fated Mates, each other's *Mo Shiorghras*, this all seems like a moot point."

"There's more," he advises. "If after the 366 days you feel that you've given your best effort to the union, but that it simply hasn't worked out, the whole *Mo Shiorghra* concept not excluded, you are entitled to fair compensation for the loss of your time and energy during those 366 days. The amount is based on your partner's net worth and whether any children have been conceived."

It takes me a moment or two to comprehend fully the entire gist of what the Legal Eagle is saying. I forget that the man sitting across from me is a member of the Royal

House, and in essence, Declan's boss. My tone is slightly disrespectful and more than a little icy. "So…what you're telling me, Lord Knight, is that according to this contract, I would get paid for my year of acting as bed mate, social director, cook, personal assistant and baby maker, correct? Like a fancy hooker of sorts?"

I can tell I've caught the man off guard. He blinks a few times and tries to come up with an answer that won't set me off. "Excuse me for being so blunt, Dr. Parker, but I believe you're overthinking this."

"Well, do you now? Then tell me this, how much is a year of my 'services' worth to Lord *Mac Nuada*?"

Beckett slides the paperwork he was holding across the coffee table toward me, pointing to a spot at the bottom of the page. I have to do a double take. The amount reads 2.4 million dollars. "This has to be some kind of joke, right?" I stutter.

"No joke, Dr. Parker. House *Nuada* has a lot of holdings here and in the Otherworld, and Fitz has his own resources. This is the amount that would be expected in a union of this sort."

I sit back on the sofa, stunned. Never in my wildest dreams did I think any of this would be part of Declan's and my life together. I can't help but feel we are starting out with a big loophole safety net, just in case it's all been a terrible misunderstanding, and it makes me queasy. My mind flashes back to that bitch in the bathroom who mentioned that she'd hoped I would release Fitzie after his obligation was up. Do his family and friends really believe I'm in this for the cash? Is that why his father is so insistent that I get pregnant as soon as possible, so that when the 366 days are up, House *Nuada* hopefully will have their male heir and the lowly tooth fairy will take her money and run?

My parlor has gotten much too hot, and I feel like I'm suffocating. I do the only thing I can think of at the moment. I grab my purse off the table and walk out the front door without another word.

TOOTHACHE 13

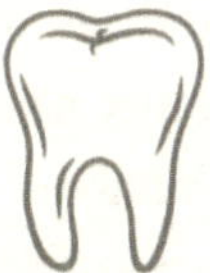

A SHORT RUN

IT TAKES me only two minutes of rummaging through my purse to figure out that my car keys are not inside it and are most likely still sitting in the glass dish next to my front door. There's no way in hell I'm going back in there to retrieve them. Not after my dramatic exit. So, without the use of my automobile, I start walking east down my block. I am not sure where I'm going or why I even left. My head is spinning with too many what ifs and a full chorus of reasons why the Tax Man and I simply won't work out. I keep coming back to what my sister said about walking my own path, yet I hear my mom's voice screaming in my ear, "Run, Rosie, run!" Seeing it all there, laid out in black and white, the actual legal deal, makes it suddenly seem all too real. It's as if the Universe is just having a bit of fun with us, but allowing for an out when we realize the party's over and I'm left with a shattered heart.

Even though it is after 7:00 PM, the temperature is in the mid 80s and the humidity is making my clothes stick to me in a most unflattering way. As I had dressed for evening company and not a five-mile hike, my feet in cute thong sandals with kitten heels begin to hurt before I've even made it three blocks from home. Every few minutes, I turn around to check and see whether my Tax Man has come after me. He apparently has not. WTF.

I'm not going to lie. I'm about to have myself a serious pity party here on the corner of Hawthorne and 5th. The lady trimming her rose bushes and the man watering his lawn are both giving me crazy lady looks as I slip off my sandals and retrace my steps home, tiptoeing barefoot on the hot pavement. It's become very clear in my mind that no one cares that I'm upset or that I've left: neither the Black Knight, which, frankly, doesn't surprise me, nor my beloved Tax Man, which, frankly, does. I imagine the two of them sitting in air-conditioned comfort, in my house, no less, on my comfy sofa, while I am out here sweating my ass off experiencing a major life crisis. I conclude this is wrong and am determined to give them a piece of my mind.

I'm still three houses away when I see Declan sitting on the top step of my front porch. I know damn well he can see me from that vantage point, but he doesn't call out or anything like that. His face is expressionless, and I can't tell whether he's angry, annoyed, or even relieved to see me. I plop down next to him on the stairs. I start off with a terse accusation and the best stink eye I can muster. "You didn't even try to follow me."

He takes my hand and I let him because I am a big, fat,

stupid idiot. "Yar a grown woman, Rosie, not a runaway puppy. I'm not gonna chase ya don the street as if ya wer one. I assumed ya needed some space, so I gave it to ya. I was pretty sure ya would not go far. Not in those shoes anyway."

The puppy comment kinda pisses me off, and I attempt to pull my hand away, but the Tax Man holds tight. "Truth be, Lass…I don't exactly understand why yar upset. Beck explained that ya wer kinda in a huff about the amount of money in the contract. If ya feel it isn't enough or is insultingly low, we can talk, though I have to say it would be considered a vera generous amount among the other Houses."

I am absolutely horrified that he thinks I'm out for more of his money, and now I really do pull my hand away, and thus accidently bang my elbow against the porch post. It hurts like shit, making my eyes water, and causing me to spit the words out with much more venom than I had planned. "How could you ever think that about me? I don't need your 'pay off' money, Declan Fitzpatrick. Not a penny of it! I was doing just fine before you showed up. Sure, maybe I didn't handle my finances like you would have, but I paid my bills, most of them on time. Believe me when I say that I didn't even realize you had that kind of insane money - just another one of the shit-load of things I don't know about you. I believed you when you said you loved me. Hell, all I ever wanted from you was a life together, forever, with all that that means, both the good times and the bad. I'm heart sick over the realization that once our obligatory year is up you expect me to say 'adios' and go merrily my own way, like it wouldn't kill me to leave you." Saying these words out loud hurts me, and now I can't stop the tears from rolling down my cheeks. I swear I've done more crying since I've met this man than I've done in the past five years.

It's my Tax Man's turn to look horrified. He pulls me into his embrace. "Rosie, Love, how could you ever think that's what I would want? Where would you ever get that ridiculous notion? You're my *Mo Shiorghra*...my True Soul Mate...my one and only. I don't know how to make my feelings and intentions any clearer, Lass. I have been waiting far' ya to come into my life far' twenty damn years!" He suddenly goes still, looking at me oddly, and I realize that because I'm in this highly volatile emotional state, I'm probably not shielding any of my thoughts very well, including the memories of the run-in I had with those bitches on Saturday. I can tell that my Fae Tax Man is picking up on some of that. "Feckin' hell, Rosie, who told you this garbage?" he demands. "I want to know who said that to you. They're gonna need to answer ta me far it."

I make a very determined effort to tighten my mental hold and wipe my eyes. "I gave my word that I wouldn't say anything, Declan. Please don't make me break my promise. As long as I hear directly from you that this contract thing doesn't mean you really want your 'freedom' after the 366 days are over, then I'm okay with it, even if it's an insane amount of money to give someone. I probably should have just asked you about it and not run off like I did. My...imagination...just got the best of me. I've been really emotional the last few days, like I'm always ready to fall off a cliff. Too much going on." I don't mention that my mother's voice from the far beyond is telling me to run for the hills.

It's easy to tell that Lord *Mac Nuada* is not completely satisfied with my desire to keep the story about Saturday from him, which is kind of a bad thing since he's supposed to be this hot shit intelligence officer. I work to strengthen my shields and change the subject. "Is the Black Knight still here? I have a few questions about this contract."

"Aye, Love," my *Mo Shiorghra* replies. "I wasn't sure when ya'd come back home, so I suggested to him that maybe we could do this another night after you and I talked it over. He laughingly explained that his Lady was down with a terrible summer cold and that his wee daughter was cranky and teething and that if we didna mind, maybe he'd just hang around awhile and see if he could be of any help when you returned. I get the impression our Knight is in no hurry to return to his domestic life. He's inside watching the ballgame and eatin' yar bag of Doritos."

TOOTHACHE 14

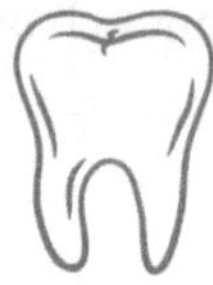

SHOP TILL YA DROP

THE TAX MAN decides we can't put off our trip to *I Idir* and *Dun Siorai* any longer and dictates that we're leaving the morning of June 30th. He's received two more strongly worded raven-grams, both from his father, reminding us that proper arrangements still are pending and that our arrival should be imminent. The excuse bruise on my cheek has faded from vibrant purple to an ugly yellow, gray, and green color that easily is covered by make-up or glamour magic, and my residual, generalized spy-shet soreness has diminished to an almost imperceptible degree. The date for our handfasting is at the three-week mark, and we have planned absolutely nothing, including confirmation of the date itself. We've mostly spent our time together as a lovely, pre-handfasting, bedroom-focused honeymoon, basically skipping over the dating part. Realizing that now I'm going to have to face my future in-laws again puts a real damper on my libido.

To say that I'm not riddled with anxiety over the impending trip would be a lie. To begin with, traveling to *I Idir* has always been difficult for me. It usually takes about an hour for my body to adjust to the different dimensional elements, and the physical effects can range from nausea or dizziness to just a bad headache. These symptoms usually dissipate on their own, unlike the culture shock that lasts the entire time I'm there.

I try to explain this to my Beloved, whom I've discovered has no patience for what he construes as whining. He responds to my worries about traveling to *I Idir* with a long-winded, boring dissertation regarding the physics of crossing over, followed by the trite advice that if I went more often, I'd be able to cross over with more ease. Duh. Like I wasn't already aware of that.

For me, it's not only the physical changes that bother me…it's the whole freakin' atmosphere there. Visiting anywhere in the Otherworld is like attending a totally immersive Renaissance Faire…on steroids. Although the Mundane and Otherworld share similar temperatures, weather patterns, fauna, and time measurement, the resemblances end there. The manner of dress, commerce, social norms, and such are like those of the Mundane World seven hundred years ago. There is no technology and no enlightened thought regarding gender roles, ethnic hierarchies, politics, family structure, or religion. Everyone adheres to a strict set of traditional protocols, and though the Ruling Houses are, in name, part of the governing system, all of the kingdoms of the Otherworld, *I Idir* included, are straight-up monarchies. Throw in all types of magic being used at every turn and I find myself experiencing a mind-bending adventure each time I'm there.

I try not to be overly critical. Although Declan went to school in the Mundane world, I've learned enough about him to know that he has spent every summer and every Otherworld holiday at his ancestral home in *I Idir* and that for all intents and purposes, his heart lies there and not in the Mundane world. But he also is a man of practicality, especially when it concerns business and personal finances. The Handfasting Contract Debacle has taught me that many of the super conglomerates in the Mundane world also have roots in the Otherworld. This is the main reason why it's essential for these powerful families to have offspring who can move comfortably between the two dimensions.

It's a bit more difficult for me. I was raised here in Salem, a computer-using, cell-phone-carrying, free thinking radical in the eyes of my Fae counterparts. My mother crossed over regularly in her tooth fairy position, but she never encouraged me to tag along, nor did we travel dimensionally to celebrate any of the Fae holidays. I knew nothing of the Solstice, Mabon, or Beltane traditions until I studied them on my own as an adult. I now consider that maybe my interest in learning about the spiritual aspects of magic later in life, which was so out of character for me, might have been a push by the Universe to help prepare me for what was coming. If that's the case, I'm grateful I didn't meet my magically gifted *Mo Shiorghra* as a complete ignoramus.

Furthermore, traveling to *Dun Soirai,* the home of

Lord and Lady *Nuada*, requires not only an entirely different mind-set than the one in which I'm most comfortable, it involves an entirely different wardrobe. Besides my Corps mandated tooth fairy uniform, which is hot pink and black and still very much frowned upon in *I Idir*, I have approximately one potentially acceptable dress that truthfully has seen better days. It's the same dress I bought seven years ago when I took my mother's ashes back to *I Idir* as she had wished. Declan has said that we might be in the Otherworld for a few days and suggests that I possibly could wait and buy some things when we arrive there, but that's a no go for me. With my figure, finding something that fits is not always easy, and there is no way in *Dubnos* I'm facing his mother wearing that washed out, plain, cotton dress.

Believe it or not, there are places in the Mundane world that sell traditional, Otherworldly attire, if one knows where to look. In my case, I need to travel to Boston to do so. Naturally, I take my Lady Maiden (similar to a Mundane world Maid of Honor) with me, and we make a day of it, catching the MBTA 11:24 AM out of Salem. It's only a 34-minute ride, and since parking is such a bother in Boston, it's a much better alternative to driving. We stroll the five-block walk from the train station to Festive Boutique, a shop that, upon first appearance, looks like a tiny place but in fact is home to one of the East Coast's largest selection of handmade apparel for interdimensional travel. Mel is talented enough to make her own travel wear, but I am not good with a sewing machine, and I haven't been to this store since I purchased that dress years ago. I cross my fingers that they haven't changed the protocol.

I tell the clerk at the counter I'm looking for cross training apparel, the code for Otherworldly shopping. I can tell she's already reading our auras to verify that we are, in fact, who we say we are, a sad reminder of the need for security the *Sidhe* face in the Mundane world. She smiles at us warmly and points us to the back of the store. "Third dressing room to the right," she explains. "The one with the red curtain."

The store is mostly empty, and no one pays us any mind as we head to the dressing rooms. We find the correct one, and Mel and I step in. A second later, the back wall evaporates and we find ourselves in an expansive showroom surrounded by a circular array of dressing rooms. We immediately are met by an older woman, obviously *Sidhe*, who oddly knows who I am and why I'm there. I instantly recognize the Tax Man's hand in this.

"Dr. Parker…it's so very nice to meet you." She turns to my BFF. "And you must be Miss Sparks. Welcome to Festive Boutique. My name is Jacy Woodly. I'm head stylist, and I'm here to help you find everything you need for your trip to *I Idir.* Don't you worry about a thing, Dr. Parker. I am up to date on all the current Otherworldy colors and styles. We'll have you properly outfitted in no time at all. His Lordship has directed that you should purchase whatever you feel you need. He's supplied me with a list of events you'll be expected to attend between now and your handfasting, so that will help guide us in your selection. I also was told specifically to inform you that you are not to worry in any way about the cost, and if

Miss Sparks finds anything that she fancies, she should purchase it as well."

I feel like I've stepped into Pretty Woman, as a much curvier Vivian Ward. I hear my BFF in my head. *"Holy Shit, Rosie! It's like winning the frickn' lottery. I promise not to go overboard."*

Before this gets out of hand, I feel the need to set everyone straight. "That won't be necessary, Ms. Woodly. I can pay for my own purchases. Billing...his umm... Lordship...isn't necessary."

Ms. Woodly isn't backing down. "I'm afraid that's something you'll need to work out with your intended, Dr. Parker. I am not crazy enough to go against a specific order from Lord *Mac Nuada*. It would be disastrous for my future business, as I'm sure you can understand. Word travels fast in *I Idir*. You wouldn't want to put me in that situation, would you Dr. Parker?"

There's nothing I can say or do standing here in the shop, but it's pretty obvious I've been set up, and I feel my blood rise. It's Mel who does her job as my Lady Maiden by putting things into proper perspective *"Don't let your stupid pride ruin what should be a happy occasion, Rosie. The Universe has given you this gift. You need to learn to accept it gracefully. Being gracious and grateful doesn't mean you're any less the Rosie Parker we all love and respect. Let Declan do this for you. It's obviously important to him."*

Mel is right. I can't keep fighting my *Mo Shiorghra* at every little turn. He knows how anxious I am about this trip, and he's a follower of rules and protocol. The correct attire is always important to him. Maybe this is his way of helping me build my confidence for my meeting with his parents. After all the misunderstanding created by the contract, I don't want another go-around with him. I push my self-doubt away and smile through my teeth. "Well, in that case, Ms. Woodly, shall we begin with a few day dresses?"

TOOTHACHE 15

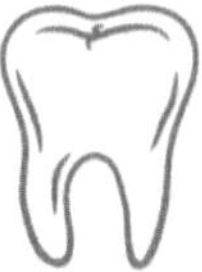

HOMEWARD BOUND

THE DAY of reckoning has arrived. I'm sure I've packed far more clothes than I will need for only three days, but as I'm limited to night time magic use (and even then my skills are pathetic), I don't want to get to the Otherworld and find that I've forgotten something I absolutely need. My shopping trip to Boston has supplied me with enough Otherworldly attire to cover whatever situation might arise, including riding gear. It seems that the members of House *Nuada* are big equestrian people from way back when, and my *Mo Shiorghra* apparently is quite the horse-man. I hold off telling him that not only have I never ridden a horse, I can't even remember ever touching one.

All my belongings and a handful of Declan's are packed in a large wooden trunk Declan bought specifi-cally for this trip. Modern Mundane luggage made with its metal parts and processed plastics have a tendency not to travel well inter-dimensionally, often ending up in some damaged form on the other side, so natural materials like wood and cloth are a better choice for crossing over. It's assumed that we will be expected to go directly to his parents once we arrive, so we have pre-dressed in the proper attire. I have selected a soft green linen overdress with Celtic designs embroidered at the sides and hemline, worn over a plain, ivory, silk chemise. My matching corset is a shade darker green than the overdress and repeats the same designs. Though it took me the better part of an hour to braid my hair in a complicated series of Celtic knotwork, it looks top-notch and is a boost to my confidence.

In the short time the two of us have been together, I've never seen my intended in Otherworldly garb, and for a few seconds, it takes my breath away. It's a given that the Tax Man looks good all the time. He's a hottie. That's all there is to it. But dressed as he is, Declan is obviously in his element. Lord *Mac Nuada* looks like he's just walked off the cover of a best-selling, bodice-ripping, romance novel. He's sporting fitted tan breeches with leather laced boots to the knees, topped by an ivory belted tunic that comes to mid-thigh; the sleeves, cuffs, and neckline are worked in gold and maroon embroidery, the colors for House *Nuada.* This all works to make D.P. Fitzpatrick look very Fae, and not for the first time do I wonder how I never saw it that very first day.

"You look amazing," I babble.

"Thank you, my Love, though I'm sure I donna hold a candle to ya. Yar quite fetchin' in that gown with yar hair all knotted. 'Tis vera beautiful."

I still blush under my Tax Man's compliments. I'd much rather forget this dreaded trip and instead spend the rest of the day playing Prince Charming games, but I know this isn't possible. I switch up my thoughts. "Do you get your clothes made here as well, or mostly in *I Idir?*" I ask.

"Both," he says, 'though I get all my breeches done here in Salem. There is a tailor I know who will put brass-free zippers in for me instead of the usual toggles or ties. It's a Mundane luxury I'm not willin' to give up." He raises his tunic to show me, and this doesn't help one bit to get rid of my naughty, romance-novel thoughts.

"Zipper's quicker," I say, while I bat my eyes in an exaggerated fashion and purse my lips coyly.

The Tax Man laughs, but it doesn't stop him from drawing a large chalk circle around the two of us and the trunk. Because it's daylight, my tooth fairy magic is useless, so Declan will have to move both of us and the luggage as well on his own. He doesn't seem worried about his ability to do this, so I hold his hand, close my eyes, and let the magic move over me.

* * *

Crossing over feels akin to free falling out of an airplane before engaging a parachute. Not that I have ever tried to do such a thing, but from what I've heard the feeling is similar. Both have an experience of sensory overload, but when crossing dimensions, one's mind can watch the body move itself through the veil on a cushion of magic. Many people report hearing a popping noise when they leave the Mundane side, while the whole event usually is over before their brains fully can register that the trip is completed.

When I travel by myself, I'm never too good at mentally steering myself to the exact spot where I want to land. I'm always a few meters off, and more often than not I arrive on my butt. With Lord *Mac Nuada* at the helm, we arrive directly in the courtyard of his ancestral home, and because my *Mo Shiorghra* is holding me up, my dignity remains intact and I land in *I Idir* standing erect. People see us arrive and come to greet us and fetch our trunk. I think more of the staff join the welcoming committee than is necessary simply to get a sneak-peek at his Lordship's Intended. I also get the impression they are fonder of my Tax Man than are either of his parents, but that might just be my own prejudices.

Several of the ladies curtsey, and I'm super uncomfortable with that. I've never been the type to put on airs, and this whole Lady and Lordship thing will be a hard adjustment for me to make. But right now, I don't want to embarrass my *Mo Shiorghra,* who for the past week has tutored me relentlessly on Otherworld protocol, so I nod and smile like I'm supposed to, all the while hanging on to Declan's hand as if he's my anchor in a storm.

I finally look around and absorb the full scope of *Dun Soirai*, Declan's ancestral home. The original fortress supposedly was built on this site by *Nuada Airgeadlamh,* who is said to have been the first King of the *Tuatha De Danann*. He's the guy in Otherworld history with the silver arm. According to what I've gleaned from Declan, the current building was built about four hundred years ago by his great grandfather. It can best be described as a cross between a chateau and a castle. It has the mansion look of a chateau, but its many turrets with bridged walk-ways between them give the impression of a fairytale castle straight from the Brothers Grimm. I've heard it rumored that Jacob and Wilhelm Grimm actually were half-blood *Sidhe* who easily could cross over, thus rendering the stories published in their 1812 fairy tales factual Otherworld occurrences and not highly imaginative stories as most Mundanes believe; but this has never been proven.

A short gentleman with the extremely pointed ears of the elvin people and a noticeably sour looking face exits the home and walks towards us. Declan leans down and whispers, "That's Master Hobart, my Lady *Mathair's* page. I assume he's here to direct us to my parents. He's always been a dour fellow, so don't be surprised if he's a bit unfriendly."

Master Hobart ignores me completely and offers a cursory half bow to my *Mo Shiorghra*. "Welcome home, your Lordship. Lord and Lady *Nuada* await you in the solar parlor. Best not to keep them waiting. Her Ladyship has other plans for the afternoon and does not wish to be detained." Without another word, the page turns on his heels and heads back toward the house.

"I guess it's best we follow him, Lass. Master Hobart will insist on announcing our entrance, and he'll consider it bad form for us to be several steps behind his proclamation." My mental angst probably is leaking out all over, and seeing this my Tax Man stops and kisses me. Here in the magic of the Otherworld, this makes me instantly feel better. He then whispers in my ear, "We will get through this, my Love, I promise ya."

TOOTHACHE 16

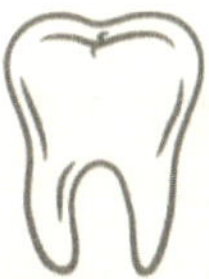

TIME WITH THE FOLKS

DECLAN and I follow Master Hobart through the halls of the house like small dogs on a leash, doing our best to keep up with the diminutive elf's hurried pace. I try not to gawk at my surroundings but find it difficult. The Tax Man's residence looks like a museum of Renaissance design with mathematically precise ratios of height and width, symmetry, proportion, and harmony. There are columns, pediments and arches everywhere I look. It's no wonder that after growing up here D.P. chose to work in the accounting field. This place lives and breathes numerical calculation, which somehow makes me even more uncomfortable than I already was. For the first time I can ever remember, I appreciate the long gown style of the Otherworld. At least its length covers my knocking knees.

When we finally reach the end of a long hall, the Page opens two wooden doors, stops at their entrance, and announces in a voice too loud for his size, "His Lordship,

Declan *Mac Nuada*...and his Intended." Under normal circumstances, I'm not big on calling attention to myself. However, in this case I find the way this Hobart character announces my presence more than a little annoying. I mean...I do have a given name. And a title. One I worked very hard to achieve. At the very least, I'd like to be addressed as Dr. Parker.

The two of us enter what apparently is the solar parlor; a large, round room with a domed, glass ceiling from which the afternoon sunlight pours through like a golden blanket. In a space full of green plants, both of Declan's parents are sitting in low slung chairs near the center of the room. My throat tightens with anxiety. My *Mo Shiorghra* senses this and squeezes my hand in reassurance. He's taught me all the protocols beforehand so I know to drop a short curtsy that matches his half bow from the waist. I look up into the face of Lady *Nuada* and easily recognize absolute disdain in her pinched expression, not only for me, but for her only son as well. For the life of me, I can't understand how a mother cannot love her child on even the most basic of levels.

It's left to Declan's *athair* to acknowledge our presence. "Welcome home, Son, and welcome to you as well, Miss Parker. My heart is joyous over your impending union."

I can't tell whether these are his honest feelings or whether this is just the expected greeting. Everyone in the room is shielding their thoughts so tightly, it feels like we're conversing in a mentally sealed vault. I bite my tongue to keep from correcting his use of Miss in place of Dr.

Declan addresses his mother. "Hello, *Mathair.* You're looking well."

"I find it quite amazing you think so, *Deaglan* (Declan). My disappointment in your poor choices has put far too much stress on my weakened heart," Lady *Nuada* says. I check the strength of my mental shield because I am thinking it's nearly impossible to damage a heart one does not possess.

I notice the beginnings of a smirk on my Tax Man's face, and I guess he's thinking the same thing. He adds, "Then it probably is fortunate, *Mathair,* that Rosalinda and I have chosen a date only three weeks away. It would not be the same if you were not with us on such an auspicious day. Given that your heart is so weak, of course.'

It's becoming very apparent from whom my Tax Man gets his snarky side. When they are standing side by side, I can see so much of his mother's DNA in the angles and planes of his face, in the way he tilts his head when he speaks, and in the raise of his eyebrows when he's being sarcastic. They match mommy's so clearly, which is a sobering thought.

"Well, I do hope you haven't made any firm plans, *Deaglan* (Declan). Your date needs the approval of Her Majesty and the House Mages, as well as that of your parents. I wouldn't engrave your chosen date on any wedding cups yet," Lady *Nuada* says, her eyebrows matching those of her first born.

"Enough of this banter between the two of you," Lord *Nuada* interjects. "Our son and his *Mo Shiorghra* have been here less than an hour, *Siobhan,* and your claws already are out and sharpened. I tire of your constant vitriolage."

Turning to Declan he asks, "Do you have the contract, Son?"

I know he means the contract I signed with the help of the Black Knight. I slide off the leather handbag slung over my shoulder and pull out the document. Remembering protocol, I hand it first to Declan, who then hands it to his *Athair*. Lord *Nuada* quickly scans the document, nodding approval, until he reaches the last page. He reads it twice and then laughs, directing his next question to me. "Let me guess, Lady Rosalinda, this addendum to the Handfasting Contract is your idea?"

I hope I'm not blushing too much. "Aye, your Lordship. It was imperative to me that this be part of my agreement."

"Whatever are you talking about, my Lord?" his wife asks. "There are no traditional addendums to a Handfasting Contract. What more is this tooth fairy trying to steal from us?"

"As a matter of fact, Lady Wife, this addendum states that in the event the union is dissolved following the 366-day period, the stated amount will not go to Lady Rosalinda but instead will go directly to the Mundane charities listed here below, including a grand portion to one that protects the lives of abused and homeless animals."

I take satisfaction in the look of absolute horrific shock on Lady *Nuada*'s face. The words out of her mouth are strangled. "You plan on giving 2.4 million dollars of our money to Mundane livestock? Are you stupid girl, or are you perhaps testing my resolve?"

"The ASCP cares for the rights of all types of animals,

my Ladyship. Surely with your love of horses you can respect my desire to care for them, too?" I say innocently. "Of course, this only comes to pass in the case that I exercise my right to break the union between Declan and me. The fact is, Lady *Nuada,* that I trust in the wisdom of the Universe and love your son very much; we intend to build a happy...and fruitful...life together."

It's pretty obvious I've scored a direct hit. At the word fruitful, she tenses up, and for a second I feel her anxiety over the thought that Declan and I might provide an heir for House *Nuada.* An heir that would be part tooth fairy. She sputters her frustration. "How can this be my Lord? Surely this is not a legal and binding contract! I am quite sure there is a way to negate such a thing."

His Lordship hands his wife the document. "It is all properly signed and sealed, Lady Wife, by the Black Knight himself. If you wish to contest this, I warn you that you will do it on your own with no backing from me. I will not question the legal expertise of Her Majesty's Number One. I do not need the wrath of The Morrigan on my head nor that of my House."

The Dragon Mama is spitting mad now. She glares at me. "Hear me now...you will rue the day you crossed me, tooth fairy." She looks at her husband with an angry scowl. "I wish to be excused, your Lordship. I have duties to attend to and have no more time to spare for this nonsense."

Declan's father waves his hand in approval, and his mother rises from her chair. "Dinner is in the Grand Hall at eight," she snarls. "Your sisters and their families will be present. Do not be late or embarrass me by coming in anything other than proper attire." She turns and gives me a hateful look. "I have had your things sent to the guest chamber in the east wing. Marissa will attend to your requests, as I have no desire to spend an extra minute in your company."

Before she can escape the room, my Lord *Mac Nuada* stops her with a direct order. His voice is several octaves lower than usual, and I can hear the anger in every word. "Rosalinda will be staying with me, *Mathair*. I want her trunk sent to my quarters."

Lady *Nuada* turns so quickly on her heels it appears as if she's doing a complete pirouette. The vitriol in her voice matches that of my *Mo Shiorghra*. "Is it your intent to shame this House in every way possible, Son? Do you have no respect for the protocols and traditions of our people, Lord *Mac Nuada*? Handfasting couples refrain from sharing a bed before the ceremony."

"I am perfectly aware of all Otherworld protocols, *Mathair*," Declan states. "That tradition only refers to the two nights before the ceremony. I know for a fact Tessa and her intended shared a chamber for months before their Handfasting. The entire household could hear their nightly lovemaking. Are the rules different for me then?" he growled at her.

"I am your Lady *Mathair*. You will do as I say."

"No, *Mathair*. I am heir to House *Nuada,* my *Athair's* only son. You will do as I say," my *Mo Shiorghra* counters.

Dragon Mama makes a weird hand signal, and I can feel Declan stiffen beside me. Then she flounces out the door and down the hall, her heels clicking on the tiled floor as she leaves.

Declan's father sighs. "Tis my hope that the Universe has chosen a happier match for you, my son. Your Lady *Mathair* has been my stone to carry for more years than I can count."

"I am grateful for the gift the Universe has bestowed upon me, Lord *Athair*," my Tax Man says. "It is true that good things come to those who wait."

"That is fully the truth, *Mac Nuada*," his *Athair* says. "This match has been a very long time in the making. It is finally good to see it come to fruition. Now, Son, I would like some time alone with your intended. The Lady Rosalinda and I have important things to discuss between us."

TOOTHACHE 17

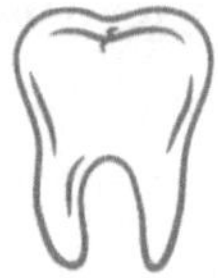

FULL CIRCLE

IT IS clear that Declan doesn't want to leave me alone with his father. He lingers a few seconds too long and is prompted again. "The Lady will be fine," Lord *Nuada* scolds. "Go and leave us."

I don't want to make things any worse, so I give my head a slight nod and pull my hand from his. My Tax Man gets up to leave and I can read the apprehension in his face. "I will wait for you just beyond these doors, my Love," D.P. states. His back is ram rod straight, his jaw is set, and it's evident that he's mightily pissed and more than a little embarrassed to be ordered around by his father as if he were a mere child. I can't say I blame him. Lord and Lady *Nuada* are hard to swallow.

If I had any common sense, I should be more concerned than I am. Currently, I'm more angry than anything else. Rudeness just rubs me the wrong way, and rudeness combined with a hoity-toity, privileged attitude really gets me going. As a visitor to their home, House *Nuada* hasn't provided me with much of the hospitality protocol the Fae are always going on about. Truthfully, the people of the Otherworld claim to be so much more civilized than their Mundane counterparts, but if you take magic out of the mix, we're all cut from the same cloth.

With Declan gone, Lord *Nuada* just sits and stares at me. Like for a really long time. It makes me very uncomfortable. Finally, I can't bear it any longer and say, "Is there something you want to say to me, Your Lordship?"

Even then, he doesn't jump immediately into conversation. Another three or four minutes go by until he sighs and says, "Where to start?" He leans forward in his chair and puts both hands on his knees, and I realize he's uncomfortable as well. These *Tuatha De Danann* types never lack confidence. It's as if they have giant egos wired into their DNA, so his attitude is extremely curious. Sighing again he adds, "You look a bit like her you know."

I don't have a freakin' clue as to what he's talking about, and I wonder if Lord *Nuada* doesn't suffer from the same illness as my father because he's making zero sense. "I'm sorry, your Lordship. I'm very confused."

He smiles, but it's a sad smile, not a happy one, and my anxiety level rises a notch or two. "You look a little like your mother, Rosalinda," he says.

I can't imagine in what world the reigning head of one of the Otherworld's most powerful Ruling Houses would know my mother. Mom did her civic duty for *I Idir* as a tooth fairy. She came and went as she had to in regards to her job, but as far as I knew, she had no personal connections or any family left in the Otherworld. Her life with us in the Mundane World was everything to her. What in the Universe could my tiny, tooth fairy mother possibly have done to cause someone like Lord *Nuada* to take notice of her? "You knew my mother, Sir?" I ask, the words sticking on my tongue.

"Aye. I knew *Aine* very well," Declan's father replies.

Aine is my Mom's Fae name, the one she was given at birth. When she began to live permanently in the Mundane World, she changed it to the more common Anna. My dad always called her "his little Annie". I search the Lord's face for better understanding, and then, the light bulb goes on in my head. I suddenly understand how Declan's father knew my mother, and the realization cuts me sharper than the best knife in my kitchen. "You're him, aren't you? You were the Fae boy who broke my mother's heart."

Lord Callum Fitzpatrick *Nuada's* face crumples in response, and I have my answer. I'm not sure how to feel. My Mom's whole attitude towards her life was negatively shaped by the relationship with the man across from me. A man who just happens to be the father of my own *Mo Shiorghra*. I literally can feel the weight of the Universe shift for me in that very second. I know he is waiting for me to say something in response. If his damn Lordship is looking for some kind of absolution, he won't get it from me. "You broke her heart, you know. She never was the same. My mother spent her entire life teaching me to hate Fae males. That's all on you."

"Aye," he admits. "And still the Universe has found a way to bring you and my son together. Fate will not be denied."

His spiritual cliche annoys me. "Is that supposed to make me feel better? The idea that my mother had to suffer a broken heart so I could win House *Nuada's* prize?"

That statement makes him angry, and he rises from his chair. For a second, fear replaces annoyance. I've seen glimpses of Declan's magical strength. I can only imagine what his father's power is like. "You make judgements without knowing the whole story, Rosalinda. Your mother wasn't the only one who suffered."

I don't speak. Instead, I make an overblown, sarcastic act of looking around at the opulence in the room. I realize I am pushing my luck, but I can't seem to stop myself. My poor mother's honor is at stake. His Lordship understands exactly what I mean.

He waves an arm around the room. "Do you think all of this makes up for a lifetime of living with my son's mother? You have experienced only a taste of her negative energy. Imagine a lifetime of it."

He does have a point. I don't understand how he puts up with the Dragon Mama's nonsense. "Then why are you with her?" I boldly ask. "Are you saying the Universe made an error? That Lady *Nuada* wasn't your *Mo Shiorghra?*"

Declan's father begins to pace the room. "No. *Siobhan* Donnely is definitely my fated mate. The ink work on her left hip is proof of that, and despite her sour disposition, there has always been enough lustful pull to create six children. The Lady *Nuada* claims our son is cursed. She is wrong. It is I who bears the malediction." My face must register my confusion. He continues. "If you can listen with an open mind and heart, I will tell you exactly how we have gotten to this point."

I nod my head. I have a burning need to understand how I came to be sitting in the ancestral home of House *Nuada* three weeks before I am to marry its heir. "I will do my best to keep judgements from forming."

His Lordship takes this as a signal to begin his story, though he continues to pace the room. "Declan has explained The Ritual that all House heirs must undergo?"

"Yes," I reply. "I think it is barbaric and cruel, but that's a discussion for another time."

"The welfare of many must outweigh the suffering of one," he states. "A return to The Dark Times would be disastrous. Though, if I had begun The Ritual when I was supposed to, perhaps three lives would not have been so miserable."

"You didn't undergo your Ritual when you were fourteen?" I ask. "I was led to believe it was a mandatory thing."

"It is," his Lordship says. "But it was the time of the Fomorian Wars across Asgard and Avalon. My father was sent to fight and was gone from *I Idir* much longer than anyone had anticipated. I was two months shy of my 16th birthday when my father finally returned, and by that time I was already very much in love with your mother."

I can see where this is heading, and part of me wants to cover my ears in deference to my mom's privacy. The other part has a deep seeded need to know. "But you obviously were already the named heir. How would you and my mother have even met? You certainly didn't move in the same circles."

"My *Mathair* tried to keep me at home," Lord *Nuada* explains, "but with four other children and a missing husband, she didn't always know where I was. I would sneak out dressed as a common laborer. Your mother and I met in the market square. In the beginning, *Aine* didn't know who I was, and by the time I revealed that knowledge, we were strongly bonded." He turns and looks at me with such intensity that I involuntarily shrink back into the sofa cushions. "You must understand…I was so sure *Aine* was my *Mo Shiorghra*," Declan's father continues. "I even gave her a promise ring in the belief that once The Ritual was completed, this would be proven true and that we could start our life together. We met in secret after the inkwork and magic was complete. The next morning, we both expected that she'd be marked with House *Nuada's* wolf sigil as you have been." Lord *Nuada* paused, looking deeply distressed. "She was not. We tried a few more times but…"

I put up my hand to stop him. I know exactly how that ink work gets transferred and there is no way in hell I want to see pictures in my head of the Tax Man's father and my mom doing the nasty. My mouth is dry, and my heart is beating twice as fast as it should. You would think at this point I'd have enough sense to keep my mouth shut. But no. Nosey Rosie has to ask more questions. "What I don't understand is how you still had feelings for my mom after The Ritual? Declan told me he had no emotional connection with anyone until me. That's the whole purpose of the damn thing. How can you say that you did?"

Lord *Nuada* shrugs. "I cannot explain it," he says. "Perhaps because I was already so in love with *Aine* before The Ritual, I didn't fully commit to the magic? I truly don't know. I surely do not have the answers, Rosalinda. This has haunted me my entire life. When it was clear that she wasn't my *Mo Shiorghra*, your mother gave me back my ring and disappeared into the Mundane World. I never saw her again. A few years later, I met Declan's mother. I was attracted to *Siobhan* instantly, more in lust than love. No one was more surprised than I when she woke the following morning with my inkwork etched on her body. She is, of course, a beautiful woman, and as you can see, my son gets his handsome appearance from his mother, but unlike my son, her beauty does not reach to her spirit, and I surely have never felt about *Siobhan* the way I felt about *Aine*. I have been puzzled for years over why the Universe presented me with a woman I couldn't have. Then, when I met you for the first time that morning, it became clear. The Universe had come full circle. *Aine's* daughter and my son."

My hands are shaking when Lord Callum Fitzpatrick *Nuada* takes my right one. He gently places a large gold and ruby ring in my palm and curls my fingers around it. "This belongs to you now, Rosalinda Parker. It's meant to close the circle."

TOOTHACHE 18

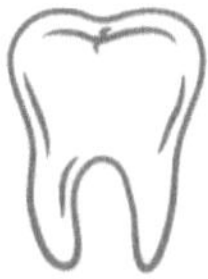

JUST GET THAT OUT OF YOUR HEAD

AFTER PLACING the ring in my hand, Lord *Nuada* wanders toward the floor to ceiling windows and stares out. I assume I'm being dismissed, but before I can ask permission to leave as protocol dictates, Declan's father says, "You should go now, Lady Rosalinda. My son paces like a caged beast in the corridor. I feel his angst and anger radiating through the closed door. I shall see you both at dinner."

I stand and curtsy, though I am not sure he can see me unless it's in the window glass's reflection. My hands are shaking, and I feel a tiny bit faint. I'm not afraid to admit it. Lord Callum Fitzpatrick *Nuada's* revelation has rocked my world, a world that already was hanging on the brink of uncertainty even before his shocking confession. I open the heavy wooden door and exit the solar parlor. My face must register my feelings because when Declan sees me, his own complexion turns several shades lighter and he practically sprints toward me.

"Lass, what's wrong? What did my *Athair* say to you that has ya looking as if ya've seen your dead ancestors? If he has hurt ya in any way, I need to know! I will handle it immediately!"

Little does my Tax Man know how on the mark he is when he mentions dead ancestors! I don't want to have this conversation here in this public space; I can see Master Hobart off to the side, and I have no doubt he's eavesdropping, hoping to carry a choice nugget or two back to his Mistress. "I'm fine, Declan. He didn't do or say anything bad. I'm just a bit…surprised at what he told me." The ring is still in the palm of my hand, and it might as well be a thirty-pound lead brick because the thought of it weighs heavily on me. "Is there somewhere we can go that's more private so that we can speak freely?" I mentally add, *"Not here, Sweetie. That Hobart creep is listening. I'm sure it's by your mother's orders."*

The Tax Man shakes his head in understanding. He links his arm in mine, and we walk down the corridor. As we pass him, Master Hobart gives a slight bow and smiles, but his expression is not friendly. I shudder involuntarily. I've been in *I Idir* less than two hours, and I already am counting the minutes until we can go home.

* * *

Lord *Mac Nuada's* quarters are on the complete opposite side of the building and consist of an entire wing housing a very large bedroom, an Otherworld style bathroom, a study, a parlor of sorts, and a huge outside balcony over-looking the rolling green hills south of *I Idir*. We both remain quiet during the walk over, but the very second we are behind closed doors Declan pulls me into an embrace. "I was afraid he would upset ya. Lord *Nuada* can be quite intimidating." His hold on me is uncomfortably tight. "Please, Love, what has you so rattled?" he asks. "Your face is as white as new snow, and I can see your hands are shaking."

I pull out of my *Mo Shiorghra's* embrace, and I can tell that this upsets him further. I don't mean to cause him more anxiety, but right this minute I'm overwhelmed and need some space to think. I move across the room and perch myself on an upholstered bench at the foot of the bed, patting the spot next to me. "Come sit, and I'll tell you what happened."

Once he's settled, I remind him about my mother's prejudices regarding Fae men and my own attempt to avoid them at all costs. I know we talked about this before, but if he doesn't understand how much this life event changed my mom, and, ultimately, me, then it will be difficult for him to understand my ambivalence regarding his father's revelation. His face registers some impatience because I think he thinks I'm simply repeating myself, but I can't be rushed. Not with something of this magnitude. As my story progresses, I see the reality of what I'm saying in his alarmed expression. Before I even get to the ring part, he gets up and begins pacing the room, running his hand through his hair over and over again.

"I knew havin' ya in ma life was too good to be true,

Rosie. It is exactly as my *Mathair* says...I am cursed. No good shall ever come of my life. Ya must walk away for yar own good. I canna let ya attach yourself to such misery. I'll get ya back home as soon as possible and then ya never have to see me again. I'll leave Salem and move ta Boston and..."

It's my turn to jump up from the bench. I stop my Tax Man from moving by physically stepping in front of him and grabbing his shoulders. "Declan...stop! Please! This has nothing to do with you! This happened long before either of us were born. Besides...you don't get to decide when I should or shouldn't walk away from you! My feelings for you are mine alone. And you should know that I would never simply walk away from you just because things might get difficult. I get that it's super weird...how it all worked out, but it just convinces me more than ever that us being together has been in the works for a long time. We are meant to be with each other! Can't you see that? Our parents sacrificed their own happiness for ours!" I open my hand and show him the ring his father gave my mother. "Your dad said that by giving me this he's closed the circle. Things are the way they are meant to be. And we can show the Universe our gratitude by getting through these little...bumps in the road...in the most positive and peaceful way possible," I say, hugging him. Then I add, "But whatever you do, don't think about your father and my mother...uhmm...getting like all down and dirty...'cause it's real hard to get that thought out of your head once it's in there."

Lord *Mac Nuada* makes a face that resembles someone sucking on a sour lemon. "Feckin' hell, Lass. Why did ya have to bring that up? I donna think I can ever get that vision out of ma head now. It's gonna be stuck there forever. How will I be able to look at my *Athair* at dinner this evening without…"

I smile. "You need to replace it with other thoughts," I suggest.

He shakes his head and gives an exaggerated shudder. "It will take some mighty strong thoughts to sweep out something that…unsettling, my Love."

"And I know just the thing, Tax Man," I say, taking him by the arm and pulling him toward that giant football field of a bed. "We've got at least two hours until dinner. Just enough time for sweeping away bad thoughts and replacing them with happier ones."

TOOTHACHE 19

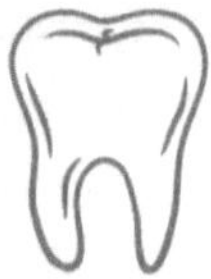

SHOWER POWER

THE SHADOWS GROWING LONGER in the west end of the room indicate that it's later than we think. The Fae generally don't rely on clocks, and of course we've left our cell phones in the Mundane World because they are absolutely useless here. I stretch and run the tips of my fingers over Declan's naked back, the scattering of freckles over his shoulders making me grin as they always do. "I think it's late," I say. "Would you happen to know what time it actually is?"

I receive only a muffled grunt in response. The Tax Man lets me scratch his back for another five minutes before rolling over and answering me. "It's a few minutes before seven, and dinner is at eight. We probably will have to shower together to save time."

"Well, boo hoo," I joke. "It's a dirty job, but somebody's got to do it."

Declan laughs and turns to me, propping himself up

on his right elbow. "It is a blessing that you can remain so upbeat through all of this. I hope you are strong enough to keep your positivity through dinner. I will not lie. It is likely to be an ordeal."

I do the complete opposite and fib like hell. "I'll be fine, Sweetie. I'm still sad and upset knowing that our parents had to spend so much of their lives being miserable. It's so freakin' unfair. Those thoughts will be both my shield and my sword tonight."

The Tax Man gives me a second grunt to match his previous one. "That's exactly what I'm afraid of Lass. I would advise a different tactical approach...something more akin to 'head down, helmet on.' My Lady *Mathair* takes no prisoners."

"It must suck to live in her head," I reply. Then, another equally disturbing thought pops into my own. "Declan, do you think your mother knows about my mother? You know...about who she was...and who I am?"

"That, my Love," he responds, "is the million-dollar question. My *Mathair* always has made it her business to know everyone else's. I would lay odds that indeed she is aware of it all, which in my mind, makes her doubly dangerous."

Lord *Mac Nuada* and I take a quickie shower in more ways than one and then hurriedly dress for dinner. My hair is still wet, so with precious little time remaining, I settle for plaiting my hair into a long single braid that I wrap around my head in a style very common to *I Idir*. It's not as glamorous as the one with which I arrived, but it will have to do for this evening since my time and energy were spent on far more pleasant activities that I do not regret.

Per Declan's request, I am wearing a long shantung gown in a deep burgundy color with a built-in, lace up corset over an Irish lace chemise. It is a very simple but classic style, and the fabric for both the gown and the blouse under it is top notch. It makes me feel not only attractive but also comfortable, as it has no buttons or bindings poking or biting me in weird places.

Just as we are about to walk out the door, my *Mo Shiorghra* hands me a velvet box. "What's this?" I ask.

"Just a little 'Welcome to the Hell I call Home' gift, Love. I saw it and thought it would look perfect with the gown you're wearing tonight."

I open the box and blink a few times before I can begin to speak. Declan's little gift is a choker-style necklace set entirely with golden colored citrines and deep red garnets. Each individual stone is at least four carats in weight, and each one catches the light with pure sparkle and fire. Not counting my handfast ring, or the precious little porcelain dollhouse bouquet, this is my first gift from the Tax Man, and it's a doozy. "It's exquisite, Darling! Beyond beautiful. I love it. Thank you so much." I lean in to kiss him, but he beats me to it, bending me over like we're characters in some old movie.

"I am so very happy you like it, my Lady. Shall I help you put it on?" Lord *Mac Nuada* offers. I nod, and he takes the necklace from the box and fastens it around my neck. "Take a look," he says.

I step in front of a large cheval mirror and catch my reflection. Can the woman looking back at me possibly be Dr. Rosie Parker, D.D.S.? Gone from sight is the frumpy tooth fairy dentist from Salem, Massachusetts, and in her place stands a curvy, glowing, *Sidhe* princess. Truth be told, I don't know whether to laugh or to cry.

TOOTHACHE 20

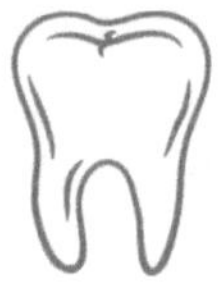

DINNER IS SERVED

THE DINING HALL, like everything else in the mansion, is as far away from Declan's quarters as it possibly could be. I think about the resulting consequences since we now basically need to run to get to dinner on time. As an outside observer, I feel that his parents, though mostly his mother, have gone to extreme measures to keep my *Mo Shiorghra* out of the family loop. I can't help but wonder whether her immense dislike of her own son goes well beyond the tragedy of what happened to Declan's twin at his birth. The look My Intended gives me is meant to remind me to stop thinking about 'shet' like that and to pull up a mental shield and hold it tightly in place for the rest of the evening.

Lord *Mac Nuada* makes for a splendid sight this evening. Fact: Lord *Mac Nuada* would look hot in a black, plastic, garbage bag. Tonight, he looks every bit the Fae prince to my princess. At home in Salem, his mostly leather attire would look more appropriate in some kink bondage club, rather than a family dinner. However, here in *I Idir*, it just screams wealth. And wowza. Lots and lots of wowza. As I might have mentioned before, the people in the Otherworld tend to dress like characters from the fantasy novel, *Game of Thrones*. And yes, George R. R. Martin is Fae…on his mother's side.

We arrive in the dining room at five minutes to eight. Of course, everyone already is seated, and there are only three empty chairs, one between his father and a teenage girl whom I guess to be his sister Meghan, one between his mother and a tall, extremely thin woman with a horsey face (Okay, I know. That was uncalled for. I'm just gearing up for battle.), and one at the far end of the table.

No one says a word. Instead, they all just stare at us. Declan leads me to the chair next to his father, pulling it out for me before taking his seat next to his mother. There are thirteen of us at a table set for fourteen; Declan's parents, his youngest sister, his four older sisters and their spouses, and then the two of us. I can't imagine who the last place setting is for, and I get this wild thought that I hope it isn't for the spirit of Declan's dead sibling, Dylan. I should have been so lucky as to have had it only be as weird and creepy as that. Instead, the truth is monumentally more disturbing and a hundred times more disrespectful.

The dining room doors open again, and Master Hobart leads a beautiful *Sidhe* woman into the room; she's a willowy, strawberry blonde with big, round, blue-green eyes and a face that launched a thousand Disney princesses. Still, it's hard to focus on her face when she's wearing a very sheer, see-through, lace gown sprinkled with some type of iridescent sequins. She's a walking, sparkling, Playboy centerfold.

I get a very bad feeling made worse when I look across the table at my Tax Man. He's wearing his very best Declan Poker face, but his slightly pointed ears have gone a definite shade of pink. Next to him, Dragon Mama is grinning like the Cheshire Cat. Lady *Nuada* claps her hands. "Lady Brigid, I'm so happy you were able to join us for Declan's homecoming dinner. I'm always so pleased to play host to a member of House *Taranis*." Declan's mother waves a hand across the table toward her youngest daughter. "Meghan, switch places with Lady Brigid and go sit at the empty spot at the other end of the table. I wish a chance for our gracious Lady and your brother to talk about old times."

Meghan makes a face, but one look at her mother and she quickly rises and obeys her Dragon Mama's orders. Master Hobart holds out the chair for the newest arrival who smiles sweetly before placing herself next to me. Even though it's after sundown and I now possess a little bit of magic, I don't need any amount of enchantment to understand that this woman and my *Mo Shiorghra* share some history, and by the ripples of amusement and excitement buzzing around the table, theirs was not a casual relationship. She turns to me and says, "Congratulations on your upcoming handfasting, Lady Rosalinda. You must be beyond happy to win such a top prize. Declan has been *I Idir's* most eligible bachelor for years. And to think he had to travel all the way to the Mundane

World to find his one and only. It boggles the mind, does it not?"

Before I can formulate an equally ambiguous and snarky response, my Tax Man jumps in. In all honesty, this sort of pisses me off because I'm quite able to speak for myself. "It is I who have won the prize, Brigid," Lord *Mac Nuada* replies. "My Lady is as brave as she is beautiful. Surely you've heard about her work with the Black Knight's intelligence unit. It is due to my Lady's courage and resolve that Her Majesty no longer need worry about the Mundane Chechens. This is in addition to her extremely successful dental practice and her generous charity work." Declan sounds like he's selling a used car, and I'm embarrassed.

Blondie doesn't seem the least bit impressed. In fact, she just looks bored. Lord *Nuada* adds to my discomfort by piping in, "Yes, Lady Rosalinda, why don't you regale us with the tale of how you helped take down those *salch bastairds* (dirty bastards)."

I have no desire to talk about what was the most awful experience of my life, and, truthfully, I was never a gung-ho participant in any of that nonsense to begin with. Strangely enough, it is Dragon Mama who gets me off the hook. "With all pardon, my Lord," Declan's mother says, "I do not think such a topic is good fodder for the dinner table. Perhaps Lady Brigid should instead tell the tale of how she and our Declan were caught skinny dipping in the sacred waters of Lake *Dagada* by Her Majesty. 'Tis a very humorous narrative that I don't think Lady Rosalinda has yet heard."

Yes, Lady Brigid. Do tell us how you and my future

husband got naked together in the sacred waters. What future bride wouldn't want to hear such a fun little ditty? Before Blondie can get too far into her story, we are interrupted by the serving of the first course. When my plate is put before me, my stomach drops. I am by no means a picky eater; in fact, I would probably describe myself as a foodie. Still, there are a few things I've tried but just can't stomach; one of those things sits in front of me. Living all my life on the east coast, I have tried on several occasions to eat raw oysters. For me, it's not so much the taste, but rather the texture. I can't get past their slimy feel in my mouth; I can't get past their slimy feel in my mouth, unable to get them down my throat no matter how much tabasco sauce I drench them with. All around me, people are picking up these snot-like delicacies and slurping them right down. I just sit and stare.

Against my better judgment, I wore the ruby ring that once belonged to my mother to dinner tonight. Something in my heart told me it needed to be on my finger for this most important of evenings. I convinced myself that my mom was speaking to me from the great beyond. Apparently, staying clear of Fae men was not the only bad advice my mother gave me.

Until now, my hands were resting quietly in my lap. When I pick up my seafood fork to poke at the disgusting oysters, the ruby flashes left and right. Both Lord and Lady *Nuada* notice it instantly, and if I had any doubts as to whether *Siobhan* Donnely Fitzpatrick knows about my late mother and her husband, they are erased immediately by a look from the Dragon Mama that would melt rubber.

TOOTHACHE 21

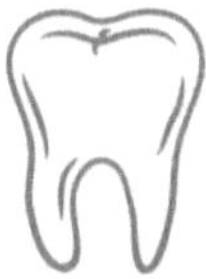

STOOP AND SALAD

ALL AROUND THE TABLE, the majority of dinner guests listen to Lady Brigid tell her silly story about the time she and Lord *Mac Nuada* left their clothes on the shore to enjoy the sacred waters and how some prankster carried them away. Blah, blah, blah. I don't really want to hear that particular damn tale. *I get it, Blondie. You and my Tax Man were lovers. Big deal. Hate to tell you, Sweetheart, but you were just one of many.* In addition to ignoring this dumb-ass narrative, I'm also working hard to keep Dragon Mama out of my head. I can feel her trying to force communicate with me, but for once in my life I manage to keep my shield intact. If this were occurring during the day, I doubt I would have enough magical power to keep her out; this certainly may be a problem going forward.

Thankfully, a member of the staff collects my still-full plate of oysters, replacing it with a summer salad that looks relatively Mundane in nature. I am happy to see something safe to eat, as frankly, despite the stress of the day, I'm starving. My *Mo Shiorghra* looks across the table at me, and I sense that he's concerned over my state of mind. I smile at him in an attempt to signal that I'm doing okay. I would love nothing more than to pop into his head and chat a bit, but I don't dare loosen my mental shield to do so. Instead, I pick up my salad fork and dig into the course in front of me.

The salad is surprisingly tasty, the dressing a slightly sweet citrus blend with a peppery after bite. I've never spent enough time in the Otherworld to have had a wide sampling of its fruits and vegetables, but like everything else in this dimension, they are similar in taste and appearance to those in the Mundane World. Blondie has finished her skinny-dipping story and, at Declan's mother's insistence, has launched into another boring tale about how she and my future husband won some hunting competition. I am sure I am frustrating Lady *Nuada* to no end with my obvious indifference to her attempts to make me jealous. After the whole Declan-used-a-whole-box-of-condoms-boinking-half-the-female-population-of-Salem discovery, I either had to accept his past or end the relationship. I chose to move on from the knowledge. I believe him when he says his prior relationships were empty encounters, and I can no better control what went on in his life before we met than he can control mine. Nor is it his fault that my history is dull and his is not. I eat my salad and listen to Dragon Mama go on and on about Lady Brigid's excellent horsemanship skills. I don't give a rat's ass that Blondie can sit a horse better than me. The Playboy

Princess can go ride her damn horses while I just keep riding the Tax Man.

I am busy secretly congratulating myself for remaining cool, calm, and collected when I see something move on my plate. The same damn plate I've been eating from for the last five minutes. I use my fork to move aside a lettuce leaf and thus reveal a couple of dark antennae and leg-type things with pinchers at the ends. Everyone, including My Intended, is listening politely to his Lordship explain a change in the rules for the next year's Beltane games while they eat their second courses. No one notices that Dr. Rosie Parker has a frickin', big ass, monster bug on her salad plate. I consider my options and decide to move it off said plate with my fork and discreetly crush its yucky bug body in my napkin. Things don't go as planned.

The bug takes offense at being poked with my fork and decides to leap from my plate and onto the center of the table. Lady Brigid sees it first and reacts by simultaneously squealing and erratically jumping up from her chair. Her arms flail out, knocking over her glass of wine and thus covering her dress in a big red stain and making the see-through material even more revealing. Everyone then follows suit, and I'm a little confused by their seemingly over-blown reaction to a damn bug.

Before I can make sense of it, my *Mo Shiorghra* has moved to the other side of the table and is pulling me away from it by my waist. Then, he gingerly swipes Lady Brigid's empty wine glass and slams it over the still living insect. The bug goes crazy inside its glass prison, banging itself against the sides and releasing a strange, yellow liquid that smokes and sizzles under the glass. I watch in absolute shock as the venom dissolves the table cloth beneath it.

"Well done, my son," his Lordship mutters. "You were able to trap it before it released its poison. I cannot imagine how it made its way into the house."

"Nor onto my Lady's plate," Lord *Mac Nuada* growls. I don't need to lower my shield to feel Declan's rage or obvious fear regarding what might have happened. My *Mo Shiorghra* is making his feelings very known.

"What is it?" I ask, not caring whether I sound ignorant.

"It is called a *Diabhal Bas,* or 'Death Devil.' They are extremely volatile and very dangerous," Declan's father explains. "Their venom is highly toxic and causes all types of symptoms, up to and including paralysis and death. They are not easy to catch and require extreme precautions in handling. It is beyond my scope of understanding to explain how one arrived at my table."

"A very good question, my Lord *Athair*. One I have every intention of answering," Declan mumbles between clenched teeth.

The Parkers didn't raise any dumb daughters. I know exactly what my Tax Man is implying. The deadly insect was put on my salad plate with the intent to harm me. Perhaps even the more sinister intent to do away with Lord *Mac Nuada's* tooth fairy once and for all. I look around the table and wonder who would want me dead. Guess what? This is a larger group than those who wouldn't.

TOOTHACHE 22

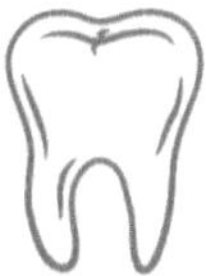

PLAY IT AGAIN FITZI

IT IS Lady *Nuada* who prevents chaos from erupting. An entire team of staff members quickly arrive in the dining room to whisk away evidence of the crime. And yes. I do think that what just happened was a crime. At least an attempted one. I can tell my Tax Man thinks so as well by the way he is glued to my side, squeezing my hand so hard that it hurts. The table is reset with new linens, china, crystal, and flatware, and then the Dragon Mama invites all guests to sit again to enjoy the rest of the meal. When we reassemble Declan takes the seat next to me, glaring at his *Mathair* and daring her to object. This relegates Lady Brigid to the other side of the table between Lady *Nuada* and the horse-faced girl. Her new position at the table does not make her happy; it's not often one gets to see a Disney Princess pout and scowl.

The waitstaff again fills everyone's glasses with wine,

and the main entree is served. It is some type of fish baked in a pastry shell. All around the table, people tuck into their food. It's inconceivable to me how everyone is able simply to ignore what just happened. Someone put a poisonous bug in my salad. It was more than just bad hospitality. This was an attempt on my life. Or, at the very least, a strong attempt to intimidate me.

I pick up my fork, but I can't make myself eat. My mind keeps seeing those wiggling legs peeking out from under my lettuce leaf. My Intended has his hand on my thigh, as though I will disappear if he lets go. He actually is eating his fish, confident, I suppose, that no one wants to see the heir of House *Nuada* dead; his inconvenient tooth fairy *Mo Shiorghra* is another story.

Next to me, Lord *Nuada* tries to make polite conversation. "So, Lady Rosalinda, you are a Mundane dentist? Is this a job you enjoy?"

"It is, your Lordship. I'm specifically a pediatric dentist. All my patients are children," I explain.

"Then I take that to mean you are fond of children," says Declan's father. "Are you hoping for *wee bairns* of your own?"

Next to me, the Tax Man stiffens, and his fingers grip my thigh a little tighter. I personally don't find his Lordship's questions rude. He is, after all, my future father-in-law, and I am a virtual stranger to him. It's an honest question for someone about to marry his son. "I would love to be a mother, Your Lordship." The rule against tempting the Universe then occurs to me, so I add quickly, "It is my hope that the Universe's path for me includes this opportunity."

It is the answer Lord *Nuada* wants to hear. He pats my hand. "Excellent, my dear. I hold the same hope." Before pulling his hand away, Declan's father looks at me with a tilt of his head and an odd expression. "The Universe always finds a way," he says.

His comment doesn't necessitate a response, so I just smile and nod, and his Lordship abruptly turns his attention to Lady Brigid.

* * *

People barely have finished their last bite of dessert, a fruit tart sort of thing, when Declan stands up and announces that he and I are retiring for the evening. It's not like I want to spend any additional time there than is absolutely necessary, but even I understand that proper protocol requires we not be the first ones to leave.

Lady *Nuada* waves her hand at her son. "Nonsense, Declan. I have made arrangements for you and Lady Brigid to entertain us with a few songs in the music room. Your sisters have been waiting for months to hear you play again. Surely you can spare another hour for your family?"

Lord *Mac Nuada* hesitates, and his *Athair* interjects. "Humor your Lady *Mathair*, son."

My Tax Man looks at me and asks, "What is your desire, my Lady?"

I'm not thrilled he's passing the buck and putting this decision on me; since our mental shields are up, I don't know whether I'm supposed to agree with his decision to return to our room or to comply with his mother's request to stay and show off his musical prowess. Truthfully, I've not yet had an opportunity to see Declan's musical side, so I am a bit curious. On the other hand, I've also grown tired of pretending not to mind Lady Brigid's blatant flirtations towards my *Mo Shiorghra*.

I decide that conforming to proper protocol probably is the best scenario. "I would love to hear you play, Declan…if you feel up to it." *There you go, Tax Man. Right back at ya.*

Mr. Poker Face doesn't give any indication of his feelings; instead, he gives a slight bow of his head towards his mother. "If my Lady Love wishes to hear me play, then play I shall. But I warn in advance, I am only committing to a piece or two."

Triumph registers on Dragon Mama's face. "Excellent." She waves everyone from their chairs. "We will gather in the music room." It's clear that Lady *Nuada* feels as if she's won this round. Honestly, I can't tell whether I've made the right choice for either Declan or his mother, but at this point I'll just have to live with the fall-out.

The music room is adjacent to the dining room, so we don't have far to walk. Declan leads me to a chair to the left and slightly behind the piano and takes a seat at the keyboard. Lady Brigid attempts to sit next to him on the bench but receives such a frosty look from Lord *Mac Nuada* that she quickly moves to a spot in front of the piano. Disney Princess isn't holding an instrument, so I guess she intends to sing while my *Mo Shiorghra* accompanies her. Suddenly, I'm very self-conscious. Lady Brigid is front and center with My Intended, while I sit by myself behind them. I wish now that we'd just returned to Declan's quarters like he'd wanted.

My Tax Man and his old flame speak quietly in Gaelic, and then he helps her find the correct key. Settling in, Lord *Mac Nuada* begins to play. One doesn't need to be a musical virtuoso to realize that Declan is an accomplished pianist. His fingers move across the keyboard with expert skill and grace. Then, the Lady Brigid begins to sing along with the piano in a voice that is hauntingly beautiful. There's no doubt that the woman is exceptionally talented, and together they are a delight to listen to. I think of all the times during the past few weeks that the Tax Man has heard me sing along with my Alexa, and I'm filled with embarrassment. It must have been sheer torture to listen to me when he himself is so musically gifted.

They finish the piece, and everyone claps wildly, myself included. Lord *Mac Nuada* looks at me and smiles shyly. Then, he speaks to Lady Brigid in Gaelic. Whatever he says to her, she doesn't like it much. She turns and takes a seat on a small divan across the room. Then, Declan says to the crowd, "I would like to play this next one especially for my Lady." He pats the bench next to him.

Everyone watches me as I slide next to My Intended. My *Mo Shiorghra* turns to me and says, "This is a very old song, My Love…about a young man who squanders his youth on women while he's away from home, and when he finally finds the one he wants, his family stands between them."

I can't help but gasp. This is a very gutsy move on his part, his choice of song mirroring his own life. I don't need to look up to feel the entire room's eyes boring into us. He leans over and kisses me and then begins both to sing and play.

TOOTHACHE 23

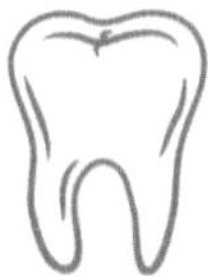

CUT TO THE CHASE

DECLAN FINISHES his song to a handful of polite applause. The energy in the room is tense and isn't helped when My Intended abruptly stands up, wishes everyone a pleasant evening, grabs my hand, and walks out. Our trip to his ancestral home in *I Idir* has shown me a very stubborn, prickly side of Lord *Mac Nuada* that I've had only glimpses of during the past few weeks. I'm not sure how to react. However, I am sure about one thing: The *Nuada* clan is one of the most dysfunctional families I've ever met and such a far cry from my own that I wonder what the hell I've gotten myself into.

Because I know we can't talk unless we're alone together, I lower my shield and say, *"Your song was beautiful, Declan. You have such a lovely voice. I didn't understand all of the words but it sounded hauntingly moving."*

My *Mo Shiorghra* responds minimally. *"I am vera glad you enjoyed it, Love."*

Clearly, my *Mo Shiorghra* is not in the mood to chat. Part of me is more than a tad annoyed. It isn't like someone tried to get his Jr. Lordship to eat a poisonous bug. It was Rosie Parker who was the nearly deceased party here. If anyone should be pissy, it should be me. I hold these thoughts until we finally reach Declan's quarters.

I swear it's nearly a mile walk to get there, and when we step inside, I'm surprised to see Declan's cousin, Duncan, waiting. He stands and gives a half bow as protocol dictates. "A pleasant evening to ya, my Lord and Lady. How fares the happy couple this fine evening?"

"Dispense with yar kowtowin' bullshit, Dunc. I am in no mood," Declan says.

I'm shocked at the Tax Man's rudeness toward his cousin, but Duncan laughs it off. "Dinner surely has gotten your *giumar* (mood) in a knot, *col ceathrar* (cousin). Is yar dearest *Mathair* twistin' yar *magairli* (balls) again?"

His Jr. Lordship grabs his crotch in a rude gesture, and the two men laugh, acting like a couple of twelve-year-old boys. Frankly, I enjoy seeing my Tax Man happy, and I'm now grateful for Duncan's arrival and his ability to lighten the mood. Ever since the night he was shot protecting me, necessitating my removal of a brass bullet from his groin, his relationship with my *Mo Shiorghra* has changed for the better. Coming so close to losing his cousin forced the Tax Man to reevaluate what is truly important. Thus, I wasn't surprised in the least when Declan asked the *gancanagh* to be his *Finne* (witness/best man) for our handfasting. However, Lord *Mac Nuada's* choice undoubtedly will not make his social-climbing parents happy.

"Did ya procure the things I asked ya ta bring?" the Tax Man queries his cousin.

Duncan picks up a wicker basket that is sitting at his feet. "Aye. Everything you requested. I had to do some heavy name-droppin' to get the shopkeeper to bother with me this late in the evening."

Declan takes the basket from Duncan and hands it to me. "This is for you, My Love. I guessed that you would be hungry after that debacle. I hope there's enough har' ta please ya."

I get all gooey inside over such a thoughtful gesture, and my Tax Man is right; I am rather peckish since all I've eaten since leaving the Mundane World is the few lettuce leaves I managed to ingest before things started moving on my plate. I kiss the Tax Man on the lips. "Thank you so much, Sweetie. And you too, Duncan. I actually could use a little snack." I take the basket to a small table and chair combination and unload its contents. There are warm, fresh-out-of-the-oven rolls, a hunk of some kind of white cheese, a few slices of thinly sliced meat resembling Mundane ham, a few apple look-alikes, and half a dozen cookies that smell heavenly. It's a fine late-night snack. "Would you gentlemen care to share? There is more than enough here."

Both men politely decline, being heavily engaged in a rather intense conversation in Gaelic. I find it rather rude, because they're both aware that I don't speak the language, and I have heard my name mentioned several times during their conversation. I interrupt. "Excuse me, gentlemen, but do either of you happen to have a knife I can use? I'd like to slice this cheese into smaller pieces."

Both men react at the same time. Declan pulls a vicious looking knife with a three-inch blade from inside his boot and a smaller one with a deadly point from the sleeve of his tunic. Duncan offers some kind of serrated dagger from inside his vest. I stare at the weapons for several seconds before I take the smaller of my *Mo Shiorghra*'s blades. "That's a lot of 'slicing' hardware for *I Idir*, gentlemen."

Duncan looks at his cousin but doesn't say anything. I look directly at my Tax Man. "Care to explain, Sweetie?"

Lord *Mac Nuada* makes a face. "You know what it is we do, Lass. You canna expect us ta go around unarmed." Then he wanders over to the table and helps himself to one of the cookies. "I am glad to see that Master Cobos has not altered the recipe for his *fianain* (cookies). They are by far the best in *I Idir*."

"Aye," Duncan agrees. "They surely are always worth a visit home."

It's one hundred percent clear to me that the subject of the knives officially has been changed and that I'm not going to get any further explanation as to why it is necessary for them to carry a selection of weapons in a place that's supposed to be devoid of danger. After what happened at dinner, I wonder just how safe I really am here in the Otherworld. And, in that moment, I vow to myself that as soon as we return home from our honeymoon, I will hire a private tutor to teach me to understand and speak Otherworld Gaelic.

TOOTHACHE 24

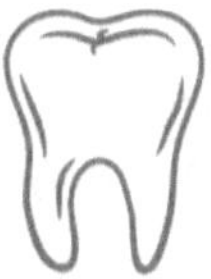

SADDLE UP, WE RIDE AT DAWN

WHOMEVER SAID things always look better in the morning must have had the opportunity to wake up next to my Tax Man. (And hell…I already know there are a lot of those ladies out there with that particular experience.) He always looks so relaxed and peaceful when he's sleeping (if you don't count the lumberjack-snoring I'm slowly getting used to), but when he finally arises, he's perfectly wide awake: clear eyed, smiling, and almost always amorous. This morning, his Jr. Lordship also has several more inches of hair and an oh-so-perfect layer of ginger stubble, thanks to a strange, fast-growing hair anomaly that occurs in the Otherworld. It's such a beautiful, fiery color I can't help but want to run my fingers over and through it.

Me? I don't wake up pretty. Not in the Mundane World and definitely not here in Fae LaLa Land either. I know for a fact that I have eye boogers crusting all around my eyes, that my hair is a tangled mess, all knotted up in the back where it rubs the pillow, and whereas the ginger stubble on Declan's face looks sexy hot, its counterpart on my legs…not so much. Plus, I'm pretty sure after nearly twenty-four hours in the Otherworld, my unmentionable locations further south as well as under my arms resemble Sasquatch after a long, hard winter. I congratulate myself for having the foresight to bring along my trusty Lady Schick on this short trip. There will be plenty of much needed deforestation this morning, so showering by myself is a must.

Declan told me last night that he intends to return to the Mundane World later today, having had as much of his parents' hospitality as he can stand. I remember our early days when I thought it was rather odd that a 35-year-old man literally had to hide from his parents. Now I understand fully and wonder whether there's some kind of in-law ward we can place on my house to prevent them from showing up uninvited. I'm disappointed that things have gone as badly as they have. Ever the optimist, I had held out a small amount of hope that maybe…just maybe…Dragon Mama and I might have been able to call a truce, but after her attempts last night not only to humiliate me but to harm me as well, all bets are off. And yes, there's no doubt in my mind that Lady *Nuada* was behind the bug incident.

Nevertheless, before we can return home, we must meet with the House Mages to set our handfast date formally. Plus, my *Mo Shiorghra* insists that I meet his childhood *Buime* (wet nurse/nanny) before our big day. Though I really want to meet the woman that was so kind and loving to my Tax Man growing up, I just wish he'd change his mind about us riding horses in order to get to her. I tried explaining to him as politely as I could that I've never been on a horse in my whole life and that the size of the ones in the Otherworld frighten me more than a little bit. His response? "I'll find ya the gentlest nag in the stables, Lass. We'll have my Lady comfortably sittin' a harse in no time. I taught Meghan to ride when she was a wee *tachran* (child/kid). I will do the same for you." He then changed the subject, which I've come to realize is Declan's way of not compromising. At some point, I'm going to have to address this issue.

But it won't be today. There's already enough tension between the two of us and his folks. I don't want to start a big relationship brouhaha at this particular moment, so instead I set my mind on conquering my horse dilemma. Everyone rides horses in the Otherworld; there are no automobiles, scooters, or even bicycles. One either transports magically or they ride. Horsemanship is a cultural thing with the Fae, especially within the upper echelons of Otherworld social circles. It's the only time a female wears pants in the Otherworld, as women do not ride side-saddle here. Ladies are expected to ride just as well as their male counterparts. Young girls are put on ponies at a very early age right alongside their brothers, wearing the same style of riding gear, though the feminine versions are often more embellished for aesthetic reasons.

I take care of my deforestation needs during my solitary shower and then dress in my riding attire after I'm dry. I miss being able to hide my less than perfect figure in a gown this morning. Normally, lady's clothing in the Otherworld is very forgiving to curvy women...not so much the riding gear. The breeches and tunic are designed to fit close to the body to keep from getting tangled in the saddle or stirrups. With my considerable curves I look like an over-blown, chunky, Dolly Parton. Most Fae females generally are willowy and not overly endowed on top. I get my big boobs from my dad's human side of the family, a throwback to his good, solid stock of our Eastern European gene pool. My Tax Man claims he adores my curves, especially my Double D's, but dressed as I am these body-hugging clothes makes me feel extraordinarily self-conscious. It actually doesn't help much when Lord *Mac Nuada* takes one look at me and whistles.

"I will need to put blinders not only on the harses, Lass, but on Duncan and Mac as well, otherwise they might fall off their saddles tryin' to get a better look at ya," my *Mo Shiorghra* teases.

"Stop, Sweetie. I'm already terribly self-conscious. I've seen smaller udders on the cows in your pasture," I mumble as I walk past him.

He grabs my arm and pulls me onto his lap. "I dunno why ya always say things like that, Love. Yar a vera beautiful and desirable woman. If we were not so pressed for time, I'd show ya just how much."

When my Tax Man talks like this, I wish I could sit back and simply bask in the feeling it begets. No one in my entire life ever has made me feel as special or desired as Declan Fitzpatrick does. It makes my *Mo Shiorghra's* sometimes stubborn, prickly ways a minor issue. Suddenly, it registers in my lust-saturated head that we won't be riding alone. "Mac O'Kelly is here in *I Idir?*" I question.

"Aye. Home to take care of some business," Lord *Mac Nuada* says with a bland expression.

"And he and Duncan are coming with us to see your *Buime?*" I ask. I find this especially odd as D.P. never mentioned they would be coming along until now. "Why?" I question, knowing full well I won't get a straight answer.

"Duncan knows my *Buime* vera well and has not seen her in some time. Mac is ridin' along in hopes of purchasing some herbal remedies for his indigestion. Mundane food does not always agree with leprechauns," Declan explains.

I'm pretty sure he's lying to me to hide the real reasons they're joining us now. I haven't yet learned all of the Tax Man's tells, but I detect a slight raise in the pitch of his voice when I think he's being less than honest with me. I know that if I push him, he'll immediately change the subject, so I decide to keep quiet and stay on my toes.

Lord *Mac Nuada's Buime* has invited us for an Otherworld version of brunch, so I don't have to worry about being poisoned during breakfast. We munch on left-over cookies from last night as we walk to the stables. I carry the little gift I made for My Intended's nanny; it's a china tea cup on its side, with a miniature woodland scene in its bowl portion. There are miniscule flowers, a small fawn drinking from a little pond, and a willow-style tree hanging over him. I consider it one of the best tiny scenes

I've ever created, and I hope Declan's *Buime* finds it special.

The horses are saddled and ready to go when we arrive at the stable. Duncan and Mac are there waiting for us. D.P. introduces me to my ride for the day, a gray dappled mare that my Tax Man says has the sweetest disposition in all of *I Idir*. "Her name is *Milsean*. It means Sweetie," he says. "Though I hope ya won't be thinkin' of this ole harse when you call me by the same name," he jokes. He puts his hands around my waist and begins to lift me up into the saddle when he abruptly stops and puts me back down. Looking closely at the horse's underbelly, he lets loose a nice, long, venom-filled, stream of obscenities.

His Jr. Lordship calls Duncan and Mac over and points out that the girth, the under strap that keeps the horse's saddle in place, has been cut nearly through. I may not know much about horsemanship, but logic tells me that should the strap come apart, as I'm sure it would after a few minutes of active riding, there would be nothing to keep the saddle, along with its rider, from falling off the horse.

The three men alternate between swearing and discussing, none of it in English, and then Duncan is sent off to find the stable hand who dressed the horses this morning. He returns with a middle-aged man whose face is white as a ghost. Beaulark, the Stable Master, insists on his mother's soul that when he dressed *Milsean*, he checked every part of the equipment and that the girth was perfect in every way.

Duncan points out the obvious. "The girth is not worn,

my Lord. It looks to have been cut almost all the way through with something sharp." My Beloved's cousin hasn't said anything I didn't already know. It's become very clear to me that a second attempt on my life has been made.

TOOTHACHE 25

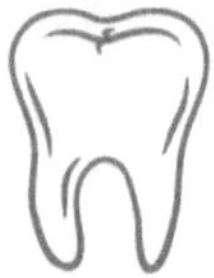

GIDDY UP LASS

I WOULD HAVE THOUGHT that after a second attempt on my life, my Tax Man would have had us safely locked in his quarters until the House Mages arrive so we could finish our business in *I Idir* and return the hell home. But no! That is not how his Jr. Lordship rolls. Instead, D.P. dresses my horse himself, using a saddle he's personally examined thoroughly. I consider hypothesizing how much nicer it might be if we went to the music room, where, instead of bopping around on horses, My Intended could perform a few more delightfully romantic songs for me; but I decide against saying this. Lord *Mac Nuada* is more than a bit cranky, muttering under his breath and slamming things around. Even Duncan and Mac give him a wide berth.

When he's satisfied that old Sweetie is saddled properly, he calls me over and lifts me gently onto the horse's back. "Just hang on to the reins with one hand, Love, and the pommel with the other," Declan says. Then, he calls over a young stable boy and hands him a long lead attached to my horse, dictating what sounds like a series of directly worded instructions. The boy nods vigorously and practically is bouncing on the balls of his feet with excitement. The men sit their own horses, and we begin moving forward; my *Mo Shiorghra* is in front of me, Duncan and Mac are behind me, and the stable boy is on the ground to my left. I feel like some kind of weird Fae sandwich wedged between them as I am. It's awkward and cuts me off from communicating verbally with my Tax Man.

After a mile of traveling this way through beautiful, rolling countryside, I start to feel guilty about the stableboy having to walk all the way to Declan's *Buime's* house. I've gathered that it's nearly six miles over rather hilly terrain. I try to apologize to the boy, whose name is Cotts, but he stops me. "Oh no, my Lady! You need not worry. His Lordship has bestowed upon me a great honor entrusting me with his *Mo Shiorghra's* mare. The other lads will be envious of my good fortune." He grins, revealing teeth in desperate need of dental care and hygiene. "Besides," Cotts adds, " 'Tis a much better job than the one Master Beaulark assigned me this morning."

His exuberance is contagious and makes me smile. "And what job was that, Cotts?"

"I was to shovel *cac* (shit) out of the stalls, my Lady. This be a much better way to spend my morning," the boy pure-heartedly admits.

I'm glad to know that leading my horse around for six miles on foot is preferable to shoveling shit and happy simply to be conversing with anyone. Declan has communicated with me only a few times since we've left the *Nuada* manor, mainly to check on my welfare. Other than that, he is shielding his thoughts tightly, which I'm guessing are focused on the two attempts to harm me. I understand that now is neither the time nor the place to discuss things of this nature, but my feelings are still a bit hurt that he's shut me out completely. I'm worried that such behavior from a future spouse might not be the most conducive for building a long and healthy relationship.

By the time we are three quarters of the way to *Buime's* home, my ass is sore and my inner thighs are chafed from constant friction. Plus, I have to pee. I have had to pee for nearly twenty minutes, but I don't relish making everyone wait while I go into the woods to relieve myself. Instead, I hold it despite my discomfort. I also pray that Declan's nanny has a regular, run-of-the-mill outhouse, not the Otherworld's version of modern indoor plumbing, which requires magic to operate that I don't possess during daylight hours. Somehow, it takes the glamor out of a budding relationship when one has to ask their lover to flush the toilet for them.

Suddenly, I hear the sound of additional horses and people shouting. Declan brings our little group to a halt, and I see a retinue of other riders ahead of us. I do a double-take at the sight of the banner that is being carried at the front of the procession: a black Raven on a green and gold background. It's the standard for Her Majesty, Queen Maeve, also known as The Morrigan.

"Is that who I think it is?" I ask with my mouth hanging open.

TOOTHACHE 26

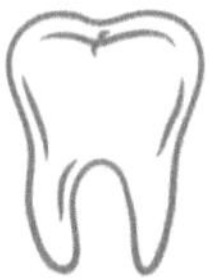

ROSIE GETS A BOON

I HAVE NEVER SEEN Her Majesty up close. In fact, before today, I can count on three fingers the number of times I've seen The Morrigan at all. She is a legend, not only for the people of *I Idir* where she reigns, but of the entire Otherworld. If it were not for The Morrigan, the Fae population still would be fighting amongst themselves while the Mundane World continued scheming to wrest control of this other dimension. She is absolutely brilliant, stunningly beautiful, extremely gifted in both white and dark magic, and entirely ruthless. Or so I am told. Everything I know about Her Majesty, Queen Maeve, has come from reading books and word of mouth, with not a shred of first-hand experience.

Declan dismounts from his horse and lifts me off mine. The men behind us do the same. Declan speaks directly to my mind. *"Do you remember the proper protocol for meeting Her Majesty, Love?"*

"I do. Full curtsy, though it's a little more awkward while I'm wearing pants, look her straight in the eye when she is speaking...and only speak if she specifically asks me to do so. Got it!" I answer with more confidence than I feel.

"Good Garl," My Intended says. *"The Morrigan is not nearly as...overwhelming as most people believe, but she is a stickler for proper Otherworld protocol. She has always been most pleasant towards me."*

Shielding my thoughts, I think to myself that even though Her Majesty is pleasant to the heir of one of her Ruling Houses does not mean she will bestow the same camaraderie and easy-going goodwill on a tooth fairy. As I previously may have mentioned, my kind of Fae background doesn't lend itself to hob-nobbing with Royalty.

We wait until Her Majesty's retinue gets closer to where we have stopped. I recognize the man next to the Queen as her consort, The Lord Warrior, *Cu Chulainn*, who himself is equally intimidating. At Declan's signal we curtsy and bow as gender dictates. I instantly note that what I've heard about Her Majesty's beauty is one hundred percent true. I note that she is gorgeous, even dressed in her leather riding gear, then I double check that my mental shield is in place, as I'm pretty sure I'm not supposed to be thinking about any of her many attributes.

"A Good Morrow to you Lord *Mac Nuada*," the Queen says. "Where do you head this fine day?"

I am thrilled Her Majesty has chosen to speak in English. This is a conversation I finally can understand. Inside my head I hear a small peal of laughter, which sounds like tinkling bells, and I realize that Her Majesty is privy to my thoughts even with my shields in place. I try to think of non-descript things that won't offend, like how pretty the green and gold ribbons braided in Her Majesty's horse's mane appear and that the hills to my left look like they are covered in a blanket of violets.

"We journey to *Na Glaschnoic* to visit my old *Buime*, Your Majesty," Declan says. "I am anxious for her finally to meet my long-awaited *Mo Shiorghra*."

"Yes. I had heard that the Universe finally has blessed you with your Forever Mate, young Lord. My Black Knight has relayed that it is a fine match, indeed," The Morrigan states.

Declan bows again. "Thank you for your gracious words, Your Highness. I feel too blessed entirely. My Lady is everything I could have hoped for and surely worth the long wait to find her."

I feel my face get hot over the words of my *Mo Shiorghra*. It is one thing to say these things to me and another entirely to say them in front of one of the most powerful beings in the Fae Otherworld.

"That is good news, indeed, Lord *Mac Nuada*. I have great hope that your offspring will bring renewed blood and spirit to your ancestral line," says Her Majesty. Then she adds, "Step forward, Lady Rosalinda."

My knees are knocking, and I have no long gown to hide them. At my obvious nervousness, the Lord Warrior smiles at me and winks. I stand in front of The Morrigan's horse and try not to look like the top-heavy bowling pin that I am. This causes me once again to hear the sound of laughter in my head. It is very disconcerting but not unpleasant.

"I have been told of your brave service to the people of *I Idir*, Lady Rosalinda… of how you were instrumental, at great personal risk to yourself, in capturing the vermin who thought to steal from my people's blood lines. It also was quite intriguing to hear the tale of how you saved the life of Master Duncan using a fish boning knife from your scullery. My Lord Warrior especially enjoyed that narrative," Her Majesty related.

"Aye," chimed the Lord Warrior. "'Tis always a wonderful thing to hear of a Lass handlin' a blade so adeptly. Master Duncan assured me that he's missing none of his manly parts." Then he winked at me again.

I feel I'm about to combust into a firestorm of embarrassment while I attempt another clumsy curtsy in tight pants. "Thank you very much, Your Majesty. I am very happy to have been of service to the Crown and to the people of *I Idir.*" Seriously, I just want to disappear. This is a lot of praise for something I did because I felt I had no other choice. A silky voice in my head says, *"The Universe will have its way, Lady Tooth Fairy. Do not think that your path has not brought you to exactly where you are meant to be. What you have been given is a gift beyond compare. As you are aware, some Fated Mates are not as lucky as you and your Beloved in finding a true connection."*

Now I just want to cry. That's all I do lately. My emotions are vibrating at supersonic levels, and The Morrigan's words resonate deeply within me. This thought makes Her Majesty chuckle again, but her next words are spoken out loud. "Allow me the pleasure of presenting you with a boon, Lady Rosalinda. I know you have no family here in *I Idir* to help with the necessities of your handfast. I would like to gift you your gown for the occasion. Anything that pleases your sense of fashion."

I am so shocked at this offer that I'm lost for words, but I quickly remember the proper protocol. In the Mundane World, humans always seem to have trouble accepting gifts. Their first response is to tell the giver that their gift is unnecessary or downplay the giver's generosity by saying, "oh…you shouldn't have…." This attitude is considered a huge faux pas in the Fae Other-world, especially towards one's Queen. Therefore, I offer another dumb curtsy and say, "I am most humbled and extremely grateful for your generous offer, Your Majesty. You have brought much joy to my soul."

The Queen gathers up her reigns. "Excellent! Then it is settled. I shall send my dressmaker to you for further discussion. I look forward to seeing what you have chosen, Lady Rosalinda, on the day of your handfasting. Now, we must depart. I have been away from *Crann Bethadh* longer than expected. Travel well, good people."

The Morrigan and her group move past us, riding south toward the center of *I Idir*. I stand glued to my spot, hearing my Tax Man talking next to me but not registering his words. Wait. Did The Morrigan just say she'd be attending our handfasting? Well, knock me down with a feather! This tooth fairy is beyond stunned.

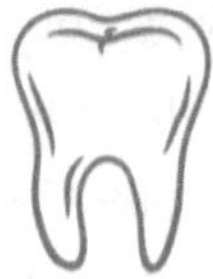

THE NANNY KNOWS

I RIDE the last three miles to Declan's *Buime's* house in quiet shock and reflection. My *Mo Shiorghra* was nonplussed regarding the news; he confided that he'd rather expected Her Majesty to attend our handfast but that her offer of the gown was a pleasant surprise he had not foreseen. He added that he hoped I would enjoy the dressmaking experience but that he was sure I would look just as lovely wearing my "harse's feedbag." Sometimes my Tax Man says the most beautiful things. Other times…not so much.

No one is happier to see the little stone cottage appear over the last hill than me. My bladder is about ready to burst, and my butt cheeks are sore in places I didn't know could hurt. We are met at the property gate by a teenage boy who greets My Intended warmly and takes our horses for food and water. As D.P. helps me off my horse, I whisper to him: "I really need to use the lady's room, Sweetie. Do you know where it is?"

He smiles as he puts me down, teasing, "I don' think my *Buime* has one for the exclusive use of 'Ladies,' but if yar willing to be less picky there is a 'necessary station' right over there." His Jr. Lordship points to a small wooden building about 50 yards away. "We will wait for you here and go in to greet my *Buime* together."

Two things are fact: The Fae have silly names for some of the same things we have in the Mundane World, and Declan is not as funny as he thinks he is. I try not to run across the field to the outhouse, and because I know everyone is waiting on me, I also try not to dawdle once I get inside. The temperatures in *I Idir* during July are similar to those back home, and the humidity makes my riding breeches stick to me and hard to pull down. I manage to peel them off, then groan when I see a spigot for water but no handles to turn on the flow, not unusual here in the Otherworld where magic rules. No sooner is this thought formulated in my head than a basin of water, a bar of scented soap, a small towel, and a hand mirror appear before my eyes, courtesy, I am sure, of my Tax Man. Okay. So he may not be much of a comedian, but he's the most thoughtful, caring man I have ever met.

Taking a few extra minutes, I freshen up the best I can and tuck back into place a few stray hairs that have come loose from my braids. Suddenly, my stomach is doing flip flops over meeting Declan's nanny. I know how fond he is of her and of the important role she played in his child-hood. I worry she might find me lacking as a mate to the man she has cared for and loved since infancy. Doubts swirl in my mind that the gift I made for her is silly and unsuitable. I hear my *Mo Shiorghra* in my head. *"Tis all well, my Love. She will love you because I do. Now hurry, she is waiting at the door."*

I tug my tunic into place, take a last look in the hand mirror, and head back outside. Lord *Mac Nuada* takes my hand, and we walk toward the cottage. "My *Buime* doesn't speak English, Love. So I will have to interpret for the two of you," he confesses.

Well, isn't that just dandy. This is another example of Declan's less than stellar relationship habits. He often waits until the very last minute to drop important news on me under the guise of not wanting me to worry. What he doesn't understand is that I need worrying time to process my emotions and get my head in order. He's now just added a huge stumbling block to this meeting that I wish I could have prepared for in advance; perhaps I could have memorized a phrase or two in Otherworld Gaelic to use during our initial introduction. Now I'm going in cold and definitely annoyed. There's no doubt my Tax Man is perfectly aware of my feelings, but he continues smiling, walking with me hand in hand as if nothing is amiss. Grrrrr.

I work to clear my head of all negative *I want to sock you in the arm* thoughts before we reach his nanny. I desperately want this woman to like me. When we reach her, Declan drops my hand and takes both of his nanny's hands in his and kisses her on both cheeks. She does the same to him, then runs her hands over his face, feeling its shape. It's then I notice a milky white coating over her eyes and realize she suffers from some type of Fae cataracts and has very limited eyesight. It dawns on me that my miniature tea cup scene with its tiny field and fauna is the silliest gift I could have brought and wonder why in the hell the Tax Man didn't say something ahead of time. I tell myself not to cry as tears begin to burn in the corners of my eyes, and I vow that when I get home, I will seek out Dr. Brannigan to ask whether there are any Fae-safe, anti-anxiety meds I can take for what I believe to be PTSD from my Chechen adventure.

His Jr. Lordship pulls me closer and introduces me to his nanny, at least that's what I think he's saying in Otherworld Gaelic. The only words I understand are my name and *Mo Shiorghra.* His *Buime,* whose name is Magda, Declan informs me, takes my hands in hers for a moment and then runs hers over my face like she did with D.P.'s. "Magda can feel things and then see them clearly in her mind, despite the physical condition of her eyes, Love," the Tax Man explains.

Magda's hand lingers on my cheek while suddenly tears begin running down her own. She speaks words in rapid Gaelic, and I look to my Tax Man to translate them. His wistful expression demonstrates that he's very emotional about what she is saying, and his words come out choked. "My *Buime* says that you are perfect in every way...beautiful inside and out...and that her soul is joyful that the Universe has allowed her to live long enough to see this match fulfilled." Between the look on my *Mo Shiorghra's* face and the elderly woman's words, I can't keep my own floodgates closed. Pretty soon, Magda and I are hugging and rocking each other and crying ugly tears while the three men stand by, awkwardly grinning like three happy, confused clowns in a Ladies Only Circus.

TOOTHACHE 28

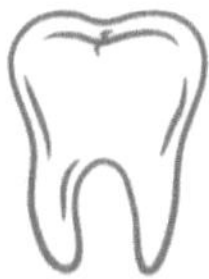

ROSIE NEEDS A NAP

BRUNCH WITH MAGDA is a lovely affair. We enjoy cold sliced meats, assorted cheeses, fresh baked rolls, a variety of fresh fruits, and a delicious selection of tiny pastries, all washed down with a peach-like sparkling wine and herbal tea. This is the first meal during my current trip to *I Idir* in which it is a pleasure for me to partake, made especially so because I have no need to worry that someone is trying to poison me. The mood is relaxed and welcoming, and I see a positive change in both my *Mo Shiorghra's* body language and his aura.

As we eat, Magda tells humorous stories about my Tax Man's childhood that Duncan gleefully translates and Declan heartily denies. There is so much goodwill and community here that I don't want the visit to end, but a long ride awaits us back to the *Nuada* estate, and our appointment with the House Mages hovers over us like a wet, wool blanket. I give my little teacup token to D.P.'s

Buime, who runs her fingers carefully over each part of it and professes it to be the loveliest thing she has ever owned. My Intended proudly tells his nanny that I created it and many things like it with my own hands without the use of magic, and the old woman genuinely seems moved by my craftwork. She then presents me with a gift as well: it's a large bundle wrapped in thin paper that I unwrap with admittedly shaking hands.

Beneath the paper is the most beautifully needle-pointed bed coverlet I've ever seen. It's a handfast blanket with a beautiful scene of a couple that strangely enough resembles Declan and me resting in some woods. There also are a scattering of pink and white French knots that Magda says she only recently added. She explains these were done to incorporate my House colors. Oddly out of character, I feel none of the shame I usually do when my tooth fairy status is mentioned. Declan's *Buime* says that she began stitching this coverlet the very day after her *gille gaolach's* (beloved boy's) Ritual in preparation for the day that the Universe would reveal his *Mo Shiorghra.* She teasingly adds that she is grateful the Universe took its time because she always has been a mite slow with a needle. I am overwhelmed by her gift and filled with deep gratitude for the love she showered on the unhappy boy my Tax Man once was. I barely think these thoughts before tears again begin for us both, prompting Mac O'Kelly to joke that if we don't leave soon the whole valley will be flooded with women's tears.

We say our long goodbyes, with Magda promising to attend the handfast. The blanket is secured carefully to Duncan's horse, and Declan helps me onto mine. I honestly can't say that I'm looking forward to the three-hour ride back to *Dun Siorai*; it's been an emotional morning, and I am physically and mentally drained. This, perhaps, is why forty minutes into the trip I feel overwhelmingly fatigued and lightheaded…so much so that I begin leaning in my saddle so far left that I nearly fall off the horse. The stableboy notices immediately and calls for our little party to halt.

The Tax Man is at my side immediately with the intent to call for Robyn Brannigan. I convince him that such an extreme response is not necessary. "Don't bother Robyn, Declan. It's nothing serious; it's just a very warm day, I'm not used to horseback riding, and I had an extra glass of Magda's fruit wine. Nothing more. I don't need medical attention." He eyes me suspiciously, not believing my nonchalant explanation. "Seriously, Sweetie, if I were really ill, I'd tell you. I am a medical professional, remember?"

The Tax Man mulls this over, then nods. "Perhaps you are right, Love. It has been a trying visit. The sooner we return to the Mundane World, the better it will be for you. In the meantime, you will ride with me for the remainder of the trip. 'Tis not safe to ride in a compromised condition, inexperienced as you are."

His Jr. Lordship informs the other men of the change and promotes the stableboy from guide to rider, which puts a huge smile on the young lad's face. Declan transfers me to his much larger stallion and climbs on behind me. Trust me. There are worse ways to travel than to be tucked firmly between your lover's thighs. I mention this fact to the Tax Man, who chuckles and adds, "I'd advise ya try and not wiggle yarself around too much, Lass, lest you wish to be ravaged in the woods while the others stand by and listen."

This statement raises my already warm body temperature several degrees, but the prospect of wiggling ends up moot. Lord *Mac Nuada* is a much better rider than I, and the gait of his horse is smooth and rhythmic. This, combined with the excitement of the day and the wine at brunch, puts me out like a light somewhere along the trail. I awaken only when Declan's horse comes to a full stop and I hear noise all around me.

"Did ya have a sweet nap, Love? Dreaming of me I hope?" the Tax Man asks as he slides off his horse and puts up his arms to help me off.

"Hell…I'm sorry, Declan. I didn't mean to fall asleep like that. It was very rude of me, but I couldn't keep my eyes open," I apologize.

"No worries, Lass. It was pleasant enough holdin' ya peacefully in ma arms. The rest no doubt will have done ya good. I cannot foretell how our meetin' with the House Mages will go, though rest assured, it matters little to me what they say. You and I will handfast. That is an absolute certainty."

We kiss, maybe too ardently by the wolf whistles it elicits, then head inside towards Declan's quarters. All I want is a nice, hot shower and some alone time with his Jr. Lordship before tackling our late afternoon meeting with the dreaded Mages. Unfortunately, like everything else during this visit to *I Idir*, my hopes are dashed. We are met by the icky Master Hobart just outside D.P.'s rooms.

He gives a curt bow and informs us that the Queen's

dressmaker is waiting in the solar parlor, hosted by Lady *Nuada*. We are expected to go immediately there.

I am sweaty and grimy from the long, round trip, my hair is a mess, I'm wearing badly wrinkled pants, and I have dried drool on my cheek. There is no way I am meeting anyone from the Queen's staff or D.P.'s Dragon Mama in this condition. My *Mo Shiorghra* instantly dons his Lordship attitude. "Surely you jest, Master Hobart. We obviously are unprepared for a meeting of this importance dressed as we are. The Lady and I will freshen up first and then will join the others in the parlor. In the meantime, serve a bottle of my Special Reserve *Uisce na Beatha* (Water of Life) whiskey. I am sure the Queen's man will appreciate that while he waits." With that, Declan takes my arm and ushers me toward our rooms without another word to Master Hobart.

When we are far enough away, I whisper to my Tax Man. "The Queen's dressmaker is a man? I had heard Her Majesty prefers only female staff members in her personal entourage."

"Aye. Master Tyler usually presents as male, but he is a *Bogie. Bogies* are shape-shifters who frequently change genders as it suits them. I have seen him only a handful of times and always as a 'Master.' He is said to be the best designer in *I Idir*, if not the entire Otherworld. He usually limits his work to the Royal Circle, so his making your handfast gown is a very big honor, Lass. Though I don' expect my *Mathair* to be very happy about your good fortune."

Well, that prediction certainly proves to be a gross understatement.

TOOTHACHE 29

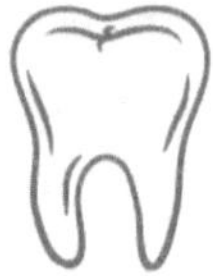

DRESS DOWN

ONCE AGAIN, my Tax Man and I shower together to speed up the process, but sadly there is no time for any slip and slide activities. Still, a naked, wet Jr. Lordship is quite easy on the eyes; and if nothing else, I imprint these delicious images in my head to help bear me through what's to come next. Because Her Majesty's dressmaker awaits us in the parlor, and also because we are scheduled to meet with the House Mages later this afternoon, I put on the nicest of all the gowns I've brought with me. It is a cobalt blue silk blend with a soft, full sleeved, ivory chemise underneath, and even I, a non-fashionista, can see that it makes for a very striking combination with my coloring. I work my still damp hair into a simple, single braid and pin it up with a jeweled comb. Then I add a bit of blush and some lipstick to my face. I am as ready as I ever will be.

Though he tries acting casual and pleasant, I can tell

Declan has significant anxiety about the decisions the Mages will make regarding us. I can't blame him; his path until now has not been easy, and he has said at least three times today that absolutely nothing will stop the two of us from committing to each other. Strangely, I don't share any of his doubts. I have known from the moment I was abducted by the Chechens and feared for my life that I am fully and deeply in love with Declan Fitzpatrick. Despite the hurdles, the inhospitality and lack of support of his parents, as well as the threats against my person, I am as sure as ever that we are meant to be together. I trust with my whole heart that the Mages will agree.

Frankly, I have more angst concerning the choice of my handfast gown. I previously had assumed I would go back to the boutique in Boston and have my BFF, Mel, and the confident Jacy Woodly help me say yes to the dress. I haven't the slightest idea how a personal dressmaker works. Will Her Majesty's dressmaker wave his hand over me and poof the right dress will appear? Will there be fittings? Do I even have a choice in any of this, and if so, what the hell is the right choice? I squeeze the Tax Man's hand, and he squeezes mine back. He gives me a smile, but he doesn't offer any of the answers I seek. Perhaps he's just as clueless as I am about this stuff.

We enter the solar parlor to find Lady *Nuada* and Declan's sister, Meghan, along with a dapper looking, middle-aged man dressed impeccably in tailored breeches and a tunic, enjoying sips of whatever goes as his Jr. Lordship's Private Reserve whiskey. The gentleman stands when I enter the room and kisses my hand as I am introduced by my *Mo Shiorghra*.

"Lady Rosalinda, it is such a pleasure finally to meet you. I have heard so much about your bravery from those in the Queen's inner circle." I watch Dragon Mama cringe at this compliment, and I only can guess how much it galls her that my name is bandied about at *Crann Bethadh*. Master Tyler adds fuel to the fire by turning to Declan's Lady *Mathair* and saying, "You must be so happy and proud to be welcoming such a beautiful and accomplished young woman to the family, Lady *Nuada*."

Dragon Mama flushes a deep red, and even her youngest daughter can't help but hide her amusement behind her hand. "Quite, Master Tyler," is all the Lady of the House can muster. Instantly, she changes the subject. Raising the crystal decanter she asks, "May I pour you another finger of *Uisce na Beatha?*"

The dressmaker shakes his head negatively. "Thank you, gracious Lady, but I think I must get on with the order of business." He turns and speaks to me. "What are your visions for your handfast gown, Lady Rosalinda? Are you a traditionalist or more a fan of the Mundane style dresses for joinings?"

Before I can answer, Declan's *Mathair* interjects. "I have been trying to explain to Master Tyler, Rosalinda, that House *Nuada* is quite capable of providing you with your handfast apparel...as tradition dictates, and though it is a very generous offer by Her Majesty, we couldn't think of accepting a gift that so far exceeds your...station."

Master Tyler looks annoyed at being reminded of this. "And as I have explained to you already, Lady *Nuada*, Her Majesty's wishes supersede that of House *Nuada's*. I am sure your own Lord would tell you the same thing.

Perhaps we should get his Lordship's opinion on the matter?"

At the mention of her husband, Dragon Mama backs down but throws the burden of being the bad guy onto Declan. "You understand what I am saying, don't you, Declan? It would be a major embarrassment for House *Nuada* to have your *Mo Shiorghra* dressed in the type of gown meant for...*Tuatha De Danann* royalty. People will think you are putting on unwarranted airs, particularly since it has taken such an unnatural amount of time for your match to be revealed, and neither you nor your Lady is in your prime."

This is where my bitch of a future mother-in-law makes her big mistake. I was ready to agree to allowing House *Nuada* to deal with the trappings of the handfast ceremony and celebration in order to keep peace between Declan and his parents. The two of us truly would prefer to handfast alone, with just our witnesses and a Druid official in my living room at home without any of this pomp and circumstance garbage. I look over and see that Dragon Mama's words about the ceremony embarrassing his House have cut my *Mo Shiorghra* deeply. Bad move on her part. My Tax Man's aura has changed to a deep purple-gray color, all the goodwill from this afternoon evaporating like rain on a hot summer sidewalk. This riles me up. Plus, this psycho woman has just implied in front of a complete stranger that Declan and I are too old to produce offspring. For some reason, this especially infuriates me. What the hell! I am a healthy, 33-year-old woman...not the crypt keeper's sister!

I stand up and face Lady *Nuada*. "I'm sorry you see this

as an embarrassment, My Lady *Mathair*." (Yes. I admit it: I hope that me calling her mother when she hasn't asked me to will piss her off enormously.) "However, Her Royal Highness offered me this generous boon in return for my service to *I Idir*. Proper protocol and good upbringing require that I graciously acquiesce to such a prestigious honor. As I already have accepted Her Majesty's offer and refuse to dishonor my *Mo Shiorghra* or either of our Houses by going back on my word, I suggest you let Master Tyler proceed with his duties."

I don't need to read Lady *Siobhan*'s aura to know that she's full of rage towards me, but I ignore her reaction and smile sweetly at the dressmaker. "I'm afraid I am unaware of how high fashion works here in the Other-world, Master Tyler. Perhaps if I show you some of the gowns I already have selected you might be able to determine the styles and colors I lean towards?"

The dressmaker stands, happy, I believe, for a chance to escape the venomous company of Lady *Nuada*. "That is an excellent idea, Lady Rosalinda, and a very good place to start." He holds his arm for me to take. "Shall we proceed, good Lady?" he asks, whereupon the two of us stroll purposefully from the solar parlor, leaving three very shocked Fitzpatricks in our wake.

TOOTHACHE 30

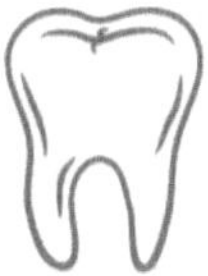

MAGES AND OUTRAGES

TRULY, I had no concept of the process involved in having a gown made specifically for oneself. It turns out that Master Tyler's initial visit with me solely is to learn of my personal tastes and to see how different fabrics and colors work with my aura. I try on every gown I've brought to *I Idir*, and he quizzes me on my favorite go to pieces back home. He takes my measurements (I swear I have never been as top heavy as I am now; maybe it has to do with *I Idir's* unique gravitational pull) and makes a few quick sketches, but he doesn't offer to show any of them to me.

Undoubtedly, the dressmaker sensed the animosity between my future mother-in-law and me, so he suggests we conduct our future business at Festive Boutique in Boston in the Mundane World. It's a perfect go-between spot because it is physically safe for Fae with only small traces of human DNA like him. Master Tyler assures me he will have no trouble finishing my dress in time for our planned date of July 18th, and we arrange to meet in one week for me to select a gown from among the final sketches and fabric he will bring with him. I can't lie. I am extremely relieved that I won't have to return to Declan's ancestral home until the actual handfast ceremony. To say that these past two days have been extremely stressful would be putting it mildly, and I am looking forward to going home and staying there until our big day.

During the entire time I'm with Master Tyler in Declan's quarters I expect My Intended to join us. He does not, and I begin to worry that I've upset the family apple cart beyond repair and that perhaps he is avoiding me. I try focusing on the dressmaker's conversation but can't because part of my brain is concerned that I screwed up. When I finally hear the Tax Man chuckling in my head I am more than a little relieved. *"Yar worried for no reason, Lass. I am mar than fine, though I am glad we are leavin' this evening. My dear Mathair is in a most foul mood, and I would not be shocked to find snakes in our bed if we were to stay."* He laughs again and adds, *"It's just that I don' wish to intrude on the secrets regardin' yar gown. I am lookin' forward to bein' enchanted by the vision of my Mo Shiorghra on our handfast day."*

Declan's words are quite a relief, though I do wish that he hadn't mentioned the possibility of snakes in our bed. I eye the tempting piece of furniture from where I'm sitting in the drawing room and remind myself to stay clear of it in the few remaining hours we are here. So much for any last minute *I Idir* hanky panky!

As Master Tyler and I are just finishing up our business, we are interrupted by Lady *Nuada's* page, Master

Hobart, to inform me that the Mages have arrived and that I am to return immediately to the solar parlor. He stresses the word immediately with a flourish, and when he leaves, the dressmaker shakes his head. "A totally disagreeable fellow, that Hobart is. I mean no insult, Lady Rosalinda. The Universe has blessed you with a kind and honorable spouse, but you have not been so lucky with your gift of his extended family."

I can't help but laugh at his comment. Her Majesty's dressmaker is one hundred percent spot-on. "I am far from insulted, Master Tyler. I couldn't agree more. House *Nuada* is in a category of its own and is a far cry from my own ancestral lines. But I have faith that the Universe has made a wonderful match between Lord *Mac Nuada* and me, and it is my greatest hope that time will smooth my relationship with his family."

Master Tyler gives me a bow. "You are truly a special soul, Lady Rosalinda. Beautiful inside and out. His Lordship is a very blessed man."

This is the second time someone has said that to me today, and I feel the floodgates behind my eyes begin to open again. This crying shit is getting ridiculous! Never in my life have I ever been such a crybaby. I admonish myself to stop. I refuse to meet House *Nuada's* Mages with red eyes and a snot-filled nose.

Dragon Mama's flunky shows Master Tyler out and leaves me to find the solar parlor on my own. Of course, I am the last one to arrive there, and the entire group is seated and waiting for me. When I enter all the men rise, including Declan's father, who now seems even larger and more imposing than I remember from last night. He is decked out in his House's colors of maroon and gold, and there is no way one could miss that he absolutely is the Lord of House *Nuada*. For a split second I try to imagine my Tax Man in this role, but I completely erase the thought from my head lest anyone get the wrong idea.

"Lady Rosalinda," his Lordship greets me, "I hope your meeting with Master Tyler was successful. 'Tis quite the honor you bring to House *Nuada*." I am careful not to look at Declan's *Mathair*, afraid I'll see a look of disgust on her face while his *Athair* brags to the Mages about my boon from The Morrigan.

Theirs are the faces I am interested in because they hold the keys as to how the next few weeks will go. Like Declan, I am committed to sealing our commitment one way or the other, but it would be a more peaceful and positive start to our life together if the Mages give us their blessings. Unfortunately, the two men and one woman, dressed in the traditional hooded robes of their profession, sit completely stone-faced and unreadable. Much like that of my *Mo Shiorghra*.

I take a seat next to his Jr. Lordship, and he takes my hand in his. I feel the tension rolling off of him, but I am afraid to let down my mental shield lest something leak out that's not supposed to be shared.

The female Mage stands up. "We have done a thorough exploration of all the signs surrounding this match between the heir of House *Nuada*, Declan Phineas Donnely Fitzpatrick, and the daughter of House *Fiacail* (Tooth), Rosalinda *Aine* Rogan Parker."

I'm so nervous now, I can barely stand it. In fact, I actually feel a bit lightheaded again. I force myself to breathe: in through the nose; out through my mouth. I'm sure I look ridiculous, but not anymore than I would look with my head between my knees.

The Mage continues. "Though it has taken an unusually long time for the Universe to bring about this match, we three are secure in the knowledge that this is a blessed union under every tenet of Sacred Law, and, in fact, may prove to be one of the most fruitful and successful unions House *Nuada* has witnessed in several generations." My Tax Man is squeezing my hand so hard it hurts, and he attempts to lean over to kiss me. Unfortunately, despite this amazing, wonderful news from the Mages, my vision has gone rather wonky and my head feels quite strange. The next thing I know, everything goes black, and the only thing I'm kissing is the hard, wooden floor of the solar parlor.

TOOTHACHE 31

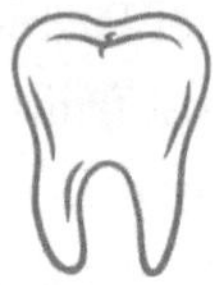

SIGNED AND SEALED WITH A SISTERLY SEND-OFF

I HAVE no idea how long I've been out of it. When my eyelids flutter open, I'm looking up at several sets of eyes staring down at me, with Declan and the female Mage kneeling next to me. The Tax Man is holding my hand, calling my name, and looking absolutely, white-faced terrified. The Mage puts a cool hand on my forehead, and I immediately feel better. "Step back and give her air," the Lady Mage instructs. She and Declan help me to a sitting position, and now that I'm fully conscious I feel like a total idiot for flopping on the floor like I did in front of everyone. "Do such things like this happen to you often, good Lady?" the Mage asks.

Declan hovers over me, and I can sense his heart racing. "Are you well, Love? I will call Robyn immediately, and if he says it is safe, then we will travel home. You can rest there easier."

His Lordship interjects. "You must both sign the final

handfast contract before leaving so that preparations can be made for the ceremony."

His son gives him a look that would freeze whiskey. "Your concern for My Beloved overwhelms me, *Athair*."

"There is no need to fuss, young Lord. The Lady is in no dire situation and does not require Lord *Spideog* (Robyn's) intervention," the female Mage states. She looks me in the eye and smiles. "All is well, Lady Rosalinda. Too much excitement, I believe." Then, she gives me a wink, and I'm more than a little confused. "When you return home, be sure to get plenty of rest and eat as cleanly as possible," she advises. "Limit your intake of processed Mundane foods and enjoy an abundance of fresh fruits and vegetables." The highest-ranking Mage of House *Nuada* stands up and says to the group, "Blessed be the Universe and its wisest of directions. We shall meet again when the Luna begins her wasting time and The Warrior and the Serpent align in the night sky." Then, the three Mages silently glide out the room.

His Jr. Lordship picks me up under the knees and announces to no one person in particular, "I am taking my Lady back to our quarters. We will be leaving to return to the Mundane World as soon as our things are packed."

"I am afraid I must insist that you complete the necessary protocols, Son. It is not a suggestion," his *Athair* threatens.

I'm pretty sure my Tax Man is gearing up for a response that includes a wide selection of Gaelic obscenities which certainly will not help the already tense mood of the room. "Really, Declan, I'm fine," I argue. "You heard the honorable Lady Mage. I'm just overtired. Let's get this finished so we can move forward and return to the Mundane World knowing we're all set for the 18th."

It's obvious My Intended does not want to back down, but he also doesn't want to add to my stress level. He sets me down on the sofa with my feet up, insists that someone fetch me herbal tea, and sits in the armchair next to the sofa, arms folded across his chest, just daring someone to cross him. "Let us proceed then with these ridiculous necessities," he snarls, looking so much like his mother in this pose it makes me shudder.

I don't really want any tea, but I sip it anyway, unwilling to rock the boat in any manner. A group of men enter with all types of documents rolled on scrolls and a feather ink pen as if this were 1624 and not 2024. I sign my name in a half dozen places despite not understanding a word of what I'm signing. I figure that with the Black Knight as my legal representation, no one in their right mind would try to take advantage of me. When all the signatures are finished and the documents are folded and sealed with wax, Lord *Mac Nuada* stands up, scoops me up off the sofa and heads out of the solar parlor in the direction of our rooms without a single word to anyone.

As I have mentioned, it is a long walk to the other side of the mansion, and I am not a lightweight, little thing. "Seriously, Declan, I'm fine now. I can walk the rest of the way," I profess.

"Hmmm," is his only response, and he doesn't set me down until we've reached our quarters. He lowers me onto the bed, which I sincerely hope is free of the snakes he mentioned earlier. "Would you like more tea, Lass?

Something to eat before we leave? I can have Duncan bring something from the marketplace," the Tax Man offers.

Truthfully, I'm not crazy about being treated like an invalid, especially since I'm feeling perfectly normal. But I also don't want to hurt my *Mo Shiorghra's* feelings any further. "No. I'm good. I'll wait until we get back home," I state.

Declan nods his head in approval, and then there's a knock at the door. He looks at it with a sense of weariness but goes to open it, letting in two female staff members followed by his sister Meghan. The servants give a quick curtsy and head straight for the large armoire in the bedroom where they begin to pack my things back into the trunk. D.P. leads his sister into the far end of the sitting area, a spot from which I barely can hear their conversation.

They are speaking in a mix of Gaelic and English and far too fast for me to understand the entire conversation, but I pick out a few words here and there. Meghan has come to plead with her brother to stay in *I Idir* for a bit longer so that she can spend some time with him. His Jr. Lordship's words in response are sweet, but he is adamant that we are leaving as soon as my things are packed. I can't fully hear his sister's response, but from the sound of her voice she is upset.

I see through the doorway into the parlor that Meghan rejects her brother's offer of an embrace, instead flouncing out the door in a huff, and not for the first time do I think that this entire group of Fitzpatricks is in desperate need of family therapy. When Declan returns, I originally pretend not to have any idea of what transpired between him and his sister, but the expression on his face is so distraught that I forget that plan and instead quietly ask, "Why is Meghan so upset?"

The Tax Man sits on the end of the bed and sighs. "She has hurt feelings because I didna' spend any time alone with har during this visit. Usually when I'm in *I Idir*, the two of us plan a day ride up into the mountains. But thar's ben so much goin' on…" His voice trails off, and he stands up and offers me a hand.

My trunk waits packed and ready. Lord *Mac Nuada* draws a circle around it and the two of us. "Are ya ready to go home, Lass?" He asks. I nod, no words left to offer. I hang on to my Tax Man with both arms, close my eyes, and breathe deeply.

TOOTHACHE 32

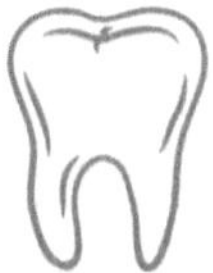

HOME FOR THE KNIGHT

THANKFULLY, after returning from our contentious trip to *I Idir,* the Tax Man and I settle into peaceful cohabitation. There's little doubt Declan thinks of my home as his space as well, as I see more of his things appear daily in this little nest we are building. I don't mention the keyboard that suddenly takes up residence in my parlor nor the weights and exercise equipment that's found a new resting place in my garage. As long as he doesn't expect me to use them, I'm thrilled to have my house become our home.

Unlike most couples in the Mundane World, Lord *Mac Nuada* and I have very few responsibilities regarding the planning of our handfast ceremony or the party afterwards. Those duties traditionally fall to the House sponsoring the match, which in this case is obviously Declan's. I have an appointment with Master Tyler tomorrow in Boston to view the sketches for my gown. I'm usually not a girl who gets excited about clothes, but damn…this is MY HANDFAST gown after all. Other than that, our biggest role is to show up in *I Idir* no later than the 17th for any pre-celebrations or last-minute issues.

Between then and now, I'm taking full advantage of the freedom I've given myself from my demanding work schedule. I've been passing a lot of this time in my garden, and when Declan goes into his downtown office, I often work on some dollhouse projects in the loft space he's taken over. I've also been enjoying cooking marvelous candlelit dinners, taking long evening walks with the Tax Man, and cuddling in front of the TV. I cannot remember ever being happier, and if I find having the bed completely made thirty seconds after I'm out of it or the towels picked up and hung before they even hit the floor somewhat annoying, I cheerfully smile and write it off as a small price to pay for communal bliss.

It's for this very reason that when the Black Knight shows up on our doorstep, I smile sweetly and invite him in instead of turning off all the lights and pretending we're not home. That, and because he's the Black Knight and there's no running from the long arm of *I Idir* law. I can't think of any logical reason why Sheriff Beckett would show up unannounced on a Thursday night, but that doesn't mean a thing. Even the Black Knight's #1 Super Spy doesn't appear to have had previous knowledge that his boss was planning a visit. My biggest concern is that Beckett is here about some kind of legal snafu that might delay our handfast. That would really suck.

Though I'm not as intimidated by the Black Knight as I once was, there is no way one cannot find the man imposing. There is an indisputable air of authority about him, even when he's casually dressed in worn jeans and a faded Rolling Stones t-shirt. I suppose it comes from being born into magical royalty. When one's father is the reigning Merlin, undoubtedly some of that magical hierarchy must seep into one's disposition.

I offer refreshments but the Knight refuses. After a few moments of polite chit chat about our upcoming handfast, he gets right to the point. "Actually, I'm here on official business with Dr. Parker," he begins.

My heart sinks to my feet, and I wonder what the hell kind of trouble I'm in now. I also have forgotten to shield properly, because the next words out of his mouth are, "No worries, Doctor, I'm not here to cause you any undo stress. Truth is, I'm here with a job promotion and an offer."

I pull up a proper mental shield before responding. "Please, Lord Knight, call me Rosie. I'm sorry, but I don't understand what you mean by 'promotion.' Perhaps you better explain," I say, working to keep the tremor out of my voice.

"Absolutely…Rosie. I am aware that you have taken a leave of absence from your practice and from your Corps duties, and that's perfectly fine. But once you resume both positions after your honeymoon, you'll find that in recognition for your brave work with the Chechens, you have been promoted from Tooth Fairy Cadet to the rank of Lt. First Class and assigned a supervisor role within the Corps. You'll be tasked with instructing new Cadets, a job that requires actual retrievals only as part of the training procedure."

Sitting as I am among *I Idir's* ruling circle, my minor promotion is no great shakes, but it's a nice little bone for a tooth fairy. I cast a thought over to my *Mo Shiorghra* to see whether he's had something to do with this, but I get nothing from him. "Thank you, Sir Knight. I am happy for the honor. I only hope I can be of service to the Crown in this capacity."

The Black Knight smiles, all perfect white teeth and dimples, but all I can think of is a large shark: a very handsome shark, but a predator nonetheless. "I'm so glad you mention 'service to the Crown,' Rosie. I was hoping to add another role to your job within the Tooth Fairy Corps."

The best I can spit out is a strangled question. "Another 'role,' Sir?"

"I'm anticipating that I can convince you to sign on as a member of our growing Intelligence Community. You would be our eyes and ears during your work for the Corps. Nothing overtly dangerous. No actual field work, or anything like that...unless, of course, something like that becomes necessary. But the general idea is for you to make us aware of anything that seems suspicious before it gets out of hand...like it did with the Chechens. You'd be an 'early warning' system."

Shit! I didn't see this coming! As Mel would say, "Buttons to bagels, Rosie...they want you to be a spy!"

TOOTHACHE 33

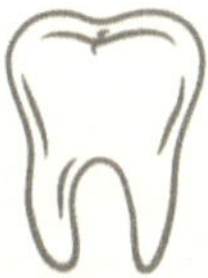

LOOKIN' OUT FOR HIS LADY

I TELL Sheriff Beckett that I will think about it. Seriously…what other options do I have? One does not simply say "nope…can't do it" to the Black Knight. Not without first having a well- prepared speech that suggests you will be a spy for the Crown when hell freezes over. (That would be the Mundane, Judeo-Christian Hell, not the Otherworld one called *Dubnos*; the two actually are quite different.) It appears that Beckett expects this reaction from me. He gives me a nonchalant answer in response, thanking me for considering his offer and instructing me to let him know my decision after the handfast ceremony.

After Beckett's departure, the Tax Man admits that he knew about the promotion and the offer before the Black Knight's visit but insisted it wasn't his place to tell me. He also said that the decision to accept the position, one way or the other, was totally mine, and that he would abide whole-heartedly with whatever decision I make. This response is typical of Declan when he's not sure how I will react to a given situation; his Jr. Lordship is not a fan of drama.

Today, however, is a new day and a big one for me, so I refuse to let the Black Knight's little James Bond-esque project ruin it. Mel and I are going into Boston this afternoon to meet with Master Tyler about my handfast gown. The Royal dressmaker is bringing several sketches and various fabric samples from which I will choose. Despite offers from both Declan and me to gift my BFF her attire for the event, Mel insists that she wants to create her gown herself. She's a wonderful seamstress, so I have no doubt it will be gorgeous, though truthfully Mel would look stunning in a burlap bag.

We girls had planned to take the train into the city like we did before, so I am shocked when a black limo pulls up in front of my house, a treat from My Intended. "I thought ya might enjoy goin' in style, Love," D.P. says. "A little champagne, some berries while ya travel…something special." This is followed by all kinds of kissy faces and would have been terribly romantic if I wasn't just a tad suspicious. For all his wealth, D.P. is first and foremost a numbers guy. Yes, he has an expensive home and car, and yes, his attire is definitely not from T.J. Maxx. But for the most part, he is not pretentious or showy, tracks his spending, and I distinctly remember him making fun of clients who used livery service.

I don't have to wait long for my doubts to be justified. After a big show of saying goodbye, Mel and I climb into the waiting limo, champagne already poured and waiting for us. We are about a half mile away when the little panel between the driver and us slides back, and I see Duncan Fitzpatrick in the front seat. He turns around with a sheepish expression and says, "'Tis obviously ma lucky day to be escortin' the two most beautiful ladies in all *I Idir.*" Mel is tickled. I am not. *"Sonofabitch, Declan! You sent your cousin along? I thought something was funny about this whole limo thing. It's not your usual style."*

There is dead silence for nearly a minute, then I hear his voice in my head. *"T'was easier to beg forgiveness than ta ask permission, Love. I knew ya'd be disagreeable ta the idea. But after the incidents in I Idir, I could not help but take precautions. The boutique is an open portal between this world and the Otherworld. I felt the need for some extra security. I swear to you, Duncan is only there for extra measure. He will not be privy to any discussions regarding yar gown."*

"This is ruining my day, Declan."

"Only if you let it, A Mhuirnin (my Darling.) After all we have been through, and all the mistakes I've made regarding your safety, how ken I feel otherwise? I ask you to accept Duncan's presence as a love gift to me. I would spend the whole day anxious for your safety if he were not there. You would not wish that for me, I hope?"

Grrr. My Tax Man's a smooth operator. It's times like this that make me realize what a great spy he probably is. Lord *Mac Nuada* always knows the right thing to say. Of course, I wouldn't want him to spend all day worrying. And he's asked so little of me, how could I not want to give him this gift. Double Grrrr. *"Fine. Duncan can stay. But you and I are gonna talk about this when I get home."*

"Of course, Darling. For now, try and enjoy this happy and exciting day. Make lovely memories. I'll be here at home... waiting for you."

I'm sure he will be...with another major distraction up his sleeve.

TOOTHACHE 34

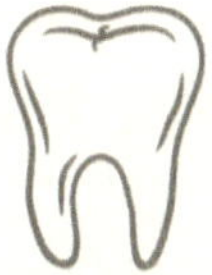

ROSIE'S GOWN

DECLAN IS RIGHT ABOUT one thing. I will not let Duncan's presence ruin this special day, though he certainly has commandeered my BFF's attention. I press the button that closes the window between the sections of the limo. My Handfast Maiden makes a face at me. "I'm not trying to be a 'Bride-zilla,' Mel," I assert, "but I want you all to myself today. No doubt Duncan will ask you out when we return home later, so save your flirting for then, 'K? Pretty please?" I shamelessly beg.

Melanie smiles, her annoyance forgotten. "You're right, Rosie. No boys allowed. We're shopping for your frickin' handfast dress!" Then she squeals with excitement, and I can't help but join in her exuberance.

I take a sip of champagne, but for some reason it tastes unbearably sour and I put it down. I think instead how nice it would be if these plain strawberries were covered in dark chocolate, and instantly they are. I laugh to myself. *"That means you too, Tax Man. No boys allowed... even Mo Shiorghras."* Then I pull up the tightest mental shield I can. His Jr. Lordship will just have to hear about my day directly from me when I return to Salem.

We cause somewhat of a commotion when we pull up in front of Festive Boutique in our limo, and I am sure people are trying to figure out who we are and why we're visiting this tiny little shop in such a spectacular way. Duncan opens my door, and the driver opens Mel's, and we make our way inside, my shadow right behind me. The same sales clerk who helped us before is standing behind the counter. She greets us with a smile of recognition and much more formality than the last time. She also does a double take when she notices Duncan in our entourage and instantly flushes a slight pink. Yes, Declan's cousin is that pretty. This does not please Mel, whom I'm sure already has staked her claim to the gorgeous *gancanagh*. My BFF makes sure the sales clerk sees her touch Duncan's shoulder, a risky venture that makes Mel's eyes glaze over, but she recovers quickly enough to declare, "I hope you won't be too lonely out here by yourself, Master Fitzpatrick."

He gives Mel the most dazzling smile, and now I'm pretty sure that there's some lustful thoughts exchanged between Declan's cousin and my best friend. The saleslady sees it too, and her cheerful demeanor drops a bit. "Time will seem to go slower without your loveliness to occupy my mind, sweet Lady. But I shall bear it the best I can until you return," says the love talker to Mel.

I take my Maiden by the hand, and we wander through the store to the dressing rooms at the back, choosing the one with the red curtain. The wall once again evaporates, and we are met by a very excited Jacy Woodly, who offers us yet more champagne. If I were actually to drink all of the champagne offered me, I'd be unconscious for the ride back to Salem.

Master Tyler is seated on a low divan with a stack of sketchbooks in his hand and surrounded by bolts of beautiful fabric in a wide assortment of colors. I want to hop up and down and clap my hands in excitement but realize that proper protocol is required of me in the Royal dressmaker's presence lest I somehow embarrass his Jr. Lordship. Master Tyler kisses both of our hands. "Tis so good to see you again, Lady Rosalinda. And this must be your lovely Maiden?" he asks.

I introduce Mel, and the four of us seat ourselves around the raised platform in the center of the room. The dressmaker explains that he has created several designs and that once I have decided on a style, we then can discuss fabrics and colors. Fae handfast traditions don't follow the modern Mundane custom of white or ivory for a bride, unless, of course, the bride wants those colors. Thus, I am free to select whatever color suits my fancy and which I think looks the best on me. With a wave of his hand, Master Tyler's gowns spring to life on a magical, virtual model of me atop the platform. This allows me to see how I might look in each of the various styles. Once I get used to the idea of seeing myself from every harsh angle, I must admit this is a marvelous way to help me decide. At least that is the goal. I am able to narrow down my choices to five gowns, but no matter how hard I try, I'm unable to make a final choice.

The dressmaker suggests an old magical solution. He gives me a small swatch of fabric from each of my final five selections and instructs me to put them under my pillow at night until I dream about one specific dress. Then, I should send word to him by raven-gram as to which one has been revealed to be my heart's true desire. Master Tyler has no doubts this will happen as he describes.

It seems a little silly and something out of a fairytale, but who am I to discount his magic? Surely not someone who has found the love of her life through magical intervention. I thank him for all his kindness, and I can tell he is excited to be part of Declan's and my special day. He even convinces Mel to allow him to create her gown as well, with the promise that hers will complement my own perfectly. Of course, my BFF knows better than to refuse the Royal dressmaker's very generous offer, and when we leave the shop for the ride home, we are giddy and giggly like a pair of school girls without imbibing a single drop of champagne.

TOOTHACHE 35

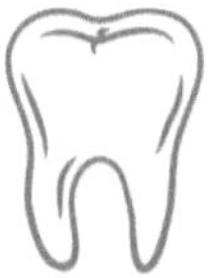

Home Is Where my Heart Is

BOTH OF MY earlier predictions are correct. First, Duncan joins us in the back of the limo for the ride home so he can flirt outrageously with my BFF unhindered by the car's driver window. Since I am in a very merry mood, I don't complain. Mel is in her glory, and I'm happy for her. We have discussed the crazy hot Fae at length, and I am confident that my friend understands that Declan's *gancanagh* cousin is not long term, committed relationship material. If Mel is to have the fling that I had expected with Declan, then I'm more than willing to be her cheerleader.

After we arrive back at my home and Duncan and Mel head together toward his car parked at the end of the block, my second prediction is confirmed. I'd guessed that my somewhat sneaky, part-time operative *Mo Shiorghra* would have a distraction waiting for me so as to avoid the conversation I'd wanted regarding his tendency to withhold important information in advance of my needing it. I was not wrong.

Upon entering my home I find the living room filled with fragrant flowers of every kind. I stress the word fragrant. The smell is overwhelming, like a funeral parlor on a warm afternoon, and the stifling odor makes me queasy. The Tax Man is smiling and waiting for me, looking as hot as ever in his faded jeans and white t-shirt, margaritas and tacos laid out on the dining room table. "Welcome home, Rosie Love. I thought we'd celebrate your selection of a gown." He waves a hand in the direction of the fiesta spread. "I hope this brings back good memories far ya, *Mo Anam Cara* (My Soul Mate.)"

I don't want to be a Debby Downer, but the smell of the flowers mixing with the fried taco meat makes me want to hurl. For real. I clamp a hand over my mouth and run to the guest bathroom, whereupon Declan finds me with my head in the toilet. This must be the afternoon for memories because I instantly have a sense of *deja vu* of the very beginning of our relationship. It seems like a lifetime ago, though in reality it's been barely four weeks.

Gone is any semblance of celebration. He holds my hair back while I'm busy being sick, something I didn't give him the chance to do the first time around. I'm not sure why the smell has made me so ill, but I tell D.P. that it must be because I'm over-whelmed by the excitement of the afternoon combined with too much champagne and chocolate strawberries. Frankly, this is a lie because I only had one sip of the sparkling wine and only one strawberry, but this explanation lessens the worry etched on the Tax Man's face. "I'm sorry, Sweetie. I'm sure this isn't the reaction you were hoping for…"

He hugs me even though I am sure I have vomit breath. "No worries, Love. These past few weeks have been a lot to take in. I'm sorry it's been so physically taxing for you." He gives me a smile and adds, "Me being here while yar busy bein' sick has been a trip down memory lane as well. At least this time ya didna swear at me to go away. Plus, unlike before, I'm here to comfort ya afterwards. Ya'll never know how hard it was ta leave ya like that the last time."

We return to the parlor. The flowers are gone, and the tacos and margaritas have been replaced by a pot of tea and some cinnamon toast. Because this is such a sweet, thoughtful gesture, I feel terrible for ruining the Tax Man's wonderful surprise and suddenly develop an ache in my throat that signals I'm about to cry. I force myself to stop. There's absolutely nothing to cry about. It's been a lovely, exhausting, wonderful day, and I'm letting my emotions run away with me. "Tea and cinnamon toast… the perfect thing," I say.

"And after you've had a wee bite, I have another surprise far ya, Love," the Tax Man promises.

"Gee…so many surprises today," I state, pasting a forced smile on my face. Truthfully, I'm very tired, and all I can think of is taking a nap. A real, sleeping kind of a nap, not our usual definition of napping. "Do I get a hint?" I ask.

"More than a hint. When you're done with yar snack, I thought we could both do with a nice, relaxing soak in the hot tub," D.P. suggests. "It's a glorious evening for such a thing."

I relax a little, thinking that he's just teasing, and I give a small laugh. "That's funny, Declan. Nice idea, but we don't have a hot tub," I reply.

"We do now," he says.

For a second I don't understand what he's implying, but then I realize what he's gone and done. "Declan...a hot tub can't just magically appear in the yard. My neighbors aren't stupid, and I don't have a privacy fence!"

I'm treated to a quick flash of Declan's cranky face. No doubt he's grown tired of me raining on his parade of surprises. He pushes down his annoyance and pleasantly explains. "I understand all that, Lass. That's why I've gone and veiled the whole thing. Yar neighbors won't see or hear a thing out of the ordinary. Say you're up to it, *Mo Anam Cara*. I quite believe it will help you relax."

The last thing I want is to spoil yet another of My Intended's surprises, so I quickly agree. "You know, that sounds lovely, Sweetie. You're right, a nice long soak will do us both good. Let me just run upstairs and find my bathing suit."

He grabs my hand to stop me from leaving and with a wicked grin adds, "That won' be necessary, Love. I'll veil us as well."

* * *

It turns out that my Tax Man is right. It is a glorious evening, and the hot tub is the perfect way for me to end this day. Not once do I think about any of the myriad of things that could go wrong in the next twelve days. For a little while I forget about Dragon Mama, and the fact that someone in *I Idir* wants me out of the way, and that I can't make a decision about which gown I should wear for the handfast ceremony. We spend the time just being Rosie and Declan. Later that evening, when I know for sure that Lord *Mac Nuada* has fallen asleep for the night, I slip the five scraps of fabric under my pillow.

TOOTHACHE 36

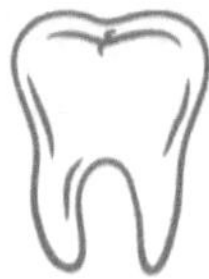

AGREE TO DISAGREE

As the days leading up to our handfast ceremony slip by, the Tax Man and I enjoy the tranquility and bliss of normal, day-to-day, domestic cohabitation. I realize that these pleasant and lazy days will change once I return to my full-time dental practice and tooth fairy duties, but in the meantime, I relish being a true Lady of Leisure. Thankfully, we hear little from *I Idir* or Declan's parents. We both assume no news is good news. As Master Tyler correctly predicted, I eventually dream about my handfast gown. Upon awakening a few days ago, there was no question in my mind which one it would be, so I quickly composed a short letter revealing my decision and sent it to the dressmaker via a nasty, old, raven-gram. I won't have my first fitting until a day or two before the ceremony, so I try not to fret about the time constraints. It is, after all, the Otherworld, where magic rules all aspects of life.

I continue not to feel one hundred percent myself, though I work hard to hide this from Declan. My bouts of nausea and lightheadedness, along with a constant drag of fatigue, has me thinking along lines for which I don't dare to hope. I check a calendar and count backwards. It's certainly possible, but unlikely, to have happened this quickly, given our ages and the fact that Declan's genetic background is nearly eighty percent *Sidhe* Fae of the *Tuatha de Danann* kind. Otherworld inhabitants have never been overly prolific in producing offspring. Maybe this has been the Universe's way of keeping a balance of power between the two worlds, or maybe there's just a biological hiccup in their genetic make-up. Children are not guaranteed to any Fae couple, and being blessed with one is considered a monumental treasure. It is the main reason why those who safely can cross over are eager to select partially human mates from the Mundane World. My being half human increases our chances, but nothing in the Universe is a sure thing, and I am too superstitious to wish too hard for something of that magnitude.

It's too early to take a home pregnancy test, and my next period isn't due until a few days after our handfast, not ideal timing for obvious reasons. I realize I probably could get an answer from Dr. Brannigan now, but I decide not to go that route. I want to enjoy living in this moment first. July 18th will be a life changing event for the two of us, and it deserves to be its own focus. Plus, I know for certain that if I give his Jr. Lordship the slightest hint that I might be pregnant, he will lose his mind and hover in even a more obnoxious manner than he already does. Until my late date arrives, I am determined to keep my mouth shut and take my physical side effects in stride while still erring on the side of caution. To be safe, I will avoid medications and alcohol and try to get extra rest.

The true test of my decision and resolve will come this evening. My Maiden BFF and my older sister have decided that I require a bachelorette party. This type of celebration focusing on wanton abandonment before marriage is an inherently exclusive tradition of the Mundane World, since the Otherworld lacks any cultural, religious or moral dictates regarding sex. In general, sexual activities are a lot looser among the Fae, so a special party allowing for lustful intentions isn't necessary. The Fae don't need justification for lust. Still, Mel is a girl who enjoys a good time, and my upcoming handfast gives her a perfect excuse to plan a girl's night out. The plural word girls basically means Mel, my sister, Claire, and myself.

D.P. is not a cheerleader for this event. In fact, I don't need any mind-share to see that he most definitely does not approve. He has provided me with a detailed lecture on how unsafe it is for three unescorted women to go to bars and drink too much. I return his lecture with my own, calmly explaining how I am a grown woman, capable of making my own decisions and taking care of myself, and reminding him that I managed quite nicely to live my life before he became part of it. I can see how the Lordship in him is just itching to forbid me to go, but he wisely tones down his rhetoric and switches to his traditional, please-make-me-happy-by-doing-what-I-tell-you, tactic.

This is not how I want to start our relationship. I've

been on my own for a long time, and I'm not used to having anyone tell me what I can and cannot do. Honestly, I wasn't really all that excited about Mel's plans, especially since I'm not drinking, but since the Tax Man basically has told me not to go, the modern woman in me has gotten her dander up.

Given my decision to go ahead with my plans, I get cranky Declan for the rest of the day; I try not to think about how much he reminds me of his Dragon Mama when he acts like this. But Lord *Mac Nuada* is not his *Mathair*. Later in the day he apologizes and insists his concern is derived entirely from his love and care for me. He tells me to have a good time and promises wholeheartedly not to send a shadow to track me for the evening. I, in return, tell him that I would never put myself at risk knowing how much he worries, and I promise to keep my activities to a nice, quiet dinner. I am pretty sure we both have our fingers crossed behind our backs as we make these bogus promises.

TOOTHACHE 37

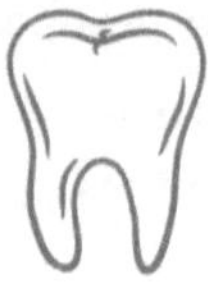

GIRL'S NIGHT OUT

I LEAVE for my girl's night out while Declan is working in his at-home office. He's cordial enough and tells me to have a good time, but I detect a bit of frost in his tone. He's made it clear he doesn't approve of the whole bachelorette party concept. I respect his opinion; I just don't happen to agree with it. Melanie and Claire have planned this night in my honor and are very much looking forward to it. I certainly am not going to tell them, "Sorry girls, his Jr. Lordship says I can't go." Not in this lifetime. D.P. gave me his word that he's not sending a shadow to track my movement, and I believe him.

When Mel arrives, she's already picked up my sister, and the three of us embark on our big adventure. My BFF mentioned earlier in the week that she had a few places in mind for the evening but never was definite about the what and where of our destination. I observe that we head south on Jefferson Avenue toward Ma-1AS, a route that leads to the city of Swampscott.

"We're not staying in Salem?" I ask.

Claire and Mel look at each other in the front seat and giggle. "Nope," says my sister. "We have a big surprise for you."

This raises my anxiety level a bit. I'd assumed that if my two gal pals had a little too much to drink I'd be their designated driver, given my decision to lay off the alcohol until I can verify certain *things*. But I'm unfamiliar with locations in Swampscott, and my night vision is not all that great. I would have preferred for us to stay closer to home in Salem rather than driving out of the city limits.

Salem's sister town of Swampscott is less than five miles away, but the highway leading to it is dark and twisty. I am again surprised when Mel pulls into the packed parking lot of a dumpy roadside venue called *The Witch Way Inn.* "This is where you're taking me for my big night out? It seems kinda...sleazy." I instantly regret sounding bitchy, but then the two of them again start laughing and now I'm annoyed at being left out of the loop.

"You'll see, Rosie Posie," Mel teases. "This is gonna be the best 'last stand' for a girl who's giving up on playing the field." Then she pulls out a plastic bag containing a silly, overdone bridal veil and a hot pink sash that says Bride-to-Be. "You need to put these on Rose, so everyone will know you're the girl of the hour," my Maiden instructs.

To be a good sport I do as I'm told; I feel ridiculous, but at least neither of my gals insist on taking photos meant for social media. For that I'm grateful. We make our way to the front entrance, and that's where I finally figure out the big draw of this out-of-the-way-shit-hole. There, next to the door, is a huge sign board featuring photos of half-naked men dressed as cowboys, policemen, and football players. The sign advertises a '**One night only! All male exotic dance revue!**' Now I understand why we're here.

My BFF pays our cover fees, and then, in a way only Mel can, charms the bouncer into giving us seats right in front of the stage. Lucky us! My feet stick to the floor, and our table has a piece missing that looks suspiciously like a bullet hole. A waiter who appears as if he's barely out of Jr. High and wearing the smallest pair of tighty-whiteys I've ever seen, comes to take our drink order. I try to keep my eyes on the drink menu because, frankly, the kid's package is at eye level, and I feel like a lecherous, old cougar ogling someone not much older than most of my patients. On the other hand, my companions wholeheart-edly enjoy themselves as they stare and wink at the young man all while ordering cocktails called Sex on the Beach with A Double and Three Way Sangria. I order a club soda, and even the jail bait waiter looks at me in shock.

When he leaves, Claire scolds, "What's wrong with you, Rosie? We're out here for a good time! I know you can toss them down like nobody's business. I watched you puke your way all through college. Why the sudden change?"

I don't know how I figured I was gonna keep my secret suspicion from either of them, but I don't want even to hint at the possibility before I tell Declan. I feel it would be very disloyal of me. "I'm just pacing myself," I lie. Lucky for me, the lights dim and music starts blasting from a speaker to the left of us making further conversation impossible. I give Claire a thumbs up which buys me more time, though I realize I'll have to order something alcoholic next time and find a way to get rid of it discreetly.

The first dancer is an extremely muscular guy dressed as a cowboy, wearing chaps but no pants, relying on a thin jock strap to keep his family jewels covered. He is very... well-endowed below his shiny bronco belt and undeniably handsome in a beardy, mustache way, but I don't find him nearly as attractive as does my married sister who shocks me by screaming up at the guy, "I'd like to ride me some of that wild bronco, sweetheart!" This encourages him to come over and wag his jewels at my sister who tucks a ten-dollar bill in his jockstrap just a little lower than necessary. He tips his hat at her and gives us all a very smarmy wink.

He is followed by a policeman who picks out a woman from the audience, also dressed in bridal gear, whom he handcuffs to a chair on stage while he then proceeds to give her a very suggestive lap dance. The Bride-to-Be looks drunk out of her marbles but clearly appears to be enjoying the performance. "Awww...too bad he didn't pick you, Rosie," Mel says. Yeah, too bad. NOT, I think to myself.

Next comes a fireman whose act consists solely of making a big deal of suggestively pulling a long hose from inside his pants. He's followed by a rockstar look-alike who continually grabs at his crotch with pure gusto. By this time, I'm starting to get bored and more than a little fatigued. I've already dumped two Lick Me All Over chocolate martinis into the fake potted palm next to me; I don't think there's enough room in the pot for a third. I wonder whether anyone would notice if I closed my eyes for a few minutes.

The music changes, and it startles me awake. A construction worker walks on stage wearing faded jeans and a white t-shirt, his tool belt hanging low on his hips. His face is shaded by shadow from the brim of his hard hat, but his movements are mesmerizing despite his being overly dressed in comparison to the previous dancers. I start to feel slightly too warm…and more than a little turned on. These feelings make me feel guilty. Then, I realize I'm probably just feeling this way because the guy is wearing jeans and a white T, which is my absolute very favorite Tax Man uniform. At least that's what I tell myself as I clap and whistle like an obsessed groupie for Mr. Construction Guy.

The lights turn back on signaling intermission. I'm about to head to the ladies room when the cowboy comes over and takes a seat at our table next to me. He presses his bare thigh up against mine while he asks whether the pretty, little bride might be interested in some private ropin' instructions. This makes the drunk Mel and Claire laugh uproariously but makes me uncomfortable. I don't want to be a bitch, so I smile sweetly and say, "Thank you, Mr. Cowboy, but I like to do my ropin' at home." This seems to only encourage him, and he puts his arm around the back of my chair and moves even closer. Over his shoulder, I see the hot construction worker taking long strides toward our table and wonder if perhaps Mel and Claire put the word out that I'm wanting to be the lap dance queen.

The construction worker never makes it to our table. Instead, the doors at the back of the venue crash open, and in pours most of the Essex County Sheriff's department, guns drawn. One of the deputies pulls out a bull horn and announces, "This is a raid. Everyone keep your hands where we can see them and don't move."

Fuck! What have Mel and Claire gotten us into?

TOOTHACHE 38

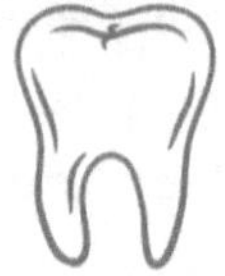

GUESTS OF ESSEX COUNTY

THIS HAS to be the most ridiculous situation I've ever found myself in. I try to explain to the deputies that I'm a pediatric dental surgeon from Salem and not involved in any illegal hanky-panky. The deputy is unsympathetic and says I can "tell it to the judge" while he zip-ties my hands behind my back. I am shuffled onto a county bus along with Mel and my sister, Claire, who is sobbing uncontrollably that her husband will never forgive her. I don't even want to think about how a certain Tax Man will react. I still maintain illusions of extracting myself from this mess without him finding out about it.

Everyone at *The Witch Way Inn* is rounded up to be sorted and investigated at the courthouse, including the exotic dancers and the still scantily dressed waitstaff. I watch the cowboy and the rock star being manhandled onto a bus loaded with people. I look around for the construction worker, but I don't see him. This is probably a good thing, since I certainly don't need to be ogling a strange, half-dressed man one week before I plan to commit to another in a permanent relationship. Plus, there's the possibility I have that *other thing* going on that I refuse to say out loud or even to let myself think about lest I jinx it.

At the courthouse, we are all placed in holding cells until our interviews, after which we'll either be processed and arraigned or simply released. Nearly two hundred people have been detained, and nothing is moving very quickly. At this rate, I will still be here in the morning and will have to tell Declan where I am, or he will go crazy trying to hunt me down. I imagine him showing up in his black tactical gear with a semi-automatic in his hand, like he did with the Chechens, and I start to sweat. Nausea rolls about in my gut; I'm not sure whether it's from the thought of hearing his Jr. Lordship's "I told you so" or the *other thing* I promised myself not to think about.

Initially, Mel suggests we disappear from the courthouse via magic. My BFF has some *Sidhe* magical abilities, and since it's after sunset, as a tooth fairy I can transport myself using my very basic magical skills. But Claire is fully human, and neither Mel nor I have enough magical skill to take her along. I would never leave my older sister to fend for herself. Plus, there are people everywhere around us. We can't just go poof and disappear in front of all their prying eyes. There are rules against that sort of stuff, and I have no doubt the Black Knight would enforce those rules, especially since it's his Mundane jail in which we sit.

My BFF then suggests she could give Duncan a mental

call to ask his help getting us out of this mess, but I put an instant kibosh on that. The *gancanagh* might be into my beautiful friend, but he is first and foremost loyal to Lord *Mac Nuada* on so many levels that I dare not trust him not to snitch on us. In the meantime, my sister alternatively cries and pukes into the single trash can that's already seen a lot of action tonight. I realize I'd better think of something fast or I'll find myself in a heap of trouble.

Several law enforcement officers walk past the holding cells. They mostly ignore our pleas, moving back and forth to usher people into interrogation rooms for their interviews. But at one point, a female deputy comes to escort another group, and by sheer luck, I instantly recognize her.

To prepare for our handfast day, D.P. has been tutoring me about who's who in the social and political upper crust circles of *I Idir*. There are a lot of people I am expected to greet and converse with, and for a half-human tooth fairy who has avoided the Otherworld for most of my life, the task has been rather daunting. We'd just gone over the *Crann Bethadh* (Tree of Life-home to The Morrigan and the Royal Court) crowd a few days ago. That's where I saw an image of this lady deputy. Her name is Roxanne Spinelli, and she is some type of Ward to Her Majesty (though I forget the particulars surrounding how she ended up in that role). I also know that in the Mundane World, she is a good friend to the Lady Dear Heart, works for the Black Knight here and in *I Idir*, and knows My Intended on a first name basis.

I frantically try to call her over, but she ignores me. I continue, and she gives an exasperated sigh and says,

"You'll have to wait your turn like everyone else, Ma'am. We're working as fast as we can to process everyone."

She turns away, so in desperation I yell through the bars, "*Rí fhada A Mórgacht, an Bhanríon Maeve!* (Long reign Her Majesty, Queen Maeve!)" This pretty much is the only whole phrase I know in the old language Otherworld Gaelic other than a bunch of swear words.

The deputy stops abruptly, and returns to stand in front of me. "Who are you?" she whispers through the bars.

"I'm Dr. Rosalinda Parker. From Salem. I'm Lord *Mac Nuada's Mo Shiorghra*," I explain.

"How the hell did you wind up at *The Witch Way Inn?*" she asks. "Isn't your handfast in like a week?" She takes in my silly sash and corny bridal veil. "Wait…was this some kind of bachelorette party outing?" I nod, and she cracks the smallest of smiles before adding, "I wouldn't think Fitz was the type to approve of something so…Mundane."

I can't help but roll my eyes because she's so spot on. "He wasn't too gung-ho about it, and now I'm pretty sure he's gonna be more than just annoyed. Is there anything you can do to get me and my two friends out of here?" I throw a thumb in the direction of Mel and Claire. "I'd be eternally grateful."

Deputy Spinelli frowns. "I personally can't… but I know someone who can. Let me see what I can do."

I sit down on one of the hard benches chained to the holding cell wall and cross my fingers, physically and mentally. Like most Fae souls, I'm forever superstitious. After nearly a half hour the Deputy returns. Unfortunately, she's not alone. She follows behind the one and only "Golden Boy of Essex County," Sheriff Theodore Beckett, aka the Black Knight of *I Idir*, who seems more than a little amused at my situation. Or my silly costume. Or both.

His deputy opens the cell door, and he signals for the three of us to exit. People around us note the Sheriff's presence and step back. The guy's like a legend in our local area. "I'm sorry you had to be rounded up like that, Dr. Parker," he drawls. "I'd ask why you were in a place like *The Witch Way Inn*, but I can see it's a bit obvious. I do suggest staying clear of places like that in the future. Witch Way has a terrible reputation."

I'm so grateful to be out of the cell that I agree, but there's a sense of smugness in his attitude I find a bit annoying. "Thank you very much for your help, Sheriff Beckett. I promise that we've learned our lesson this evening." I pause for a second, and, throwing caution to the wind add, "I'd really prefer if his Lordship wasn't made aware of my poor decisions, Sir. I'd rather not vex him this close to our handfast."

The Black Knight smiles again with his adorable dimples and shark-like teeth, and with a nod says, "Of course, Dr. Parker. I'm sure we can keep this between the two of us." Then he winks at me, and Cornhusks to Coronets, I realize I've just made a deal with the devil himself.

TOOTHACHE 39

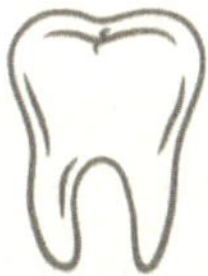

FACING THE MUSIC AND KEEPING IN STEP

DEPUTY SPINELLI IS TASKED by her boss to drive us all home. Personally, I think Mel is perfectly fine to drive, and I'm not super excited that Declan might see me return home in a patrol car, but I'm so grateful just to be going home that I don't argue. I only want this disaster of a night to be over ASAP. It's unlikely that despite the Black Knight's promises I'll be able to keep the evening's events a secret from my Tax Man. (*What does it say about you, Rosie Girl, that you feel the need to keep so many secrets from your Mo Shiorghra?*) The best I can hope for is getting a good night's sleep before having to face the music in the morning.

It's a little after 2:00 AM when I finally arrive home only to find the lights in my house still ablaze. Shit. I was holding out hope that D.P. had turned in for the night, but when I really think about such a notion it was rather stupid of me considering how over-protective of me he's been. I unlock the front door and am pleasantly surprised he's not standing in the parlor tapping his foot. The house is quiet, so I set the security alarm, turn out the lights, and go upstairs.

Declan is tucked into bed reading a novel. Strangely enough, he's wearing a pair of glasses. I realize this is ridiculous because I know he only uses them as a spy costume prop, but I don't comment. My only plan is to feign complete exhaustion to avoid the start of any long conversation in which too many questions could be asked. Seeing me, Declan looks up and says pleasantly enough, "You're home late, Love. Did you have a good time?"

I force myself to look him directly in the eyes. "Yes. It was a ton of fun. The three of us talked for hours. I never knew Claire and Mel had so much in common." I've mentally got my fingers crossed that D.P. won't ask me in what ways, because, frankly, the two of them couldn't be more different and I wouldn't know what to say in response. To give myself something to do besides lie directly to My Intended's face, I walk to the windows and close all the blinds. Then I remember I once mentioned I like to feel the sun on my face in the morning, so now I have to invent a bogus reason for shutting the blinds. "I'm probably going to sleep in tomorrow," I blabber, "because I've had such a late night."

"Good idea," the Tax Man replies. He sounds way too calm, which makes me nervous. I look to my left and notice his favorite jeans and white t-shirt casually thrown across the back of the vintage boudoir chair in the corner of the bedroom. I know he was wearing them when I left, but his Jr. Lordship is obsessively neat. He never, ever, leaves dirty clothes lying around. Anywhere. Something is wrong with this picture. I can feel it.

Declan closes the book and puts his glasses on the nightstand. Then he leans back in bed with his hands behind his head. He looks too relaxed and just a tad too smug. "I'm gonna wash up for bed; I'm bone tired," I say as I escape to the bathroom. I dive in and shut the door, glad for a few moments of privacy to compose myself. That's when I see them: a tool belt thrown over the towel bar and a yellow hard hat on the edge of the sink. Now I understand and am both simultaneously relieved and pissed. "Sonofabitch!" I shout from down the hall, not caring if my neighbors hear me.

I storm into the bedroom. "You ass! You followed me! After you promised you wouldn't! Then you have the balls to shake your shit in front of a room full of strange women...a week before our handfasting! Your dancing bordered on...on... obscene!"

His Jr. Lordship is now sitting up, arms crossed in front of his chest. I know that look. He's digging his heels in, convinced he's right. "I could say the same, Lass. A week before our handfast and my *Mo Shiorghra* willingly has taken herself off ta drool over half-naked men waggin' their private parts in har face."

I feel my face go hot, but I'm still convinced that I'm the injured party here. "I wasn't doing any such drooling, if you must know. I thought the whole thing rather... juvenile." I sniff and throw my chin up.

"Ya didn't find the cowboy sexy?" he asks.

"Ewww...no! Not at all. Truthfully, I was bored until the construc...you...came on stage," I admit.

"'Tis the first honest statement ya've made, Lass. I felt your lust crawlin' all over me. But I'm pretty sure that at the time ya didn't know it was me, did ya?" The Tax Man directly questions.

His statement cuts me deep. He's right. I didn't recognize my own *Mo Shiorghra*. And yes, I obviously was attracted to what I thought was just a random man. I've been feeling guilty about it all evening. My lip trembles and the tears flow, even though I absolutely do not want them. I don't dare think my excessive boo-hooing might be hormonal. This is not a good time to think about what I'm not supposed to think about.

The realization that he's truly hurt me blooms on Declan's face. He dives from the bed across the room and takes me into his arms. "Please Love, don't cry! I am so sorry for saying that. It was cruel and unnecessary, as was my decision to go on stage. I am ashamed of taking my teasing too far. I admit it. I was angry and jealous that ya wanted to be in a place like that, but it doesn't excuse what I did."

I try to wiggle out from his grasp but he just holds me tighter, so I have to wipe my drippy nose with my sleeve. "But you're right, Declan. That's the sad point here! I didn't know it was you. I'm a terrible *Mo Shiorghra*."

Now he's the one looking deeply upset. "Don' say such things, Love! Yar ma One and Only! There is no one else for me. Ever." He lets me go and begins pacing the room, rattling off a string of words in Gaelic I can't understand.

"Declan, please stop. Speak in English. I can't understand anything you're saying," I profess.

He comes back and takes my hands in his. "Bein'

someone else is what I do, Rosie. It's why I work in intelligence. I'm vera good at it. I didna want ya to recognize me, and so ya didn't. I am sure that the longer we are together that will change, but as we are so newly in love…" His words trail off, but then he adds, "You are my *Mo Shiorghra*. I've made love to ya enough to know what ya like, Lass, and I used that knowledge to attract yar attention and fool ya. I am vera, vera ashamed of ma behavior and I wholly regret it. I hope ya can forgive me. Where yar concerned, Rosie Lass, I seem to lose all hold of common sense."

It's crazy, but his saying all this makes me feel better. I wasn't lusting after a stranger after all. It was just my Tax Man being…well…my Tax Man. Plus, it's not like I was planning to lie to him as well. I planned to tell him about the evening…just not until morning. Still, I go ahead and push my luck. "You know I can't stay angry with you, Declan. I'm head over heels in love with you! I forgive you for pranking me like that. And…for being dishonest and following me in the first place when you said you wouldn't."

He lets go of my hands, and I see him raise an eyebrow. "I never lied to you about that, Lass."

"Seriously, Tax Man? You're gonna stand there and pretend you didn't promise not to 'shadow me' tonight?" I protest.

"That is not how the conversation went, Love. Ya made me promise I would not 'send' a 'shadow' to follow ya, and I agreed," Declan says. "I did not send anyone. I followed ya myself."

"Semantics," I counter.

"Ya should say what ya mean, Lass, and mean what ya say," Lord *Mac Nuada* states.

It is the Fae way. The *Sidhe* are Masters of Negotiation and have an uncanny ability to twist words around to suit their arguments. I'm not up for this type of battle. Not tonight. Instead, I suggest, "How about we just go to bed and forget this night ever occurred? All things considered I believe everyone involved would find that an acceptable compromise."

"Agreed, *Mo Stor* (My Darling)."

I go back to the bathroom to wash up for the night. When I crawl into bed, the Tax Man shuts off the bedside lamp and curls up next to me. In the dark, I whisper, "Will you promise me something, Tax Man?"

"Aye, Love. Whatever ya wish," he murmurs into my neck as he nuzzles it.

"Would you do that 'construction man' dance again? But just for me this time?"

He chuckles in my ear, soft and low. "Aye, Lass," my *Mo Shiorghra* says. "Ya have my raincheck on that."

TOOTHACHE 40

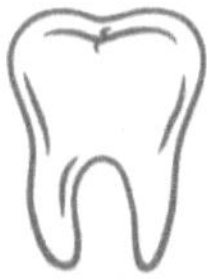

THE WAITING GAME

MY WISH for a private lap dance from my very own sexy construction worker is put on hold as time creeps closer to the 18th of July. The Tax Man is a crazy bundle of never-ending energy and nerves. His morning runs have become thirty minutes longer, and he's taken to spending a few hours a day lifting weights in my garage, leaving the overhead door open for extra air. It might just be my imagination, but there suddenly seems to be a large contingent of neighborhood ladies who have taken up afternoon walks that have them strolling past my house at approximately 3:00 in the afternoon. This just happens to be the exact same time Declan engages in his workout routine. I suppose I can't blame them. It is a lovely sight to behold.

I'd probably be out there myself, taking in the show, if I didn't need that very same time for my own afternoon necessity...a carefully planned and well concealed power nap. As soon as D.P. hits the garage, I drag my weary ass to the sofa to catch forty winks. I set the alarm on my phone for twenty-seven minutes, which is slightly less than his estimated work-out time, so that I can be bright-eyed and bushy tailed when he comes back inside. I feel some guilt over playing this covert, little game, but I am bound and determined to keep my suspicions to myself about the secret *thing* I'm not supposed to be thinking about until I can be sure that the *thing* is a reality.

Over the past few days, the local news has covered the story of *The Witch Way Inn* raid. Apparently, the dancing cowboy was offering me more than just a lap dance that night. Several of the dancers have been charged with solicitation and prostitution, while the bartender has been accused of selling narcotics. The media claims the Swampscott venue had been under investigation for several weeks before the raid, but I have my doubts that this is true. Working for the Black Knight, the Tax Man is privy to knowledge of a lot of criminal activity occurring in the major East Coast cities. If his Jr. Lordship was following me from the very moment I left the house (which I'm absolutely sure he was), saw my final destination and knew it was under investigation for such activities, I never would have made it inside. Nope. Instead, I think the Sheriff first became aware of the illegal activities occurring at *The Witch Way Inn* by an informant whom I believe was posing as an extremely sexy, exotic dancer in a white t-shirt and faded blue jeans.

This means my Tax Man knew me and Mel and my sister were in a holding cell in the Swampscott Court-house and left the three of us there to sweat it out. In addition, Sheriff Beckett, aka the Black Knight, already knew that Declan was aware of where I was and what had happened, and yet he accepted my deal to keep his supposed silence. Grrrrr. In my mind, this means our deal is null and void and I don't owe the Black Knight any additional favors. I mention this to My Intended who rattles off something in Gaelic before changing the subject. I can pick out only two words I know…*cinneadh*, which means decision, and *iarmhairti,* which translates to consequences. I don't need a translator to understand the gist of that comment. Double Grrrr.

As to my deal with the Black Knight, his Jr. Lordship proclaims that if I made any promises on that crazy night then it is entirely my business how it is handled and that I need to work it out with the man in question. There's no use being angry about it. I've always owned up to my poor decisions and whopper mistakes long before Declan Fitzpatrick became part of my life. Why should that change now that we're a couple?

Plus, today is not the day to be angry. We have just received a copy of the handfast invitation via raven-gram that has gone out to most of the population of *I Idir.* I admit to being almost faint with excitement over seeing it formally in writing for the first time. (Or possibly…I feel faint because of the *thing* I'm not thinking about.)

Tiarna Callum Fitzpatrick Nuada agus Bhean Siobhan Donnely Fitzpatrick Nuada cuireadh a thabhairt duit finne lamh a mic agus a noidhre Tiarna Declan Phineas Donnely Fitzpatrick Nuada

chun

Bhean Rosalinda Aine Parker Fiacail
ar 18 u uil ag lui na griene I n Grarran Naofa Theach
Nuada

(In English)
Lord Callum Fitzpatrick Nuada and Lady Siobhan Donnely
Fitzpatrick Nuada invite you to witness the handfast of
their son and heir Lord Declan Phineas Donnely Fitzpatrick
Nuada
to
Lady Rosalinda Aine Parker Fiacail
on the evening of July 18th in the Sacred Nuada Grove

To my mind, seeing these words right in front of my
eyes makes this whole crazy thing official!

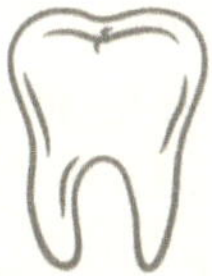

LET THE FUN BEGIN

I'M pleased to find that I'm getting better accustomed to traveling back and forth between the two dimensions. For most of my life, I've suffered from the travel bends upon my arrival in *I Idir,* symptoms usually consisting of a bad headache, some lightheadedness, and often a queasy stomach. That's one of the reasons I tended to put off delivering my Corps teeth on time. But during my recent two visits traveling with Declan, I've landed in pretty good shape. Perhaps it's been due to his Jr. Lordship's exceptional magical abilities, or possibly it might have to do with that *thing* I'm not thinking about. Whatever the cause, I'm grateful not to have to lie down in a dark room before being able to proceed with my business.

Although the physical worlds in both places are pretty similar, there is a time difference between the two that compares to traveling in the Mundane world between the United States and Asia or Africa. However, the in real time between the dimensions is much greater, 32 Other-worldly-style hours to be exact, so when we leave Salem the evening of July 15, we arrive in I Idir in the late morning of the 17th. Nothing like cutting it close. Neither of us wants to spend any more time with his family than we are forced to, especially since his parents insist on maintaining that ridiculously, old-fashioned tradition of keeping us apart before the handfasting.

This custom goes back to the ancient dark times when females were kidnapped from their intended spouses before an official handfast could be made and used as political bargaining chips or, in some cases, to procure a ransom. Things are more civilized in the Otherworld today and thus this old tradition of hiding the Lord's Lady to keep her secure is no longer necessary. Still, just as with Mundane wedding traditions, the Fae enjoy carrying on with the customs of the past simply for the fun of it. Declan and I have decided to go along with these silly high-jinxes to keep the peace, and both he and Mel have tutored me on what to expect.

Therefore, I'm not surprised when upon my arrival in *Dun Soirai*'s courtyard I am led away by Mel in one direction and Duncan teasingly leads my Tax Man in another. The two of them don't even allow us a good-bye kiss. I smile and act like a good sport, but deep down I have a tiny bit of apprehension and insecurity about being on my own within the *Nuada* estate. After all, we never did learn who was responsible for the bug in my salad or the cut in my saddle strap during my last visit.

I tell myself that if Declan thought I were still in danger, he wouldn't let me go with Mel, so I try to shake these negative thoughts from my mind and allow myself to live in the moment. My BFF leads me to the west side of the estate to a lovely room overlooking the sacred grove where our handfast will occur the following evening. I'm thrilled to see that the suite has two large beds and learn that it's also a tradition for the Maiden to stay with her Lady to meet any of her needs in the hours leading up to her joining. Apparently, I'm not supposed to leave this room until it's time for the ceremony. Both Declan and Mel have somehow left that part of the description out; I am decidedly not excited about being imprisoned in this room for 36 hours, but I remind myself that tying the knot with my *Mo Shiorghra* is the prize that awaits me at the end of all of this nonsense.

Melanie is relishing her role as my Maiden. As she unpacks my trunk, she lists all of the things she's planned for us while we await the big day. She lifts out the very sheer boudoir apparel I've brought along for my handfast night. "Oh La La, Rosie! Girl...this is mucho sexy. Your boy toy is gonna love this on you."

I snicker at the thought of anyone calling my Tax Man a boy toy. He is so NOT that. "I saw it in Boston and couldn't resist," I say. "I was going to save it for our honeymoon but I've changed my mind. It makes me feel like I'm a gift...all wrapped up in ribbons and bows."

"For sure you'll be a gift that makes your *Mo Shiorghra* want to do all the giving," my Maiden says with a big grin and a wink. She stands on her tippy toes to hang the peignoir in the wardrobe, then stops and turns around to ask me, "You did take care of getting waxed before you came here, right?"

I look at her blankly. "Wax? Wait…are you saying I have a mustache?" I shut the wardrobe door so I can check myself out in the full-length mirror. I don't see any nasty little hairs above my lip. "My lip is fine, Mel. I don't know why you have to get me all riled up like that for no good reason."

"I'm not talking about waxing your lip, silly," my BFF explains. "I'm talking about waxing your lady parts. You know…a Brazilian bikini wax."

I look at my oldest friend like she has two heads. "For Pete's sake! Of course I didn't get a bikini wax! That sounds awful, not to mention embarrassing as hell. Why would I ever do that? Besides, Declan has already seen what I look like…down there."

"That's exactly my point, Rosie Parker! Don't you want something new and exciting for your special night? Men like surprises…and they happen to like the bald look. Trust me on that. You know I have way more experience with Fae men than you do. You want to make your 'Lord' feel like you've gone out of your way to do something really sexy and special for him, don't you? The night of your handfast needs to be once in a lifetime memorable."

It's always been like this between Mel and me. From the time we were kids together, she's been the one making me try new things and escape my comfort zone. Hell…she was the one that convinced me that I could get through all those years of dental school. Maybe she's right about this as well. "Do you really think my Tax Man would prefer a bikini waxed me?" I ask.

"Oh Rosie…his eyes will pop right out of his head. You wait and see."

"But we're already here in *I Idir*. Are the Fae women into that sort of thing? Do you know of anyone who'll make house calls? I obviously can't leave this room."

"Fae women are tres chic! All the *Sidhe* ladies get waxed!" My BFF gives me a big hug. "I'm so proud of you for being brave, Rosie. You won't be sorry, I promise. Don't you worry 'bout a thing...we'll have you bald and beautiful in no time."

TOOTHACHE 42

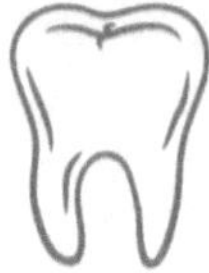

THE BARE FACTS ABOUT WICKED ROSIE

Okay. I'm just going to come right out and say it. Getting a bikini wax sucks. I may be in the minority regarding this personal hygiene choice, but my experience yesterday was so terrible that I have firmly vowed that I will never, ever, do it again. After yesterday afternoon's debacle, I can only hope that my Tax Man is willing to accept a hairier *Mo Shiorghra,* because I swear I never again will let anyone come near my nether regions with hot, melted wax.

After my concession to surprise My Intended with a bikini wax, Mel found an older *Sidhe* wax specialist who'd been recommended by a Fae friend of hers who spends half her life in *I Idir.* For someone who regularly performs such an intimate service, the waxing specialist wasn't particularly big on customer service. I was up front and honest with her that this was my first time getting a bikini wax, and I also shared that I was terribly apprehensive about the experience. I even tried to crack a few jokes to lighten the mood, but Madame Ripley (whose name is highly ironic considering her profession) was simply nothing but business and just grunted at me in response.

I'm not sure which part was worse; the application of the hot, gluey mess to my most sensitive lady parts, the constant ripping and pulling of hairs from my tender flesh, or the loud tisks and disapproving noises from the Mistress of Pain, Madame Ripley. The whole process was uncomfortable, long, and more than just a little bit embarrassing. I swear that Fae woman waxed parts of me that I didn't even know grew hair. The procedure went on for what seemed like forever, and when it finally ended, I over-tipped her hoping she would refrain from spreading the news to all of *I Idir* that Lord *Mac Nuada* was hand-fasting a Mundane Sasquatch.

When she left the room, I took a look at myself in the mirror and was, well...horrified. Not only was I very... bare...the skin down there was red and swollen. I couldn't imagine how in the hell this was considered sexy and fervently hoped that all this swelling and red skin was just a temporary reaction to the tugging and pulling, and that it would look much better the next day. When Mel returned and asked how I liked it, I tried to be upbeat with my response, but, frankly, everything below my belt felt like it was on fire. That night, I slept with no bottoms on, although even the sheets touching me in those places made me uncomfortable.

By the following morning, some of the obvious swelling had gone down, but now I'd gone and developed an ugly, blistery rash. I sat in the bathroom and cried about it for a good thirty minutes. Then, deciding that this day was too important for tears, I took a cool shower, got dressed, smeared aloe vera over my tender, bare, lady-parts, and made plans for the hours leading up to our handfast.

I had a fitting with Master Tyler before lunch, but the hair and make-up ladies were not scheduled until later in the day. This left me with nothing to do but worry and try not to scratch my privates, which now had developed an ungodly itch. I was feeling a bit sorry for myself and quite antsy, all the while also missing my *Mo Shiorghra,* something fierce. In truth, we hadn't been apart for this long since my abduction by the Chechens, and thereafter, I'd quickly gotten used to his solid presence in my daily life as well as in my bed at night.

It was all of these things that led to my plan to escape from my prison and surprise Lord *Mac Nuada* with a little special sexy time. Declan was always the one planning our memorable moments, and I decided it was high time I returned the favor. I needed Mel's help for this, and, of course, my BFF, who is always up for naughty fun, instantly agreed to offer her assistance. I had no idea where my Tax Man was holed up or where he might be found at this point in his day. Mel disappeared to see what information she could gather from Duncan, who by now seems completely smitten by my Maiden.

She returned a half hour later, flushed, disheveled and swollen-lipped, with the news that his Jr. Lordship intended to go riding with a group of friends this morning and would be in the stables around 10:00 am. Duncan promised my BFF that he'd make sure his cousin went there alone, though he couldn't promise for how long he could keep the rest of the party from intruding. He said that Declan liked to saddle his own horse and most likely would be found in the tack room.

Together, Mel and I plotted how I might get to the stables without being noticed, using the servant tunnels that ran under the house. Although it would be a rather long hike through the tunnels, it would let me out only a few yards from the stable entrance, and since I'd been inside of it during my last trip, I had a good idea where the tack room was located. Mel found me a plain, loose, work dress from the utility closet and I covered my head with an old scarf. Dressed this way, I felt confident I'd be able to pass myself off as a member of the estate's huge staff. Our joint espionage venture made Mel and me joke and laugh like high schoolers, and for the first time since I'd arrived in *I Idir* for my handfast, I felt like things were going to work out fine. Famous last words, I suppose.

Getting to the stable through the tunnels was even easier than I'd anticipated. The people I passed as I winded my way through the passages were intent only on getting to where they needed to be and paid me no mind. I felt excitement in the air, and I guessed it was due to the anticipation of the big celebration planned for that evening. I had my own extra special reason for excitement this morning.

The stable was empty as Duncan had promised. The stable hands were out and about, seeing to their chores. I let myself into the tack room and hid, heart pounding, behind a large partial wall covered with harnesses and bits. I didn't need to wait long. I heard the door open and knew immediately it was my Tax Man, the woodsy, citrus scent of his favorite soap a dead give-away. I waited until his back was turned, and went behind him and tapped him on the shoulder.

Apparently, it's not a good idea to startle someone who works for the Black Knight. Without a word, my true love spun around and put me in a complete choke hold before recognizing who it was he was assaulting. It took only a few seconds before Declan let go and turned me around to face him. He didn't look particularly happy. "Feckin' hell, Rosie, ya kennot be sneakin' up on someone like that. I coulda hurt ya!" Then, realizing I'd obviously risked scolding to come look for him, he smiled and added, "Though, 'tis a wonderful thing to see ya, Love. I've missed ya somethin' awful. Last night seemed to go on forever."

"I missed you too, Tax Man. I couldn't start this special day without telling you how much I love you."

"I love you too, Lass. Won't be long now before we are joined. I am anxiously countin' the minutes."

The two of us spent the next several minutes lip-locked and playing grabby ass. Then I remembered that we'd only have a limited amount of time before the rest of the men came in for their horses. "We don't have a lot of time, Sweetie, and there's something I need to do before I leave," I tell him. I drop to my knees and start pulling at his Jr Lordship's belt, grateful in that moment that my Fae lover has opted for the ease of modern zippers instead of the usual Otherworld toggle ties.

Above me, a very surprised Tax Man whispers, "Ya are a vera wicked woman, Rosie Lass…and I'm a vera lucky man."

Before I can get down to any real business, we both hear a shout outside the stable and the sounds of people approaching. Startled, my *Mo Shiorghra* grabs for his zipper and begins to tug it back up. Unfortunately, in doing so, he catches a clump of my hair in it. The more I tug, the more firmly the strands tangle themselves in the teeth of the zipper.

"Feck, Love! I don' wanna be found like this! I'd not ever live it down. Yah, need to get up, Lass, and hide in your same spot. I will try an' veil ya as much as I kin."

"I'm trying, Declan, but my hair is caught in your damn zipper! It doesn't want to come out!"

The voices get closer and louder and I sure as hell don't want to get caught in this position either. Anyone with eyes can see what it was we were in the process of doing.

His Jr. Lordship whips a knife from his boot. "Sorry, Love. I donna have a choice." He then whacks at the clump of my hair with his blade, cutting me loose and yanking up the friggin' zipper. I jump up to go hide, but my Tax Man grabs me by the wrist, kisses me and whispers, "I'll be expectin' a raincheck on this, Lass." I give him a wink and quickly tuck myself behind the wall just as a large group of men enter the tack room.

TOOTHACHE 43

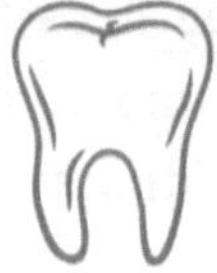

IT'S FITTING

His Jr. Lordship has some serious, top-notch magical talent. The veil spell he places over me holds firm the entire time the men saddle up their horses. Still, I'm relieved when they finally depart, as I'm sure it's getting nearer to the time of my fitting; in hindsight, I wish I had thought to ask Declan to fix the missing chunk of my hair. I hustle back through the tunnels to find Mel anxiously waiting for my return to our suite, excited to hear how my seduction went. We spend the next fifteen minutes laughing until we cry over my failed sexy time endeavor.

"I swear Rosie Posie…something that ridiculous could only happen to you! I mean, who else meets the love of their life by scalding their balls with hot coffee?"

"Yeah," I giggle, "that's a story I hope no one will tell tonight. To be honest, I'm not sure if anyone knows about that other than you."

"I agree, I wouldn't want that to be the center of everyone's congratulatory toasts," my BFF says, "though some day it will be a great story to tell your children and grandkids."

Mel's mention of kids squeezes my heart. It's been extremely difficult to keep my suspicions to myself, especially from someone who's been such a close friend since we were little girls. But I am determined that Declan be the first to know, if by some chance, my suspicions are more than just a pipe dream and we truly are going to be parents. I push that *thing* out of my mind. Master Tyler will be here soon, and I will get my first look at my handfast gown. I'm nervous, excited, and so incredibly happy that I can barely think straight.

When the royal dressmaker finally arrives, I am about ready to wet myself with excitement. He has several attendants helping him to carry the long pole with my covered gown hanging from it. "As promised, Lady Rosalinda, your dress is finished," the man says. "With plenty of time to make alterations if needed." He pulls off the covering to reveal the gown underneath.

When Mel sees it, she grabs my hand. "Oh Rosie…it's exquisite." Then she starts bawling like a baby. Of course, in the state I'm in, I quickly join her, and pretty soon even two of the designer's female attendants are wiping tears from their eyes.

"I assume the Lady is pleased then?" asks Master Tyler, himself beaming.

I forget all protocol and throw my arms around the royal designer in a hug. "Oh Master Tyler! It's everything I've dreamed of! How can I ever thank you or Her Majesty enough?"

The dressmaker gives a short bow from the waist. "You honor me by wearing this gown on yours and Lord *Mac Nuada's* special day, dear Lady. Now, shall we try it on and see what's what?"

I undress down to my chemise and the attendants help slip the multi-layered gown over my head. I still marvel at how well the design suits the person I am. It has the Celtic lace embellishments so popular in the Otherworld, yet also has the cut and style of a traditional Mundane wedding dress, perfect for a woman with one foot in each of the two dimensions. The bodice shows off my bosomy shape without making me look too much like Dolly Parton, and the way the layers fall from the waistline I don't have to feel self-conscious about extra love handles or rolls. I feel like a fairy princess whose Prince actually might ride in on a horse. I feel more tears welling up in the corners of my eyes, and I surely don't want to start with the water works again. Luckily, reality snaps me right back to attention when Master Tyler tries to lace up the back of the dress and it's obviously a tad too snug in the bust and waistline.

Master Tyler takes this in stride. He smiles at me, and I swear I can tell by the expression on his face that he knows the real reason the measurements he took only a few weeks back are now not correct. Ever the gentleman, he politely says, "No worries, dear Lady. My earlier measurements must have been off a bit. I apologize for that…Otherworldly gravity shift and all. There's no problem. It will all be fixed by this afternoon. These things happen all the time."

Across the room, I see Mel tilt her head and give me a

long, searching look, but I don't say a word. In fact, I purposely pretend to be examining the lace pattern across the front of the dress so I don't have to look at her. I'm praying she'll let the matter drop without prying. I don't want to have to lie to my BFF on the day she acts as my Maiden.

Eventually, I take the dress off, it is once again covered, and the dressmaker and his entourage leave the suite. I'm left so antsy by the too-tight gown that I literally pace the room. When lunch is delivered to our suite, I'm glad to have something to occupy my time even though I'm not in the least bit hungry. If Mel has questions for me, she's doing her best to keep them to herself. We sit down to enjoy our meal, and in my over exuberance and nervousness, I attempt to lift my glass in a silly toast and end up tipping it over. Both Mel and I immediately jump away from the table as the wine from the spilt glass sizzles and burns a large hole in the linen tablecloth. My Maiden and I look at each other in horror, as it becomes clear to us that another attempt has been made on my life.

TOOTHACHE 44

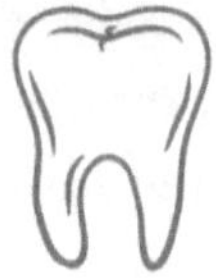

MOUSE TRAP

WE BOTH STARE at the growing size of the hole the liquid is burning into in the tablecloth. Neither of us wants to get near the caustic substance, and I shudder to think what might have happened if I had not been such a klutz. I suppose it was utterly naive of me to think that whoever had it in for me during my last visit suddenly would have abandoned all nefarious plans. If anything, their attempts seem to have become even more deadly.

"I'm calling Duncan," Mel states. "This is frickin' unbelievable."

"Stop, Mel! I don't want everyone to know about this, especially the Tax Man. It'll spoil this day for him. We only have a few more hours left. You and I can take care of ourselves until then," I plead.

"You're being silly, Rosie," my BFF scolds. "This was a blatant attempt to murder you! What makes you think that once the ceremony is over the culprit is going to stop? Do you really believe that a few Druid words and a piece of ribbon will keep them from trying again and again until they get what they want? If you and Declan ever are going to live in peace and be able to stop looking over your shoulder all the time, you'll have to get to the bottom of this…once and for all."

The logical side of me knows Mel is right, but I have a hard time letting go of my dream for a perfect handfast day. Of course, a dead *Mo Shiorghra* would also put a damper on the celebration. "Okay. You can call Duncan, but tell him he can't say anything about this to his cousin. Maybe we can look into this latest attempt without his Jr. Lordship finding out," I say.

Mel closes her eyes and seconds later, Duncan Fitzpatrick is standing in our suite. The fact that she can reach him so quickly indicates that things between them have gotten far more serious than I'd thought. My Maiden must also have mentioned why she was summoning him, because he arrives ready with his battle dirk in hand and a fierce expression on his handsome face. Mel points to the spilled glass of wine which is still eating away at the threads of the linen.

Keeping his distance, the *gancanagh* carefully examines the substance and its effects on the tablecloth, then stands and exhales a particularly colorful stream of Gaelic obscenities that include ancient magical curses and a barrage of actions that I don't think are physically possible. He takes both of my hands in his. "You are without harm, fair Lady?" he asks.

"Yes, Duncan. I'm fine, though I'll admit I'm getting really tired of this shit."

"Aye. These attempts on your life are a travesty without measure. Still, you must understand that I am unable to keep news of this atrocity from his Lordship," he states.

"Oh Duncan, do you have to tell him? You know how he gets. It'll ruin the whole day," I beg.

"And you know as well, Rosie, that if I don't tell him he will never forgive me. He is my cousin and my Liege Lord. Though I am very fond of you and owe you my life, if I were to withhold this information from Lord *Mac Nuada* our relationship forever would be broken. I hope you will not ask me to do such a thing," Duncan pleads.

Ruining the recently renewed relationship between Declan and his cousin is the last thing I want to do. Duncan is the closest thing my Tax Man has to a brother. I won't be the one to take that from him. "I suppose you're right. Go ahead and tell him, but you have to promise that you're gonna stick around and help keep his temper in line. I don't want this…this incident to ruin our handfast this evening."

"Aye, my Lady, I will do my best, but ya know as well as I do, his Lordship is more than a little stubborn," says Duncan. "I think it best if I seek him out and explain in person what has occurred. It will give him a few minutes to process the information and perhaps find a way to diffuse his temper before he examines this wretched scene. We both will return shortly." Then the *gancanagh* disappears, leaving Mel and me to pace and worry.

It takes a good ten minutes before the two men return, and I can only guess what went on before they appeared in our suite. My Intended has his jaw clenched so tightly that my own teeth hurt just looking at him, and he's wearing his cranky Declan look…on steroids. He enfolds me in his arms. "You are all right, Love?"

I suck in a whiff of the masculine soap scent that's become so much a part of my life. "I'm fine, Sweetie. I just don't want this shit to ruin our ceremony tonight. I don't want anything to delay our handfasting."

"We will tie the knot this evening no matter what transpires between now and sunset. Ya have my word on that, *Macushla* (Darling). But I ken not ignore this shet any longer. I must find this wretched soul and put an end to their black heart." The Tax Man lets go of me and turns to Duncan. "You will assist me in this quest, Cousin?"

"Aye, my Lord. As we have discussed, this traitor to House *Nuada* is undoubtedly a woman and assuredly will make another attempt before sundown," Duncan states.

"Wait," I interject, "how can you be sure the perpetrator is a woman?"

"Because, my Love, no *Sidhe* male would use such cowardly methods to assassinate someone. They would use a dagger or sword. It would be close up and eye to eye, done as quickly and methodically as possible. Poisons and subterfuge are the tools of females," my *Mo Shiorghra* states matter-of-factly.

"Isn't that a rather sexist statement?" I ask. "I don't understand how you can be so sure."

The Tax Man raises a single ginger eyebrow at me, a sign that he's not in the mood to be challenged. Sometimes that eyebrow thing is super annoying, especially because I don't seem to be able to do it. Some type of genetic quirk. "The culture here in the Otherworld is much different than that of the Mundane World," he says slowly, as if I were brain damaged. "As you spend more time here, you will see that for yourself." Declan pauses and then adds, "In fact, I am so sure of it, I propose a little wager."

Wagering on whether my supposed killer is male or female seems like a completely inappropriate thing to suggest on a day like today, but I realize it might be the way my *Mo Shiorghra* is hoping to diffuse the awful reality for me. I decide to play along. "Okay, Tax Man…I'll take your bet. What shall we wager?"

Now he raises his other eyebrow, and I think maybe I've agreed to a sucker's bet. There's the slightest hint of a wicked smile on Declan's face as he lays out the terms. "If I am correct and the perpetrator turns out to be a woman as I have said, then you must double up on your 'raincheck' from this morning."

"And if you're wrong?" I question.

"Then I will make good on two of the same," the Tax Man says with a perfectly straight face.

It's suddenly much too warm in the room, and I am keenly aware of the two other people listening. Still, I'm no chicken. "Okay, Fitzpatrick. You've got yourself a bet," I say as I put out my hand to shake.

He takes my hand to complete the deal, and when a tingle runs up my arm I think that perhaps this is a wager in which neither of us will lose. Duncan laughs and looks at Mel. "Would ya like to get in on this bet, my Lady?"

Mel puts up her hands. "Hell no! That's a sucker's bet for sure. I'm with you guys. This feels like 'super mean girl shit' to me."

I realize from his comment to Mel that Duncan must know what I had planned for Declan during our rendezvous in the stables earlier. I'm not sure who spilled the beans…Mel or Declan, but it's not something I care to get miffed about. I know the people in this room truly care about me, and I feel the same about them. I ask the only question that remains. "So…just how do you plan on finding out who's behind this nasty plot?"

"That's easy, my Love," says his Jr. Lordship. "We will set a fine trap and let the traitorous 'mousey' come to us."

TOOTHACHE 45

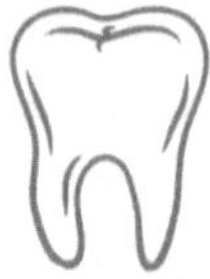

THE TRAP SNAPS SHUT

WITH ALL DUE respect to my Tax Man, I think his plan to smoke out the culprit is dumb. I get that he's a 'super spy' and has more experience with subterfuge than me, but I can't believe that anyone with half a brain would fall for something so…well…simple. According to Declan's trap initiative, I am to lie in bed and pretend to take a nap. Mel is supposed to make sure she is seen in several places around the estate, alerting everyone to the fact that I needed peace and quiet to nap and thus I am alone and most likely asleep, resting before my big evening. To D.P.'s mind, since no alarm has been sounded, my would-be killer must be aware that their poisoned wine has not led to my demise and must be looking desperately for a way to hatch yet another attempt.

Lord *Mac Nuada* is confident that the perpetrator undoubtedly will take advantage of my unguarded solitude. Of course, he and Duncan also will be in the room, magically veiled. After seeing how skillfully Declan veiled me in the stable, I am certain that whoever comes to call won't realize that anyone else is in the room. Part of me is annoyed at My Intended for being so damn confident that his plan will succeed, because I get the distinct feeling he believes this because he's quite convinced that only a woman would be dumb enough to fall for such a lame scenario. Perhaps this is not the time nor the place to have a discussion about his views regarding a woman's capabilities, but it's definitely going on my list of things to later discuss with my *Mo Shiorghra.*

Mel leaves to do her part, and I crawl into bed and pull the covers around me. Until recently, I have never been much of an afternoon napper, but the *thing* I'm not thinking about has changed that, and thus, once in bed I fight to stay alert and awake despite the fact that I'm lying here waiting for my potential killer. It seems like an extraordinary amount of time passes without anything happening, and I begin to feel self-righteous about the soundness of his Jr. Lordship's plan. Then, I hear the door creak open and I try not to squirm as I'm supposed to be soundly asleep. I hear footsteps in the room along with a strange hissing sound, something akin to a baby's rattle. My mind puts two and two together, and I suddenly realize that along with my probable killer there might be a rattlesnake in the room as well.

I use every ounce of my self-will and faith in my Tax Man's abilities not to jump up and run screaming out of the room. I am not fond of snakes. In fact, they terrify me. I hear breathing on the other side of the bed and the sound of someone fiddling with a metal latch. My heart is in my throat, and my eyes are closed tightly when suddenly I am scooped up from the bed. I open my eyes to find that I'm looking up at my *Mo Shiorghra*. The expression on his face is so grief-stricken and pained that I'm momentarily confused. If anything, I expected rage. Anger. Righteous indignation. Not a look of pure anguish.

He puts me down, and I turn around to face the person who has made multiple attempts on my life. Now I understand my Tax Man's reaction. Duncan has Declan's sister, Meghan, in a tight hold, the snake in a metal cage on the floor next to them. She is fighting her confinement and sobbing at the same time.

"Let her go, Cousin," Lord *Mac Nuada* says.

Duncan releases Meghan, and she runs to her brother, falling on her knees and grabbing at his legs in an embrace. "I am so sorry, Deckie. I had no choice."

"Did our *mathair* put you up to this, sister?" he asks. I can hear the tremor in his voice, and it makes me want to cry, but I don't. This isn't the place.

Meghan looks up at him, confusion replacing her tears. "*Mathair?* No. She knows nothing about this. She never pays me any mind. I could disappear for days and she'd not notice."

"Then who? Who made you do such horrible things against my *Mo Shiorghra*, Meghan?" Declan questions.

"No one made me do anything, Deckie. I did it for you! All for you!"

Declan pulls her up by the wrists. "For me? That makes no sense at all, sister. Why would you hurt me in this way? I thought...you and I...were fond of one another? The others I could understand, but you? I am lost for words."

"That's exactly the point, dearest brother! If you join with this ugly tooth fairy, you will spend more and more time in the Mundane World." Meghan points an accusatory finger at me. "She is more human than Fae. She would never consider making a home here. I would lose you forever. We would never go riding like we used to. Nor play draughts in the evening and tell jokes until our sides hurt with laughter. No. If you handfast her, you will prefer to spend all your time becoming more human yourself. I could not bear the thought, Deckie! You don't belong in the Mundane world! Can you not see why I had to do what I did?"

I sure as hell hope my expression is not registering my complete horror at their conversation. I realize every couple deals with the tensions of melding two families together, but truthfully, My Intended's clan is more dysfunctional than most. It's hard to comprehend that the Tax Man's sister was willing to take my life so she could go horseback riding with him on a more regular basis. Yikes!

If my face isn't mirroring revulsion, then Declan's is. He lets go of her hands. "So, are you saying to me, *Deirfiur* (Sister), that you would see me alone for all of my life...no partner, no children...no heir for our House...simply so you could be assured of more time with me?"

Meghan crosses her arms over her chest and sticks out her lower lip in a stubborn pout. I've seen that look before. Must be a Donnely trait. "You're making it all sound bad on purpose, Deckie. I did it for you. Because you are my favorite person in this family. The only one who pays me any mind around here. I don't know why you can't understand that."

The room goes deathly quiet except for the rattling of the snake in the cage. I want to hug my *Mo Shiorghra* and offer comfort, but I've learned well enough that he is not a fan of pity, so I stay silent and look at my feet. After a full minute, Declan turns to me. "I am sorry, my Love, for all that has been put upon you at the hands of my *deirfiur*. There is no apology worded fine enough for what you have had to endure." He kisses me lightly on the cheek. "After all of this, if you still feel in your soul that you desire to join your House to mine, your heart with my own, then I will see you in the Sacred Grove at sundown."

Then he walks to Meghan, kisses the top of her head, and says, "This is goodbye, Sister. It is my sacred promise in front of everyone here that I never wish to see you again." Then he turns and walks out of the suite.

TOOTHACHE 46

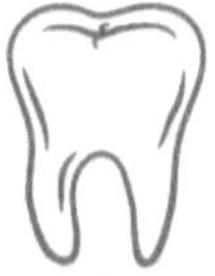

KNOCK, KNOCK

THE REVELATION REGARDING Declan's sister has left us all in a somber mood. Information relayed to Mel via Duncan informs me that after leaving my suite, Lord *Mac Nuada* saddled up his horse and went riding. That news did not put a spring in my step, to say the least. The logical side of me is confident that my *Mo Shiorghra* will, as promised, be in the sacred grove at the appropriate time, but the glass half full girl still is anxious.

The hair and make-up ladies have come and gone, and there is little to do now but fret until show time. Mel suggests a game of cards to pass the time, but even on my best days, I lose interest in keeping track of the suits. After two hands of gin rummy, I give up and go back to counting the number of geometric circles in the carpet pattern. All things considered I would have preferred that completely boring activity to the ensuing intrusion by two very much unwanted visitors.

My first visitor is none other than the Black Knight, who politely asks my BFF for some privacy. As soon as she picks her tongue up off the floor, Mel scuttles out of the room. If possible, the long arm of the law in *I Idir* looks even more handsome in the old-world garb of the Otherworld than he does in his regular clothes in the Mundane World. Unfortunately, this isn't a social call. The Black Knight apologizes for intruding on this of all days but explains he is required by responsibility to do so. He's come to inform me that Meghan Fitzpatrick had been taken into custody to await trial and sentencing for her attempts on my life. Under sacred *I Idir* law, such actions toward a fated mate is considered a capital crime, and it's within my right to ask that the death penalty be payment for her actions.

Once I recover from my shock, I inform his Lordship that under no circumstances will I request a death sentence for my future sister-in-law, and though I fully understand that life in the Otherworld is vastly different from life in the Mundane, I find the idea of capital punishment barbaric and reprehensible. The *Ridre Dubh* nods his head in understanding, but suggests that perhaps I would like to think on my decision and discuss it with my *Mo Shiorghra* before I make it final. I brush off these suggestions, explaining that as it is my decision, and since I am of perfectly sound mind to make it, I don't require Declan to tell me what to do.

At this, the Black Knight gives a short bow but I can see a half smile creep up in his expression, which, considering the situation, I frankly find annoying. Having little patience left, I add, "I'm sorry, your Lordship, but I fail to see what is amusing in all of this."

He shrugs, looking more human than he usually does. "My apologies, Lady Rosalinda. It's just that you remind me so much of my own Lady, and I find it extremely humorous to think of Fitz in a similar position. I imagine you will confidently keep him in line, dear Lady." He then adds another short bow, and turns and leaves the room, laughing to himself.

I barely have time to recover from that whole experience when there's another sharp rap on my door. "Come in," I say, wishing I could go back to counting patterns on the carpet. This time, it is Master Hobart, who announces that Lady *Nuada* would like a few words with me. After taking on the Black Knight, you would think that I would be willing and able to just tell the Dragon Mama that I wasn't receiving visitors. Not the case. No matter what I think of her, she is Lady of House *Nuada* and my Beloved's *mathair*. Therefore, I agree to see her.

Lady *Siobhan* Fitzpatrick is already dressed for this evening's celebration, and it's hard for me not to stare. She is a stunningly beautiful woman, and I can see so much of my Tax Man's face in her feminine one that it makes me catch my breath. Still, there's something different about her in this moment, and I realize she's lacking her usual complete air of haughty indifference. This evening, here in my room, she wears a definite look of wariness. Dragon Mama sees me studying her and pulls up her defenses. "No doubt you are pleased to see me in this position, tooth fairy," she mutters.

"I can assure you, Lady *Nuada*, that I am in no way pleased by the events of this afternoon. It is my handfast day, and it now carries a shadow of grief. What is it you want from me? It's getting late, and I need to finish dressing."

"Very well. I shall come directly to the point. I witnessed the Black Knight leaving your quarters. I am sure he has informed you that my daughter has been arrested and that you hold the power to sentence her to death. I have come to plead for my child's life. Take what glee you can from this, for it is surely the last time I will beg you for anything. Spare my Meghan's life, and I shall provide you whatever it is you wish," said Lady *Siobhan*.

As long as I live, I am certain that I will never understand the dynamics of this family. This woman loses a child at birth and inexplicably and viciously blames his twin for a tragic accident of nature, yet later begs for the life of a sociopathic daughter who knowingly attempted to kill someone multiple times. All I want right now is to join with my Tax Man and live our lives away from these damaged people. "I will put your mind at ease, Lady *Nuada*. I already have informed the Lord Knight that I absolutely will not seek Meghan's life in return for her attempts on my life."

Declan's *Mathair* is quiet, and I see the woman's shoulders relax, but it is momentary. She rears up and barks at me, "I do not wish to be beholden to you in any way. Name your payment, Lady Rosalinda."

"I have no price, Lady *Nuada*. My decision is based on who I am and what I hold dear," I say.

"I will not spend a lifetime knowing that you hold this

over me," Dragon Mama says. "There must be something you desire that will even this score."

The solution comes to me out of nowhere. "If you wish to provide payment, Lady *Nuada,* then do so by explaining to me why you hate him so much. Make me understand."

TOOTHACHE 47

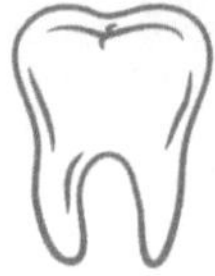

SIOBHAN

LADY *NUADA'S* face flushes pink, and she moves toward me so quickly that I take an involuntary step backward. "Do you think I hate my own child, tooth fairy? The son of my own body? Is that what you see as the truth?" She practically spits her angry words at me.

It is so not the reaction I'd expected that I stammer my response. "Yes...I...I assumed so. You speak to him so cruelly."

Dragon Mama's aura is a combination of pain and anger. It shimmers off of her with pulsating energy, giving me a good look at the power of her magic. "You stand there so smugly, Rosalinda Parker, basking in the blessings the Universe has bestowed upon you through no efforts of your own. You have no understanding of how cruel and demanding the Universe can be for those of us less fortunate. To the Universe, we are only puppets in a long tale of history, playing our parts without personal choice. You are ignorant to the sufferings of others."

I've always thought myself to be a truly compassionate person, normally atuned to the feelings of those around me. Her accusation that I'm not stings. "I DO care, Lady *Nuada*. I want to understand the dynamics of your House. Help me do so. Please, explain them to me." I plead.

Lady *Siobhan* marches to the window and looks out at the sacred grove where in a few hours I will join my life to her son's. She doesn't look at me when she speaks. "I was barely fifteen when I met Callum Fitzpatrick. Just a mere girl. Though Callum was not yet Lord, his own father still being alive, he was so commanding, so handsome and mysterious. Our attraction was immediate, and when it was revealed that I wore the ink of House *Nuada*, I was as joyful as you are at this moment. I did not know about his relationship with your mother. He kept that from me until after our handfast. Nearly four months after our joining he confessed to me in a drunken stupor that he was in love with another woman, a tooth fairy by the name of *Aine*. He tearfully admitted that though he was attracted to me physically, he had no feelings towards me beyond those of a sexual nature. I was crushed and adamant to prove him wrong. I tried everything I could think of to change his mind. I sought the advice of the mages and wise folk, tried magical potions and spells, but nothing helped. I begged for answers to explain my *Mo Shiorghra's* feelings, but all I was told was that sometimes we could not discern why the Universe acts as it does. I was the fated mate of a man who didn't share my love or devotion. It was the damned path set before me."

This was an awful and tragic story, and despite her behavior from the moment we met, part of me feels sorry for a young woman placed in a situation that could lead only to future unhappiness. A thought enters my mind. "If you were both so unhappy, why didn't you end your union after 'the one year and one day' had passed?" I ask.

She turns to face me, and by her expression I guess the answer before she gives it. "I was already pregnant, expecting twins of all things, two boys as the mages predicted. I took this blessing to mean that perhaps things would work out after all. That my Lord would see his heirs and love me for providing them. With a family of his own, maybe he'd forget about the tooth fairy woman and be grateful for what the Universe had provided him."

Having heard this part of the story before, my stomach tightens knowing what comes next. I think about the *thing* I'm not thinking about and imagine too many what ifs. The Lady continues her story, though neither of us really wants to hear it. "My pregnancy was normal all through the nine months, and I expected a day of great rejoicing when I went into labor. But then the first son was born dead at the hands of his twin. Lord *Nuada* looked at me with such blame and revulsion, as if it were my fault. Any feelings I might have had for the man disappeared that night, along with the souls of those that lost their lives in the flood. I was forever joined to a man I had no respect or devotion towards, and he was joined to a Lady with whom he had never shared an ounce of love."

I feel sick. The story is even more horrific to me now that I know the intimate details. Still, my loyalty to the Tax Man is stronger than my pity for his *mathair.* "Declan was an infant, Lady *Nuada.* To spend his whole life telling him he was cursed is an abomination to maternal instinct."

The Lady herself looks defeated, and I feel guilty for using a word as harsh as abomination.

"From the very first moments of his life, the child hated me as much as his father," she reveals.

"Maybe his sire's negative energy passed into Declan. I cannot explain it. He stiffened each and every time I tried to hold him. He cried incessantly and refused to nurse. Those around the family began to spread rumors that the child knew his *mathair* was unfit and hated him. Under my care he grew sickly, and finally his sire demanded a nurse be brought in to care for him instead.

Since those infant days, things have never been right between the two of us. The son who so much resembles my blood line has no use for his own *mathair* and after all these years, I have returned those very same feelings back to him."

TOOTHACHE 48

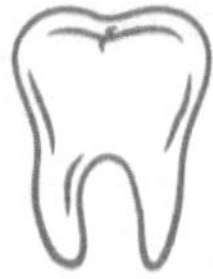

READY OR KNOT

I DON'T RECOGNIZE the reflection of the woman in the mirror looking back at me. She is not Rosie Posie, comfortably unstylish in her sweats and bunny slippers. Nor is she Dr. Rosalinda Parker, D.D.S., looking professional and in charge wearing her clean white lab coat. She's not even Tooth Fairy Cadet Parker, decked out in her ridiculous satin tooth fairy uniform. The woman in this mirror is a Celtic princess, dressed in lace, hair woven into complicated braids, a glow to her skin that defies her human heritage. This woman is no one I know, yet everything I am, on this, my handfast day.

My conversation with Declan's *Mathair* leaves me shaken. Her words were raw and truthful, and her bitterness hangs in the air around me like a perfumed scent one doesn't care for but from which one cannot escape. How can you continue to blame him for something over which he had no control?

How would I ever be able to bear it if the *thing* I'm not thinking about is real and doesn't return my love? These thoughts and feelings sit heavily on my shoulders even as the team of Fae ladies arrive to help me slip the layers of petticoats over my head. It's not until they finally maneuver the lace gown over my body and fasten its toggles on the back that my mind returns to the glorious monumental moment in my life that's about to take place.

I think about my Tax Man and wonder if, on the other side of the estate, he's thinking about me. I suppose I could open a line of communication between us, but with his mother's words still floating in my head, I decide it best to keep my thoughts private. We'll have a lifetime together to deal with his difficult family dynamics. Tonight is meant exclusively for the two of us.

My little entourage fusses with my dress, tucking and pulling and smoothing out the layers, until they all stand back and agree that I am one hundred percent completely good to go. My Maiden joins us in the room and squeals in typical Mel fashion when she gets her first look at me. "Oh, Rosie...you look like a real live princess from a Disney movie!" She moves in to try and hug me, but my dress ladies step between us to stop her, scolding in Gaelic what I'm sure is a warning not to smoosh the dress or smudge the make-up. She giggles despite the warning and says, "You owe me a hug, girl!"

Mel looks absolutely stunning in her own right, and there's no doubt a lot of male heads will be swiveling in her direction this evening. Master Tyler has designed her gown as well, and it compliments mine perfectly without looking too matchy-matchy. The royal designer has dressed my BFF in a sapphire blue, off the shoulder style that flatters her long graceful neck and delicate shoulders. The color is striking with her strawberry blonde hair, sea green eyes, and pale porcelain skin, and I'm sure that Duncan will have heavy competition for my Maiden's attention this evening.

Two men from House *Nuada's* Security team arrive to escort Mel and me to the sacred grove. I wasn't aware that I still needed security since Meghan had been arrested, but I assume this is another throwback tradition to the days when mates were sometimes kidnapped and held for ransom before the handfast could take place. I don't even want to think about that possibility. Come hell or high water, I am determined to join with my Tax Man tonight, even if I have to fight off would-be kidnappers with my bare hands.

As we walk through the halls of House *Nuada's* ancestral stronghold, I finger Declan's gifted garnet choker. Though it has been barely six weeks since I first laid eyes on Lord *Mac Nuada*, it's as if I have lived an entire lifetime since. Getting to this moment has been nothing short of a miracle, and I take the last few seconds before we arrive to send a prayer of thanks to the Universe for sending me Declan Fitzpatrick.

Our little group exits the building and crosses the courtyard before heading toward the sacred grove. We pass the stables, and I secretly grin at our little adventure earlier in the day, not to mention the bet I lost and for which I am looking forward to paying. People clap and throw handfuls of wheat berries before me, an Otherworld sign of fertility and happy new life, similar in nature to the old Mundane world custom of tossing rice at a newly married couple.

As we step into the sacred grove, a shiver runs down my spine. It's a warm summer evening, so my reaction has nothing to do with a chill and everything to do with the current of magic that fills the space. This grove has been used for a myriad of sacred ceremonies over hundreds of years, and the power of it pulses under my feet. I try to imagine a young Declan sitting here on his 14th birthday as ink is applied to his bicep; in response, a piece of that artwork tingles on my shoulder blade. Even though I have spent practically my entire life living as a human in the Mundane world, I feel the Fae blood racing through my veins in a way I have never felt it before.

There's a spot that marks the place I'm to stand on the right side of the grove. Behind me sits a large group of people representing House *Fiacail* (Tooth). In truth, I know none of them, since my *mathair* chose to cut herself off from most of her family in *I Idir* long before I was born. I now realize why that was, the past here in the Otherworld being too painful for her to bear. A ray of light from the torches suddenly catches the ruby stone in the ring on my right hand, given to my mother by Lord *Nuada* and recently passed on to me. It makes the gem appear to have fire burning beneath its facets, and I view this as a sign that my mom is with me in spirit.

Somewhere behind where Mel and I wait, music starts to play. I look at the empty spot across from me where Declan will soon stand with members of House *Nuada* sitting behind him. I feel a bit awkward positioned here alone with Mel, but when the inked wolf tattoo, House *Nuada's* sacred sigil, begins to tingle and burn in earnest on my right shoulder, I know for certain that my *Mo Shiorghra,* my One and Only, has finally arrived in the sacred grove for the tying of the knots.

TOOTHACHE 49

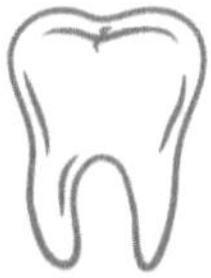

TYING THE KNOT

As proper protocol dictates, my Tax Man first greets Her Royal Highness and those seated with her, then his parents, and finally the other members of House *Nuada*. Since my own parents are not in attendance, and my House is in no way a part of the Ruling Council, none of that is required of me. The fact that The Morrigan, goddess of war and destruction and Queen of *I Idir* is a guest at the handfast of Rosie Parker is enough for me to try and wrap my head around without having to greet her in person.

As he walks across the courtyard to join me in the center of the grove, I decide that referring to my *Mo Shiorghra* as my Tax Man absolutely is inappropriate on this day. The man coming toward me is not the same D.P. Fitzpatrick, C.P.A. that I met in my office six weeks ago. This man, Lord *Mac Nuada,* looks every bit a member of ancient Fae royalty. His Otherworldly bloodline is written on every plane and angle of his proud face. How I could ever have mistaken him for a human defies logic. It shows just how Mundane my life had gotten despite my tooth fairy roots.

Declan's handfast attire matches mine in all-out finery. He is dressed in his House's colors of maroon and gold, and the luster and flow of the fabrics demonstrates that they are woven of the finest silk. His tunic is worn over tight fitting trousers of cream colored, doeskin leather, with dark brown leather boots laced to over his knees. If it weren't for the absolute huge grin on his face, Lord *Mac Nuada*'s 6'4 appearance would be intimidating. Instead, he looks like a boyish figure radiating the pure joy of a Christmas morning.

When he gets closer to me, I can feel the tremendous amount of emotion rolling off of him. It's so strong that it makes me wobble on my feet for a moment. I can tell he's feeling mine as well, and I use all of my concentration to hide my feelings about the *thing* I'm not thinking about. For a second, a quizzical look passes over his face, but whatever it is that has him momentarily curious he lets go of it and moves in to embrace me.

"This moment has finally arrived for us, Rosie, my Love. I am beyond joyful and so fully blessed. You look incredibly beautiful and so worth every minute of all those years I have spent waiting for you," he whispers in my ear.

I can't imagine how excruciatingly painful it must have felt to know that there was someone in the world who would love me like no other, but not know who she was or when she'd appear in my life. I feel doubly blessed that this man came to me as a wonderful, amazing, surprise gift from out of the blue. "Oh Declan, this is like a dream come true…a wonderful, enchanted, amazing dream. We're going to be so happy together," I gush, trying not to think too hard over the words lest I start bawling like a baby and mess up my stunning make-up job.

As we both stand there grinning like circus clowns, a Druid in full ceremonial robes enters the grove and comes toward us. A reverent hush fills the space, and when the figure comes closer, I see by the sigils on the front and sleeves of his robe that this person is the current reigning Merlin. *I Idir's* Merlin is Ambrose James Myrdynn, who also happens to be the Black Knight's father. I definitely see a family resemblance between them, despite the hood covering a portion of the wizard's face. That our handfast is being officiated by the most powerful Druid in the Otherworld is a testament to the importance of House *Nuada* and its heir to the Ruling Council of *I Idir*.

The Merlin smiles at us. "Are you ready to begin?" he asks.

"Aye, my Lord Merlin. The sooner the better as I canna bear to wait even a second longer," my *Mo Shiorghra* says.

The Merlin laughs under his breath. "As it is with fated mates, Lord *Mac Nuada*." He turns to me and asks, "And you Lady Rosalinda…are you more than ready as well?"

"Absolutely!" I answer. "Let's rock this handfast!"

The Merlin smiles at my lack of reverence and protocol before taking my right hand. He then takes Declan's left and places it on top of mine. My Mo Shiorghra's hand is extraordinarily sweaty from nervousness and we both laugh over that. Then the wizard takes my left hand and places it on top of Declan's and finally puts Declan's right hand on top of that. A young woman dressed in the white robes of a Druid novitiate steps into the center of the grove and hands the Merlin a set of cords in the shades of maroon, gold, white, and rose pink, the four colors representing both of our Houses. Lord Merlin then asks us to state our intentions in front of everyone gathered around us.

As the female, it's traditional for me to go first. Because my Gaelic is so weak, we've received permission to express our vows in English. This is preferable to me than stuttering along and mispronouncing my vows. I open my mouth and the first few words come out as a squeak. "I, Rosalinda *Aine* Parker *Fiacail*, do solemnly and of my own free will, join my life to yours, Lord Declan Phineas Donnely Fitzpatrick *Mac Nuada*, to walk the path that has been set before us by the power and wisdom of the Universe, to promote harmony among our people, to serve as we are directed to serve, and to welcome with joy any offspring that comes of our union. Let our love be the light that guides us through the dark days and fills our years together as many as they shall be."

The Lord Merlin then wraps the pink and white cords representing my House around both of our hands, leaving the two ends temporarily hanging free. He then nods to Declan, whose voice has no squeaks or cracks. In fact, he nearly shouts the words so that even the guests sitting in the last rows can hear the force behind them. "I, Lord Declan Phineas Donnely Fitzpatrick *Mac Nuada*, do solemnly and of my own free will, join my life to yours,

Rosalinda *Aine* Parker *Fiacail*, to walk the path that has been set before us by the power and wisdom of the Universe, to promote harmony among our people, to serve as we are directed to serve, and to welcome with joy any offspring that comes of our union. Let our love be the light that guides us through the dark days and fills our years together as many as they shall be."

The maroon and gold cords are then also wrapped around our hands. The Merlin then takes the ends of all four cords, tying them in an intricate, repeating knot, leaving the strands loose enough so that after the ceremony we will be able to free our hands without damaging the complex weave. When the wizard is done with the knotting, the novitiate hands him a lit white candle of pure bee's wax, and he drips the melted wax over the final knot. This symbolizes the sealing of our covenant. The Merlin hands the candle back to the young girl and raises both palms up to the sky, saying, "As your hands are now bound together, so shall your lives be bound as one. Keep this cord as a visible reminder of your promise to one another, and let no one unbind it during these days and nights of your handfast vow."

As the last of the words leave the Druid's mouth, there is thunderous applause, the blasts of trumpets, and exuberant shouts of congratulations. And just like that, with our hands tied together and our lips now firmly locked, my beloved *Mo Shiorghra* and I become Otherworld husband and wife.

TOOTHACHE 50

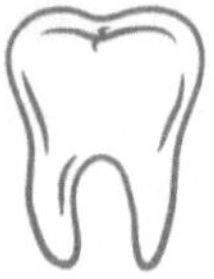

WHO'S GAME?

HANDFASTING celebrations in the Otherworld are not unlike wedding receptions in the Mundane world. There is food, drink, dancing, and general merry making. I spend the first hour of our life as joined mates in a type of mental stupor, the realization that I am now wife to my Tax Man being overwhelming. I realize this moniker I have for him is inappropriate given Declan's regal blood-line, but Declan's been my Tax Man from the moment I saw him in my office and this is my way of reconciling the reality of the man…the one who snores all night, picks the croutons out of his salad, and enjoys trashy crime novels… with the Lordly title under which he was born.

Duncan and Mel help us remove the cords from our hands without disturbing the knots, and they are placed in a satin-lined, wooden box engraved with our names and the handfast date. The box is given to the care of his Jr. Lordship's personal valet who then will deliver it safely to Declan's quarters. We spend an excessively inordinate amount of time greeting guests and accepting congratulations, so that there will be no possible way I ever will be able to put the correct names to the faces once they leave the line.

Before dinner, the two of us stop by the table holding the massive stacks of *Comharthai Gra* (Love Tokens) that our friends and family will take home at the end of the celebration. Unlike weddings back in Salem, Fae handfastings don't have the tradition of one large, decorated cake that is initially cut by the happy couple and then shared among the guests. Instead, hundreds of small loaf cakes are baked, festively wrapped, and given as favors for the celebrants to take home when the celebration is over. The treat is similar to a spice cake, fragrant with ginger, cinnamon and cloves, and studded with bits of dried apple and hawthorn berries, all symbols of ancient fertility rites. In a fun twist, one of the cakes has a large oval garnet, House *Nuada's* symbolic gemstone, baked inside for one lucky guest to find. Tradition states that whoever finds the garnet and keeps it will be guaranteed a happy, fruitful, love match, though the odds are high that the stone will undoubtedly be sold off for a profitable return. The Fae, like their human counterparts, love an unexpected windfall.

There is also one unwrapped cake on the table, left for my new mate to feed me bits of, symbolically representing the new life he will hopefully give me. We both laugh and joke during what's supposed to be a solemn ritual, the Tax Man in playful anticipation of what the "fertility" part entails, and me because I'm pretty sure the fertility ship has already left the harbor.

Afterwards, a tremendous feast is served, but I merely pick at my food, so much so that I'd be hard pressed to give an accurate account of the menu. My mind is trying to process everything at once. Even without the cords physically keeping us tied together, my *Mo Shiorghra* has yet to let go of my hand, and each time I look at him, he is staring at me with a complete look of wonderment that matches my own feelings. I also notice he's hitting the ale pretty heavily. This catches me off guard, since I haven't known him to be much of a drinker. In fact, I'd most likely describe him as a teetotaler. I guess this must be what's expected of a groom-like celebrant at an event of this kind, but I was rather looking forward to a sober lover on this, our handfast night.

There's more dancing after dinner, and of course Declan and I are expected to participate. As tradition requires, Declan must dance with as many single ladies as possible, and I am expected to dance with all the single gentlemen. This is to ensure extra good luck in their chances of also finding a perfect match like us. After several dances and near exhaustion, I at last find myself back in the arms of my husband. As we move through the reel, he grins and says, "I probably shud' warn ya', Lass, there's a game afoot."

I don't particularly care for the word warn. "A game? What kind of game? What's going on? And why are you drinking so much ale? I've never seen you drink this much before."

"'Tis not actually ale, Lass. I have made arrangements

for the steward to pour me plain cider instead. It only appears that I am imbuing more than ma' fair share," Declan explains.

"But why? Is that part of the game you mentioned?" The more I hear, the less I'm liking this subterfuge. This is our handfast night, not a Beltane tournament, and I know my Tax Man can become extremely competitive when challenges are involved. Frankly, I'd like to be his ONLY game this evening.

"Do you see that group of young gallants standing near the musicians?" Declan asks.

I casually look over my shoulder. "Yes. They've been hanging in that same group all evening. Reminds me of a high school dance." He pulls me in closer and kisses my neck. I know when I'm being buttered up. "Okay, spill it, Tax Man. What the hell is going on? I've already had enough spy 'shet' to last me a lifetime."

"This is not about spy shet, Love. It's just a little Otherworld…game…in which the single men of my House will try to keep you and me apart on our handfast night. The old tales hold that the night of a couple's handfast is the one most likely to produce offspring, so I must keep them from stealing away my chances to father a child. I know it sounds childish and silly, but it has been a tradition for centuries, and the young men look forward to out-playing the *fear na bainnse* (bridegroom). They will not miss this opportunity to tease House *Nuada*'s heir."

I am aching to tell him that I'm about 90% sure that the producing of an heir has already been accomplished, but this is not the way I'd envisioned giving My Beloved the blessed news.

On the other hand, after the Chechen incident, I'm not excited about the prospect of being kidnapped again, even if it's just for fun. Besides, I've been missing my Tax Man…a lot…and I'm not willing to give up the evening I've been thinking about since we first got to *I Idr* and were separated. I make a face, but I simply kiss him back. "I'm counting on you to outwit them, Sweetie. I'd be mighty disappointed if I was unable to pay off my part of that…rain check tonight."

Declan offers me a doozy of a kiss in return. "Have no worries, Sweet Rosie Lass. I fully intend to collect on your debt. Everyone knows that *Mac Nuada* never loses a challenge."

TOOTHACHE 51

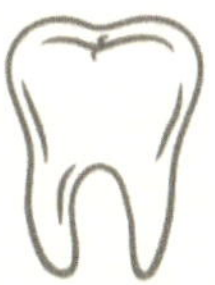

A ROSE BY ANY OTHER NAME

I SPEND the next half hour chatting with various guests and watching my husband make a complete ass of himself. Declan and the group of young gallants, as he called them, are in the midst of some silly drinking game that involves throwing knives at a marked target, with the owner of the knife landing furthest from the center required to drink another tankard of ale. It seems an incredibly stupid idea to be throwing knives around when one is inebriated, as some of the men do appear to be, but I know better than to say anything, lest I somehow embarrass my Jr. Lordship's pride.

According to the Tax Man, he's actually cold stone sober, but he's intent on making the young men surrounding him think he's totally smashed. Lord *Mac Nuada* is doing a fine job of appearing drunk, and, once again, I understand why he works in intelligence: My Beloved is one hell of an actor. He looks up from the cup, and I catch the faintest of winks he throws my way, just as his old *Buime* (Nanny) pulls up a chair next to me.

Magda doesn't speak English, and my Gaelic is virtually non-existent, so without Declan to translate, we are forced to rely on simple hand gestures. She takes my hand and puts it to her heart; in return, I do the same. It's not hard to feel the love she has for my husband, and now for me as well. *"Is brea liom go mor e* (I love him very much)," I stutter out, hoping I put the words in the correct order so that she understands.

Magda nods and smiles, so I venture that she understands well enough. She places a hand on my belly and looks at me questioningly. I freeze for a moment, wondering how she could possibly know. I've done my absolute very best to keep these thoughts shielded. If she's seen through me, has anyone else done the same? I watch as she puts her hand back on her heart and then points a finger in Declan's direction. I make a last-minute decision to reveal the truth to her, hoping my Tax Man won't mind that I've told his beloved *Buime* before him. "He doesn't know yet, " I whisper. "I wanted to surprise him…after we were officially handfasted…a special gift of sorts. Please keep my secret, Magda."

The old woman smiles wide so I assume she understood enough of my words to make sense. I see tears in the corners of her eyes, which of course threaten to set off my own. She takes my right hand and draws the Other-world symbol for new life on my palm. Then she kisses my cheek and wanders off, leaving me wondering whether I've committed a relationship boo-boo by telling her ahead of my husband. I don't have much time to fret, since one of the younger men from Declan's group comes over, gives a low bow, and asks, "May I have this dance, Dearest Lady?"

The sigil on his sash declares him the Lord Heir for House *Badb*, and a cousin to Her Royal Highness, The Morrigan. To decline his offer would be considered highly offensive, so I rise wearily and accept his offered hand. I am thankful it's a slower paced reel, as, frankly, I really am getting extremely tired. It's been a terribly long day, and part of me just wants to put my feet up. The Lord *Mac Badh* is pleasant enough, full of compliments and congratulations, but I note that with each complete circle we make, he is moving us ever so closely toward the far exit.

This causes me some alarm, so I look back to where I last saw Declan, but he's no longer there. This puts me into a general panic, and I mention to my dance partner, as casually as possible, that I've lost sight of my new mate. He smiles at me and laughs. "It seems our Lord *Mac Nuada* no longer has the stomach for good Otherworld ale. Perhaps he has gotten too familiar with the watered-down sludge the Mundanes call 'craft beer?' I saw him wander off to the trees, most likely to relieve his stomach of its contents." His tone is so pompous and demeaning that I decide I don't like this jerk very much. Plus, he's moved us almost directly in front of the archway leading to the inner courtyard, completely away from the other dancers. It doesn't take an experienced spy to deduce that he's been charged with leading me off as part of this dumb-ass kidnap game.

I can't decide what to do next. Declan has instructed

me just to play along as if I were a good sport, but the Chechen experience has made me overly cautious. I decide to pretend to twist an ankle, and if my acting is anywhere as good as my Tax Man's, the annoying heir will have no choice but to help me back to my seat. However, I never get the chance to test my theory. Declan's father, Lord Callum Fitzpatrick *Nuada,* steps through the archway, blocking our exit.

"There you are, Lady Rosalinda. I've been looking for a chance to speak privately with you all evening." He turns toward the Junior *Badh.* "You don't mind if I steal my new daughter-in-law away for a few minutes, do you, Cillian?"

The young man doesn't look happy at this unexpected turn of events, but it's evident he doesn't have the balls to say no to one of the most powerful members of *I Idir's* Ruling Council. He gives a polite bow and hands me over to my father-in-Law. "I leave you in the company of his Lordship, good Lady."

He stomps off and Lord *Nuada* puts out his arm for me to take. "Shall we, Lady Rosalinda?" I have no choice but to take his offered arm and wonder whether I've now somehow managed to jump out of the frying pan and directly into the fire.

TOOTHACHE 52

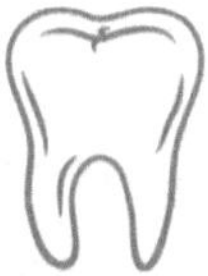

...WOULD STILL SMELL AS SWEET

My new father-in-law remains silent and aloof as we walk across the courtyard, away from the noisy exuberance of my handfast celebration. Everything about this whole scenario feels...well...weird, for lack of a better word. It gets a hundred times weirder when Declan's *athair* suddenly pulls me into a hidden alcove and backs me up against a wall with both hands planted firmly on my ass. Within this close proximity, it's easy to observe that his Lordship is...uhmm...very happy, because his happiness is ...uhmm...firmly smashed up against me. Being this close also provides me with a deep whiff of a very familiar, woodsy scent.

"Damn it, Declan! That better be you!" I whisper in outraged tones.

"Aye, Love, 'tis I," he laughs softly. "I tald ya I was vera, vera good with disguises," my Tax Man says, as he kisses my neck. With a wave of his hand, the glamour spell is gone and I'm left staring into the grinning face of my One and Only. "Ah, Rosie Lass, I'd have ya right here," he mutters, "if I thought we'd have the time to finish properly. Alas, *Badh* will soon be noticin' his mistake when he sees my father still sitting at the table with his cronies. We must make haste if we wish to escape without a chase."

"Wait...we're leaving our own reception? Isn't that rude?" I ask.

"It's what everyone expects. They'll happily go on with their merriment without us, though I'm guessing some people will be searchin' for the happy couple with renewed vigor," the Tax Man says. "But no worries, Lass. They'll never find us."

"Where are we going? I presume not back to your quarters?"

"Feck no, Lass. That'd be the first place they'd look. I have no intention of makin' it that easy. Rest easy, Love. Yar adorin' *Mo Shiorghra* has somethin' vera special planned. 'Tis a surprise. Now, hold on to me tightly, close yar eyes, and do not open them until I say it's okay," his Jr. Lordship instructs.

I wrap my arms around my happy hubby and close my eyes. One of the things I love most about my Tax Man is his ability to make everything fun and adventurous, though in all honesty I would have been perfectly happy with a just a quiet, romantic night on this particular day. I assume he's moving us magically and wonder where in the hell we're going.

I feel the initial rush of energy around us that's common when travel magic is used, and then I feel my feet hit solid ground. Wherever we are, the air feels cooler than it did at the *Nuada* estate, and everything smells fresher and greener. I can't imagine where Declan has taken me. "Can I open my eyes?" I ask.

"Aye, my Love. Ya can open them now," he says, a timbre of gleeful excitement in his tone.

I open my eyes and blink in the darkness, the only light coming from a nearly full moon. We are standing in a wooded clearing, with the sound of running water nearby and the solitary hoot of a night owl.

"Do ya recognize this spot, Rosie?" Declan asks.

That's when it dawns on me, clear as day. We are in the same spot the Tax Man took me six weeks ago, on a warm Sunday afternoon at the very start of our strange, fantastical relationship. Though that experience ended with me passing out and needing to return home, we both consider that afternoon in *I Idir* our first date.

"Oh, Declan! Of course I recognize it! This is where you took me six weeks ago! On our 'first date.' This is your all-time, favorite, secret spot in *I Idir*. Is that the stream I hear in the background? The one where you caught the fish?"

"It is," the Tax Man says. "Though I do not think I will be much interested in playing games with Master Fish on our handfast night." He leans in to kiss me, and I'm more than glad his mind is not on trawling for trout.

"This is so romantic, Declan! Thank you, Sweetie."

"Ya have not seen the best part yet, Rosie Lass." He takes me by the arm and leads me toward a large grove of oak trees. My eyes finally are adjusting to the dark when suddenly I see the most wondrous tent structure in the middle of an open space between the circle of tree trunks.

I'm loosely calling it a tent, because it's like no tent I've ever seen. It's constructed of maroon and gold bunting attached to the lower branches of the oaks and lit by a multitude of tiny candles inside ornate lanterns hanging from hooked poles. There is a large platform bed in the center piled high with richly colored bedding and multiple pillows, an overstuffed loveseat to its left, and a small inlaid table bearing wine, cheeses, fruit, and bread. It's about the most perfect wedding night spot a girl could ever imagine, and I can't help but break into tears.

This is not the reaction Lord *Mac Nuada* expects. He looks at me with concern. "If ya donna like this spot, Rosie, we can go somewhere else." He pulls out a small medicine vial. "I had Robyn give me this medicine for altitude sickness in case that bothers ya again."

I hug him tight. "Oh no, Sweetie. It's perfect! Absolutely fabulous! I couldn't ask for a more lovely handfast night! I'm just so happy it brings me to tears."

Declan sighs with obvious relief. "I am glad you are so pleased, Lass. I am vera happy as well. In fact, let me show ya just how happy I am," he says, as he starts to unfasten the ties on the back of my dress.

I lose myself in that experience for a moment before I remember that whole "disaster down under." I gently pull away from him. "It's awfully…ummm…bright in here, Hon. Do you think you can maybe put out some of those candles?"

He tilts his head and looks at me oddly. "Ya have never been shy with me before, Lass. Have your feelings changed because we are now a handfasted couple?"

The last thing I want is for Declan to think I don't

want him as badly as he seems to want me or that somehow my passion for him has in any way diminished because of a ceremony. I decide that I'd better come clean. "That's absolutely not the case, Declan. I'm like crazy-hot for you too, Sweetie. It's just…well…I have something to show you…and you have to promise me you're not going to be angry with me…or worse yet…laugh."

"I could never be angry with you, Love. Nor laugh at my Beloved *Mo Shiorghra*. What's bothering you? Just tell me. It will be okay, I promise," he says.

"Give me a minute," I respond. Then without any help, I turn around and shimmy out of the various layers of my dress and undergarments, all the while trying to prepare myself for Declan's reaction. When I dressed earlier in the afternoon, my poor, abused skin looked like stubble-covered road construction. I finally stand buck naked, so I turn around and face him.

For a second, my Tax Man stares at me confused, and then, as his view travels downward, he blinks wide-eyed, looking at the fire-engine-red mess below, and then back up at me. "Are you alright, Lass? How did this happen?"

"I had a bikini wax done to surprise you, and I guess I was allergic to something in the process, because this is what happened," I confess.

"But why, Rosie Love? I thought you beautiful just the way you were. I would never ask you to do something like that."

"I thought it would be sexy. At least that's what Mel said. And for sure, this disaster doesn't look sexy." I can feel the tears building again. Damn hormones.

Declan must hear the same sound in my voice because

he steps forward to hug my naked self. "You are still incredibly desirable to me, my Love, whether or not ya have hair on your head or down below. Besides, hair always grows back, even quicker here in the Otherworld. 'Tis nothing to worry about. Though it looks somewhat… painful. Are ya sure ya don't want Robyn to take a look at it?"

The thought of showing Dr. Brannigan my scratchy, bald, messed up who-ha makes me shudder. "Yeah, I don't think I want to be showing the Doc this mess, Sweetie. I'd be mortified. Besides, it's finally stopped itching, so I think I'm good."

He shrugs. "As ya wish, Lass, though I donna think Robyn would be very put off by it since he spends his time delivering wee *bairns*."

Hearing Declan say wee *bairns* makes me think of the thing I'm not thinking about and I quickly change the subject. "Let's forget about Doctor Brannigan and get back to what's important here, Tax Man. Like the fact that I'm naked…and you're not."

The Tax Man laughs and pulls me toward the lushly, dressed bed. "Tis a problem I'm hoping ya can help me with, Rosie Lass. Plus, thar is that little 'rain check' debt ya owe me…times two…that needs repayin.'"

"Never let it be said Rosie Fitzpatrick is a low-down welsher, Tax Man," I answer with a grin as I unlatch the buckle on his belt.

TOOTHACHE 53

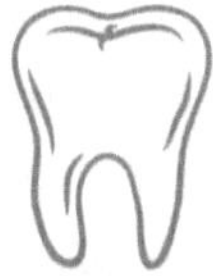

POST HANDFAST

As long as I live, I shall never recall my handfast night without a blissful grin and a very long sigh. A more romantic, joyful or passionate experience would be hard to replicate, so perfect was each and every detail. Declan and I linger in the cozy space well past sun up, sharing more cuddles, along with a little skinny-dipping in the crystal, clear stream and a simple breakfast. Eventually, reality intrudes in the form of one of those nasty raven-grams sent by Duncan, who was the only other living soul who knew where we'd snuck off to the previous evening. It seemed that the real Lordship was calling for our presence in his chambers before we returned to the Mundane world.

The plan had been for us to leave the Otherworld this morning without a lot of hassles or fanfare. Our Mundane honeymoon flight to the island of Antigua was set to depart from Boston's Logan International Airport at 9:10 AM on July 18th. Even with the time difference between the Otherworld and the Mundane, this only leaves us with 14 hours to get home, finish packing, close up both houses, and drive into Boston from Salem. The physics attached to the Mundane world make it nearly impossible for the Tax Man to move long distances magically, and although as a tooth fairy I can transport after sundown, I don't have the ability to move both of us and our luggage, certainly not the amount of miles it would take from my home all the way to Antigua. Thus, we are required to deal with the headaches of modern transportation and air travel like every other human being.

Thankfully, Declan has arranged for a fresh set of clothes delivered to our handfast suite so I don't have to appear in front of Lord *Nuada* wearing my rumpled gown from yesterday. We look adorably matchy-matchy in coordinated maroon and gold apparel, and despite being nervous about any time I have to spend with my Beloved's crazy family, I can't seem to wipe the silly grin of happiness from my face.

The staff welcomes us back to the estate with whistles and cheers, making the trek to Lord Callum's chamber less anxious. My new husband seems antsy to be gone from here, mumbling under his breath how his parents seem to enjoy turning everything into "a beg feckin' drama." His words, not mine.

We knock and are allowed entrance. Declan's father is dressed in elegant riding apparel, and he turns to greet us as I drop a curtsy and Declan gives a half bow while placing his hand over his heart, the customary greeting between a Lord and his heir. "Good morrow, *Athair*. I was told you wished to speak to my Lady and me," says my *Mo Shiorghra.*

"Aye. You disappeared so quickly last night, there was no time to offer my own words of congratulations," Lord *Nuada* says.

"I apologize, my Lord. As you may be aware, my *chiorcal cairde* (circle of friends) were determined to continue the tradition of *bean cheile ag goid* (wife stealing). I could not very well let them succeed. It required a clandestine departure for us both."

"Indeed!" said his Lordship. "It would be most embarrassing for House *Nuada* to lose such a game of cunning and deception. Well done, Son. I hope the Universe has blessed your night with new life."

I don't dare look at either of the two men, lest I somehow give something away. My Tax Man adds, "As do I, *Athair.* Though to be certain, the Lady Rosalinda and I have planned some time away to…seriously continue at that endeavor before we both return to our regular duties in the Mundane world."

Having our honeymoon described as a serious endeavor does nothing for me in the romance department. In fact, it's a tad embarrassing and makes the whole thing sound like scheduled stud service, but of course that's not what I say to my new father-in-law. "I want to thank you, my Lordship, for a most beautiful handfast celebration. I could not ask for anything better," I gush.

"You are most welcome, Lady Rosalinda. I will say that you looked much like the goddess Danu, Herself, in your handfast finery, a most appropriate match for House *Nuada's* heir. Let us hope that the goddess grants you the same level of fertility as she has done with your handfast day appearance."

What I want to say is, *"You bet your sweet ass she did! Already got me a bun in the oven, so what do you think about that, old man? Not bad for a little old tooth fairy, huh?"* What I say instead is, "Thank you, my Lord. I wish with all my heart for the very same gift."

For a few seconds, Lord *Nuada* tilts his head and looks at me, and I start to worry that he picked up on the sassy words I just thought. Or worse yet, he has an inkling about that thing I'm not thinking about. Then he gives us both a crooked smile and says, "Then off with you two on your lovers' quest. I shall expect positive news when you return home."

TOOTHACHE 54

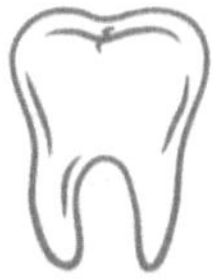

THE LOVE NEST

DECLAN and I return to the Mundane world with exactly 12 hours and 43 minutes left before we need to board our plane to Antigua. We'd hoped to be able to just sneak off after our meeting with his father but were delayed by several staff members who wanted to reminisce about last night's event and wish us bountiful blessings. My Tax Man, always the perfect gentleman, politely accepts their handshakes and kind words with genuine gratitude. Strangely enough, we don't have any communication or contact with Declan's mother which, all things considered, is probably for the best.

Still, that little bit of lost time puts our Mundane activity into high gear. My new husband uses some of his magical talent to finish his packing quickly. He offers to do the same for me, but I'm still undecided as to what exactly I want to take as part of my honeymoon trousseau. I probably went overboard buying things in advance of our trip; cute sundresses, strappy little sandals, sexy lingerie, and even a few bathing suits that don't look absolutely hideous on me. Unable to make a decision, I throw the whole kit and kaboodle into the suitcase, causing Declan to give me a look while attempting to lift the bag into the trunk of the car.

This will be my first time flying first-class, and I'm pretty excited about it. My new hubby seems amused by my exuberance. He tries to be a good sport while I take a ridiculous number of photos and selfies to record every moment of the trip, even while he's busy on his laptop taking care of last-minute business at his office. Thank goodness he was able to convince Eleanor, the "Bitch Pitch" to return to her job at his firm. Declan never told me how he did it, but I figure his PA received a sizable raise and a few extra weeks of vacation to ease her wounded pride after D.P. Fitzpatrick decided to choose the chunky dentist over her svelte self.

The flight to Antigua is four hours and 35 minutes long, during which time I desperately try to get a few hours of much needed rest and relaxation. As keyed up as I am, I'm not too successful. My Beloved fills these hours reading one of the crime novels he's crazy about, but I end up staring at the same few paragraphs of my own best-seller over vnd over again, lost in far too many daydreams. Per my tracking, I am now officially two days late. It's not really a surprise. I've been sure of my state for a few weeks, and my conversation with Magda on the day of our handfast sort of sealed that deal. I packed a few pregnancy tests I purchased before our handfast ceremony in my toiletry bag, and plan to use them for my big announcement scene tomorrow night; our honeymoon package includes a romantic private dinner on the beach, which I've decided will be the perfect setting for an announcement of such grand importance. That means I only have to work at not leaking my thoughts out for another 24 hours, which is a big relief.

I did some minor research before booking this package, but the photos online don't do justice to the actual beauty of the resort. The Love Nest, on the island of Antigua, is twelve acres of lush, tropical paradise. Our honeymoon suite is on the fifth floor of a Caribbean style building with a stunningly beautiful ocean view and a cozy hot tub on the balcony. I'm expecting that the Tax Man already is formulating a romantic afternoon interlude. I'm wrong. Declan is more interested in the little newspaper listing all resort activities and daily events.

"Look, Love," he says, pointing at the newspaper. "The resort is hosting a Honeymoon Olympics! They have prizes and everything! We shud' sign up for this as soon as possible."

I stand still, instantly frozen to the spot. Games are like opium to my Tax Man. He enjoys nothing better than a challenge he feels he can dominate, and if prizes are involved, he's like a damn hound after a fox. "Olympics, Sweetie? I'm not sure why honeymoon couples would want to spend time competing against each other."

"Tis a good time, Lass! They have all types of competitions and ya get points far each one ya win. The grand prize is a free sunset booze cruise! I think we'd have a good chance at winnin'." He gives me a classic Declan grin. "I am vera good at physical challenges, ya know."

"Yes, dear, I know you are. But I'm not. You know first-hand that I'm not very…athletic."

"Aye…but I am good enough to cover us both. I can help you with the hard parts, Love."

My hubby looks so excited by the prospect that I feel like a bitch for not trying to make this trip fun for him, so I do the only thing I can think of. I put him off. "Let me think about it, okay Sweetie? Maybe you can get some specific information on what kinds of 'games' are involved."

Ever logical, my *Mo Shiorghra* agrees. He nods and says, "Ya are right, Rosie Love. I would not want to have a significant advantage over anyone simply because I am Fae. "T'would not be vera fair."

"That's an understatement," I think to myself. *"Not just Fae…but super Fae."* "Exactly," I agree, "I know how absolutely fair you always want to be. Getting more information is a good idea." I stifle a yawn. All of sudden, everything has caught up with me and I can barely keep my eyes open. "I'm dead on my feet, Sweetie. I think a nice catnap is in order." I expect him to offer to join me. Once again, I am wrong.

"Aye. You've run yourself ragged, Love, gettin' ready for our handfast. You enjoy a nice nap." I watch as he digs a pair of swim trunks out of his suitcase. "If ya don' mind, Lass. I think I'd like to soak up some sun and surf befar lunch."

I'd be lying if I said I wasn't a tad disappointed, but the way he's pacing around the room I can tell my Beloved is antsy after sitting for so long on the plane. "No, you go ahead. Have fun and be sure to scope out the best seats at the pool."

He kisses me passionately, then goes to change into his swim trunks. I lay across the super-sized canopy bed and I am out like a light before he even leaves the room.

TOOTHACHE 55

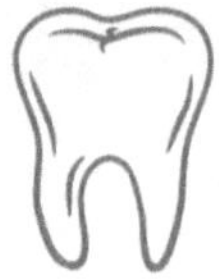

SPEEDO MARK

I AWAKE WITH A START, momentarily unsure of where I am before putting all the pieces back together. I feel as if I've been asleep for hours, but according to my phone it's been less than two. The room is empty and my new husband is nowhere to be seen. I assume he's still out and about enjoying the Antigua afternoon.

I roll out of the immense bed and grab a juice from the complimentary mini fridge, then head to the balcony to take in the view and see whether I can locate my errant hubby and coax him into some lunch. From this location on the fifth floor, I have a panoramic view of the entire resort, including the massive swimming pool below. There are people everywhere: in the water, sitting at the swim-up bar, relaxing on the loungers. It seems unlikely I will be able to pick Declan out of this milling menagerie, until I hear a very familiar male voice shouting over the steel-drum music, "Heads up, lads in the back. The lass serves ta the far right."

Not too many people nowadays use the terms lass and lad. That, and the shocking red hair, which in the sun makes his head appear as if it's on fire, is a dead give-away that it's my Tax Man out there in the pool, playing water volleyball. To find him involved in some kind of athletic activity is par for the course. What I can't fathom is why my husband of less than 48 hours has a tiny blonde wearing an even tinier bathing suit balanced on his shoulders.

I try not to let either my imagination or my hormones run away with me. I'm sure there's a perfectly good reason why some blonde bimbo has her skinny legs wrapped around my *Mo Shiorghra's* neck, with her perky boobs slapping him in the head every time the two of them move. I consider shouting at him from the balcony but quickly realize that my solution to the problem would be embarrassingly ridiculous. If I want to know what's going on I simply must march myself down there and find out in person.

I'm still dressed in my rumpled travel clothes, so I drag my two-ton suitcase over to the bed and struggle to lift it up there. Obviously, one goes to the pool area wearing a swimsuit, so I dig through its contents until I find one of the new suits I bought for this trip. They all looked really cute in the store when I picked them out, but now, compared to the one the blonde has on, they scream old lady. My answer to that is to put a cover-up over my suit and head poolside.

At first Declan doesn't notice me, involved as he is in

the game. Finally, he notices my waving and shouting and waves back, but then he returns his focus to the net. The blonde waves as well, while I stand there like a pale-skinned dummy, unsure of what to do next. I look around for an empty lounger, but as it's mid-afternoon, the pool area is excessively crowded, and I don't see an empty one anywhere. I try not to cry. This is nothing to cry about. But lately I cry over everything. Behind me, I hear someone calling my name. "Rosie? Rosie Fitzpatrick?"

I turn to find a tall man with a very hairy chest wearing an extremely small pair of Speedos standing directly behind me. "Yes. I'm Rosie. Do I know you?" I stammer.

"No," he smiles. "But I've met your husband, and he's done a bang-up job in describing you. You're just as gorgeous as he said you were." The man sticks out his hand. "I'm Mark Spanner. That's my wife, Jess, out there on your husband's shoulder. Come join us. We saved you a seat."

I'm unsure about following a stranger, but he's heading in the direction of four loungers under a large umbrella. I see Declan's shorts and his expensive sandals on one of them, so I follow behind this Spanner character. He plops down on a chair and points to the one next to him. Mr. Speedo reaches into a cooler and pulls out a bottle of chilled champagne. "Make yourself comfortable, Rosie," he says, as he pours the champagne into a thermal cup and hands it to me. "Let's chat a bit while our spouses are busy earning us points. I have a feeling we're gonna hit it off just perfectly."

TOOTHACHE 56

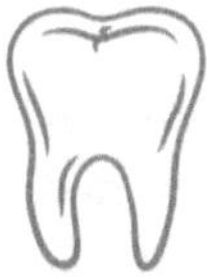

BIG FOOT ON THE BEACH

I TAKE the glass of champagne from Speedo Mark and put it on the little plastic table next to me, waiting to find an opportunity to discreetly dump its contents. In the meantime, I work at gleaning information on how Speedo Mark's bleached blonde, bimbo wife wound up on my husband's shoulders playing in this game. Yes. Declan Fitzpatrick the man can be very charming…when he wants to be and with people with whom he is comfortable. Otherwise, he is D.P. Fitzpatrick, CPA, all Brooks Brothers and polite, impersonal conversation. I've been privy to both personae, but neither is what one would call the life of the party.

"So, Rosie. Declan says you guys are newlyweds on your honeymoon," the man says as he rubs sunscreen onto his ape-like chest. He holds the sunscreen bottle up and adds, "Would you like for me to get your shoulders and back? The sun here can be brutal. I'd hate to see all that lovely, pale skin with a bad burn."

My ick factor is in full force by the thought of Speedo Mark touching me, and I muster all the willpower I have not to pick up my beach bag and run...not walk...back into the hotel. But I don't want to insult the Tax Man's new friend, so I shake my head back and forth in the negative while silently shouting in my head, "Get the frick away from me!" Instead, I just offer him a nondescript "No, thank you," then counter with a question of my own. "How did you and your wife happen to meet my husband, Mark?"

"Oh, that's just a lucky coincidence," he replies. "Declan was looking to get into the 'couples only' water volleyball game but didn't have a partner. He told us his wife had some jet lag and was in their suite resting. Volleyball is definitely my Jess's game, so she offered to partner up with him. They agreed to split the points."

"Points?" I question.

"Yes. For the 'Honeymoon Olympics.' Your hubby seemed really charged up for the competition," Speedo explains. "The two of you are a day behind the rest of us, so you're gonna have to work at catching up, but my man Declan didn't appear concerned over that little set-back, and it looks like he and Jess will pick up points for being on the winning volleyball team." He points to my Tax Man, who is busy high-fiving and fist bumping the rest of his teammates. "He sure is a competitive guy."

Competitive isn't the word. More like challenge obsessed. "Yes...Declan does enjoy...a good game." I see my husband walking toward me, and I'm relieved to no longer be stuck alone with Mr. Sasquatch.

Declan greets me with an embrace and a kiss, dripping water all over my cover-up in the process. "Yar indeed a sight for my poor eyes, Love, lookin' so fetchin' in yar cute little sun wrap."

I know he means it as a compliment, but it just embarrasses me, especially while his volleyball partner is practically naked. Her bathing suit has two small triangles covering her boobs and an even smaller one down below. She obviously is a fan of properly bare bikini waxes, and when she bends down to retrieve her towel I notice her suit is thong style. I don't dare think about those perfect little ass cheeks resting on my Tax Man's bare shoulders. "I'm glad I was able to find you down here, Sweetie. I should have known I'd find you where the action is." I mean this as a bit of a dig, but it goes right over my new husband's head.

"Aye, Lass. I was happy to find a chance to earn some points. We are sadly behind the other competitors, but I am sure if we put our minds tard it, we can catch up.'

The love of my life is sadly mistaken if he thinks I'm going to spend my honeymoon playing silly games I'm sure to suck at. Of course, this is not a discussion I'm willing to have in front of Sasquatch and Bubble Butt. "That's great, Declan. Maybe we can talk about it over lunch. The muffin I had at the airport isn't holding, and I'm afraid I'm a bit hungry. I was thinking maybe we could check out that adorable sushi place we saw when we checked in?"

Before I can stop him, the Tax Man turns to the other

couple and asks, "Would ya care ta join us?" I hold my breath. *Please say no...please say no.*

Speedo Mark raises his glass of champagne. "Thanks for the offer, my man. We're not much for raw fish. But you two love birds go on and enjoy yourselves. Maybe we'll catch you later tonight for cocktails."

Declan agrees and shakes the guy's hand, while at the same time I'm busy thinking... *Not if I can help it.*

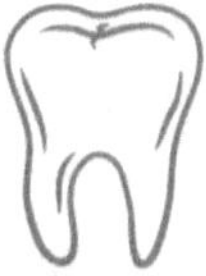

SCOLDED OVER SUSHI

Sunshine Sushi, like every other aspect of the resort, is an example of cuteness overload. We are seated at a small table next to a real koi pond, shaded by a large, paper umbrella covered in a delicate, heart pattern. The menu is extensive; we order a few specialty rolls and some sashimi to share. It's such a pleasant location that I'm more than a little annoyed when my Tax Man brings up his new friends and all of that damn Olympics nonsense.

"They seem like vera nice people, don't ya think, Lass? And both of them are vera athletic. Mark is a personal trainer, and Jess is a yoga instructor. If they're willin' to split the points, we would be mite lucky to team up with them for the rest of the games." He reaches across the table to hold my hand, and I feel like I'm about to get played.

"Declan…Sweetie…I understand that you like to keep active. And I know you love when there's a challenge…but

Hon…this is our honeymoon. I want to relax and spend time with you and not Mr. Sasquatch. Or his limber lady."

"Who's Mr. Sasquatch?" my husband asks.

I realize that there might be a cultural difference and that perhaps Declan hasn't heard the term. I google a photo of it and show him. "This is a Sasquatch, Sweetie. It's my nickname for Mark. Because he's so…hairy." I give a dramatic shudder just for effect.

His Jr. Lordship murmurs a non-committal "hmm." Then, "It does not seem vera nice of ya to dislike him just because he has an abundance of hair on his chest, Rosie. Yar usually so friendly ta people. I'm afraid ta hear what name ya've come up with for his wife."

I'm feeling as if I'm being scolded and I don't like it. Not one little bit. "Doesn't matter. Seems like you liked her well enough for both of us." I pull my hand from his, not even sure why I'm being bitchy. Maybe I'm just hangry or maybe the crazy hormonal thing has kicked into full gear.

The Tax Man raises that one solitary eyebrow of his. "Are ya implyin' that I'm attracted to that man's wife? Because I know vera well that ya know I'm crazy in love with ya, Rosie Fitzpatrick! You are ma *Mo Shiorghra*, ma One and Only. Hell, Lass, I forget ma own name the second I touch ya!"

I give him a noncommittal shrug, but his comment does make me feel a tad better. Of course, my Tax Man is still my Tax Man, so sometimes he doesn't know when to leave well enough alone. "Now I shall thank the gods and goddesses," he says, "that I have a nice smooth chest and not a hairy one, lest my Love find me distasteful."

Again, this sounds less like joking and more like scolding to me. I hate being scolded, and I spit out my words before I can stop myself. "Oh do you? I can't seem to remember what you look like anymore."

I get the eyebrow raise again, accompanied by a slight upturn to the corner of his mouth. "Ah, so that is the reason my *Mo Shiorghra* is out of sorts. Yar feelin'... neglected.' Tis easily fixed," he says as he winks at me.

Automatically, I turn a light shade of pink at being called out as a sex-crazed, horny shrew, though I am saved from answering by the waitress arriving with our food. Declan saves the rest of the afternoon by changing the subject completely, shifting the topic away from my neglect and towards the luxury of the resort and my *savoir-faire* in selecting it. The sushi is delicious, my Tax Man is being charming Declan, and most of my earlier crankiness fades away. I begin to relax and feel better about the start of our honeymoon...that is until My Beloved says, "I need to stop back at the room to get my water slippers. I thought we might try out the kayaks this afternoon."

I nearly bite my tongue in half to stop myself from starting a full-blown argument. I keep my thoughts to myself as we walk back to our room. I intend to remain in said room as hell would need to freeze over before I would consent to paddling a kayak in rough sea waters. Just the thought of it is makes me queasy. I consider telling him the big news, figuring it might derail his agenda, but then I change my mind. I still want to tell him in the grandiose fashion I have planned in my head for weeks. I consider outright seducing him instead, but it turns out neither of these plans are necessary

When we walk into our suite, we are greeted by two island women dressed in starched pink uniforms who have set up massage tables on our balcony. This space overlooks a stunning view of the Caribbean Sea. Our balcony has been shaded in sheer gauze that lets in the light and breezes but allows for privacy. There are tropical flowers everywhere, the warm air overwhelmed with their fragrance, along with the aroma of fresh cut fruit set out as a snack. The words stick on my tongue. "You had this planned?"

"Aye. I arranged for it while ya were napping," Declan says. "I wanted it to be a surprise. I thought that a honeymoon should have some surprises. I arranged for us to get a romantic couple's massage here in the privacy of ar suite. I hoped this was something ya might enjoy, Lass."

"Oh, Declan…it's perfect! Thank you," I say. I kiss him and add, "You're absolutely right! Honeymoons definitely should have surprises."

TOOTHACHE 58

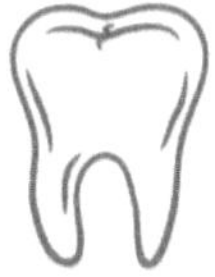

BASKET CASE

ALL GOOD THINGS must come to an end. It is the natural way of things. The philosophy of The Old Ways teaches that the Universe balances the good with the bad to allow for a full experience of life. Most of the Mundane world's religions hold similar beliefs. I've read them all: the sweet and the sour, joy mixed with suffering, the whole gamut of contradictory stages of everyday life that one must temper with faith and hope. From all perspectives, my life for the past seven weeks has been as though torn from a romance novel with a cutesy cover: crazy, wonderful and amazing. Save, of course, for those few incidents when Declan's sister tried to kill me, or when Duncan took a bullet for me, and perhaps when I was kidnapped by those Chechen terrorists, but for the most part, it's been filled with delightful sweetness. I suppose I must have been due for a mouthful of sour.

The Tax Man's honeymoon surprise was top rate. We

grinned and held hands all the way through our couples massage, causing one of the lady therapists to remark that "our marriage surely was magical." Declan and I looked at each other, and when he smiled and winked at me, I thought I'd died and gone to the Afterlife. When the ladies left, we soaked in our private hot tub, snacking on tropical fruit until my One and Only decided the rest of the afternoon should be spent making sure his Lass was no longer feeling neglected.

At some point, we must have dozed off, as it was well after 6:00 PM when I opened my eyes to the shifting early evening light in our luxurious suite. The Tax Man was still out for the count, splayed out over most of the bed and snoring in his usual rhythm. Content as I was, I thought why not add to the memory. I'd patiently waited the specified two days after my missed period. It was time. Shifting carefully from my side of the bed, I padded on tippy-toes to the spacious bathroom and closed the door. I took one of the pregnancy tests from my toiletry bag, read the multi-language instructions, and peed on the stick as directed, hitting my fingers as well. (Seriously, how can you not end up peeing on your hand?) Sitting on the toilet, on the beautiful island of Antigua, I waited for my future to unfold. Part of me thought that perhaps I should have asked my new husband to join me in the wait, but I was hell bent on my Hallmark movie moment, so I faced this part of the journey alone. Eventually, the news I had already known for several weeks stared up at me from the counter of the sink vanity. Two bright pink lines side by side marked the fact that the Tax Man and I were going to be parents. I sat there holding the pregnancy test in my hands for a long time. I considered doing a second test…just to be sure…but changed my mind. There was no need for doubt. The Universe had already decided weeks ago. I carefully tucked everything back in the box and placed it in my toiletry kit in anticipation of making my big announcement the following night.

I walked back to the bedroom to find my Beloved in the exact same position in which I left him. The urge to blurt out my news is so strong that I literally take several deep breaths before doubling my mental shield to avoid leaking out my secret thoughts. I give his shoulder a shake. "Declan…Sweetie…it's almost 7. Do you think maybe we should get up, shower, and head out for some dinner?"

I get a mumbled response from the pillow, but he doesn't move from the spot. "Sweetie…I'm gonna go ahead and jump in the shower first, okay? It'll take me longer to dress and fix my hair," I say. He answers with another vague collection of words, so I head back to the bathroom.

The gigantic bathtub for two is tempting, but I opt for the quicker rain shower option. I focus on the warm water pulsating on my skin and the fragrance of the sweet floral soap to avoid thinking about the secret I'm keeping from my *Mo Shiorghra*. As I begin to lather my hair with plumeria scented conditioner, I hear the incessant ringing of the suite's doorbell even through the sound of the running water. How can the Tax Man not hear it? I turn down the water and poke my head out of the shower and yell, "Declan, someone is at the door. Can you please answer it! I'm in the shower!"

I hear what suspiciously sounds like Gaelic swearing, but eventually the ringing stops, and I can hear the Tax Man talking to someone. Satisfied he's got it covered, I turn the water back up and finish my shower. Wrapping myself in one of the oversized bathrobes, I wander back into the suite. "Who was at the door, Hon?"

"T'was a man from guest services, Love," he says from a stretched-out position on the bed. "Mark and Jess sent us a gift. Wasn't that a nice thing to do? And here ya were, not givin' them a chance when all they wanted to be was friendly." He points to a large cellophane-wrapped basket on the table near the balcony.

I try not to make a face as I go to take a closer look, but once I get a good peek at its contents, I freeze on the spot. Inside the basket is a bottle of French champagne and a fresh pineapple, upside down, the green leafy crown of it resting on the bottom. The note attached to the ribbon reads, "When it's right, it's right. How about the four of us party tonight?"

TOOTHACHE 59

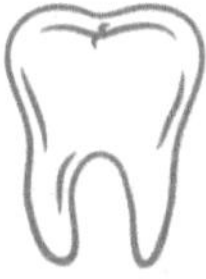

SO MUCH FOR NEW FRIENDS

I'M no woman of the world, and I certainly am no expert regarding the sexual proclivities of the human species. Truthfully, my sex life before B.T.T.M. (Before the Tax Man) was about as exciting as a plateful of Kraft Macaroni and Cheese. The only reason I have any inkling regarding the intention of Speedo Mark's and his tiny-tits-wife's special gift to Declan and me relates to a TV crime show I watched about a month ago whose topic I subsequently verified via an eye-opening Google search.

"Declan...Sweetie...I'm not sure you understand... uhm...what this gift implies," I mutter.

He gets up and stretches, perfectly comfortable in his nudity. "Ah, Rosie, I hope ya won' be angry with me far sayin' so, but I think yar being a tad unfair about yar dislike of these people. The man canna help where he grows hair. Plus, they're from 'Down Undar' ya know.

Perhaps the social culture there is friendlier than the United States."

I try really hard to not be annoyed at being scolded again. "Sweetie…it's a little more than just being 'friendlier.' I don't think you're getting the whole picture." I point to the upside-down fruit. "Turning the pineapple upside down like that…it's a symbol for couples who…uhm…like to swing."

He stares at me like I'm speaking a foreign language. "I have no idea what yar talkin' about, Lass."

For a man who claims to have completed his college education in the Mundane world, the Tax Man sometimes is clueless and often very naive regarding the social norms of fully human people. "Geez…you're not making this easy for me, Hon. I'm trying to tell you as gently as I can that your buddies Mark and Jess enjoy having sex with other couples…switching partners. It's called 'swinging.' That's what they mean about 'partying' tonight."

"I know ya don' like them, Rosie, but that is a ridiculous notion ya got in yar head," my new husband complains. "Do ya really expect me to believe that Mark, a married man and a complete stranger, expects that he will bed ya this evening? Or that I desire to sleep with his wife? If it is a joke yar tryin' to make, I ken assure ya it's not vera funny."

Now I am officially annoyed. I grab my cell phone and poke away at Google. Then I hand him the phone. "Here! Read it yourself."

I watch as he opens one article after another, his face registering more disbelief and horror with each cache of information. "Now do you believe me?" I ask. "I told you there was something snarky about them. He gives me the creeps."

He hands me back my phone, his usual easy-going demeanor replaced with a steely rage, that's akin to cranky Declan on steroids. Taking my hands in his, he asks in a low growl, "Did that man put hands on ya, Rosie?" I pause a second too long, and he adds, "Do not lie to me, Lass. I will know, and it will hurt me deeply. I canna abide falsehoods."

Panic rises in me, not because of anything Speedo Mark did but owing to the big secret I've been keeping from my husband. Would the Tax Man consider me not telling him about the baby a falsehood? This thought causes me to stammer as I answer his question about Sasquatch. "Not exactly," I say.

"What da ya mean 'not exactly,' Lass? Explain yarself," Lord *Mac Nuada* demands.

"I didn't really get close enough for him to touch me, Sweetie. It was just...well...the icky way he looked at me." I know I'm babbling but can't seem to help myself. My only goal is to keep Declan from sensing what I'm hiding from him. "He kept saying weird stuff...like he knew we were going to get along fabulously and how his wife was 'very taken with your good looks.'" The Tax Man doesn't look very convinced by my examples, so as a last-ditch effort I throw in, "Oh...and he wanted to rub sunscreen all over my body...but of course I said no thank you to that."

Had I known in advance how Declan would react, I would surely have taken an entirely different tack. Hindsight being what it is, I shouldn't have made the sunscreen offer sound as if it was a swinger come-on, like I apparently did. Perhaps if I hadn't been so intent on hiding the baby thing from him, the two of us could have just laughed off the invitation while making a pointed effort to avoid Mark and his wife for the rest of the trip. Furthermore, I absolutely should have finally come clean then and there regarding our family status even if it meant giving up my romantic Big Announcement dinner plans. As it was, I am to blame for a lot of what happened next.

TOOTHACHE 60

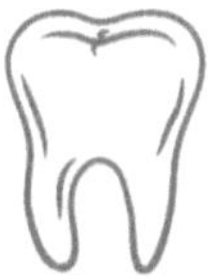

RETURN POLICY

UNFORTUNATELY, my sunscreen comment is the trigger that gets his Jr. Lordship's blood boiling. "Feckin' Sonofabitch! That dirty bastard!" he shouts as he paces the room, swearing in the rapid-fire ancient Gaelic of the Otherworld. I understand a few of these choice words, thanks to the help of Declan's espionage team who have been tutoring me in the finer skill of using insulting Fae obscenities. The Tax Man peels off a particularly descriptive passage about Speedo Mark's father having copulated with a sow. It's a top-rated insult, indicating that he is more than just a little angry.

I do my best to diffuse the situation. "Declan… Sweetie…I think you're overreacting. Really, nothing happened. He offered, and I said no. End of story."

He stops moving for a second and takes my hands again. "That does not mean he didna want ta touch ya, Lass. I understand that yar not vera experienced in the ways of men, Love, but the bastard surely wanted ta touch yar beautiful, soft, skin. Who would not want to take advantage of such an opportunity? Yar like a little lost lamb to the slaughter."

I understand that he means this as a compliment, but frankly, it's extremely condescending. My love life before Declan may not have been quite as...diverse...or as plentiful as his, but I made it clear to him that I wasn't a nun before he came along. Therefore, I interpret his comment to mean that initially he had found my bedroom skills somewhat lacking, and since I am obviously hormonal (that's my story and I'm sticking to it), I probably do not choose my words as carefully as I should. "Is that so, your Lordship? Well then, I suppose your far more experienced self didn't think it odd that the man agreed to allow his wife to squeeze your ears with her oh-so-limber thighs?"

As soon as I say these words, I regret them. His color goes a shade lighter and I can tell by his expression that my insinuation hits its intended mark. I believe this to be the exact moment when events spiral completely out of my control. "You are most correct, Love," he replies. "The bastard set me up from the start. 'Twas he who started the conversation with me at the bar and he who offered his wife as a partner for the game. I thought he was just bein' friendly." He stops and points to the upside-down pineapple in the basket. "But all the time he was plannin' his disgustin' 'feck party.' I dunno how I could have been so stupid." He looks at me and shakes his head. "This is what comes from tryin' to be Fae in the Mundane world. Humans donna' have any sense of what et means to be honorable."

In truth, the Fae generally are more open to sex than their human counterparts, lacking the moral and religious boundaries that the Mundane world has placed on the purely natural activity. Pretty much anything goes between two consenting, unattached, Fae persons over the age of maturity, which is 14 years in the Otherworld. The key word, however, is unattached. When it comes to contracts, pledges, and promises, the Fae are deadly serious, and handfasting is the most sacred contract of all. To break one's handfast commitment is a serious ethical offense in Otherworld culture. It doesn't surprise me that my husband, whose heart is one hundred percent Fae, finds Mark's breach utterly offensive. I watch with my heart in my throat as the Tax Man angrily grabs the pineapple from the basket and heads for the door. "Sweetie…where do you think you're going?" I ask.

"I plan on returnin' this damn pineapple back to the bastard that sent it to us with an answer to his filthy invitation." The look on Declan's face is reminiscent of the same look he had when he learned that Erik Ashton had taken a few swings at me.

I start to panic at what could happen. "Declan, maybe that's not such a good idea. We should just ignore them both from here on out and try to have a nice honeymoon."

"Are ya askin' me to allow that man to mock me, Lass? Because, I would hope ya would know I canna do that, no matter how much I want to please ya."

I'm not sure how to answer that, so instead I say the only thing that comes to mind. "No, Sweetie…but you're naked, Hon. I know the dress code here is loose, but you can't walk around the resort without any pants."

He looks down at himself and tisks loudly, stopping only long enough to grab his swim trunks from the drying rack in the bathroom. Then, he picks up the forbidden fruit again and storms out the door, slamming it behind him. I know I should follow him, but I'm only wearing a bathrobe myself. By the time I get dressed and get out there, World War III will surely already have started. I hustle to the balcony to see whether I can track what's going on from there.

A few minutes later, I see Declan exit our building and head to the pink structure across from ours. Following his direction, I spot Mark and Jess sitting in swimsuits on their third-floor balcony, enjoying an early evening glass of wine. I want to shout at my husband to stop, but no words seem to come out of my mouth. Declan stops under their balcony and whistles up to them. Seeing him, Speedo Mark leans over the railing and says, "Declan, buddy, I see you got our gift basket. Come on up for an afternoon cocktail. Where's your pretty, little wife?"

My husband's face goes stone cold when the stupid man mentions me. He shouts up at Mark, "I've no need of yar libations… 'buddy.' I just stopped by ta return yar feckin' pineapple and to warn ya that if ya ever put yar filthy hands on ma wife I will break every feckin' bone in both of them. In fact, I donna want to even see ya putin' yar eyes anywhere near har direction. Am I makin' maself clear enough?"

People are starting to gather and watch. I want to cover my eyes, but it's like a five-car pile-up and I can't seem to pull my attention away from the impending disaster. Mark is both embarrassed and annoyed at being called out so publicly. He puts up his hands in mock surrender. "Whoa, Mate! I'm sorry we read your signals wrong. You and my Jess looked cozy enough in the pool. I thought you'd be game for a little fun. I'm real sorry if there's been some kind of silly…misunderstanding."

Declan lifts up the pineapple. "Misunderstand this, ya feckin' bastard!" He pulls his arm back and flings the pineapple in the direction of Speedo Mark. Given the weight and shape of the fruit, a normal, human man never would have a chance of hitting the intended target. Speedo Mark is, after all, three stories, up which I'm guessing is a range of about 33 to 35 feet. Unfortunately, my new husband's DNA lies well on the Fae side of biology. In addition, he is extremely athletic and in excellent shape. Therefore, I'm not at all surprised when Mark, who hasn't moved an inch from his original spot, catches the pineapple square in the face. The guy screams in pain, and when he removes his hands at the urging of his wife, his nose appears to be broken and his face is a bloody mess. As for the Tax Man…he gives the wailing man an obscene gesture and turns to stomp off toward the direction of our building, while all around him people are staring with mouths agape and with cellphones pointed and filming.

TOOTHACHE 61

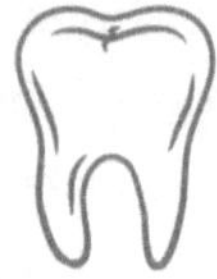

THE ONE YOU NEED

RESORT SECURITY IS NOT FAR behind my husband. Lord *Mac Nuada* stomps back into our suite muttering in a mix of old Gaelic, English, and what I think is French but I can't be sure. I try to speak calmly to him, but I'm a tad worked up myself. "Declan…what the hell were you thinking? I think you busted that guy's nose! I'm sure he's going to sue you, and maybe even have you arrested. Shit! What are we going to do now? This is a foreign country!"

My One and Only doesn't have an opportunity to respond, as immediately there are fists banging at our suite door. Before I can answer it, Declan steps in front of me. He opens it to reveal two very large men from The Love Nest's security team standing in the doorway. They ask Declan whether he was the same man involved in an incident with a guest in the building across the courtyard. My husband admits that he was but pleads his case, going as far as to show the men the note that came with the basket. The two men look at each other knowingly. They are polite but firm. They ask us to leave the resort immediately. If we refuse, the local police will be called to assist.

The officers patiently wait outside our suite as we hurriedly pack up our luggage. We arrived only eight hours ago, so most of our things are still in our suitcases. Declan alternates between swearing and apologizing. He offers to try and find us another resort here in Antigua, but I am so terrified by the thought of his being arrested that I want nothing more than to be safely back in the United States.

When we finish gathering our things we are escorted down to the lobby. People stare at us; some of the men admiringly comment about my husband's amazing pitching abilities, and the women give me looks of either thinly veiled disapproval or simmering envy. I'm sure my face is beet red. I am mortified to my core while also feeling terribly guilty about my part in the fiasco. Now, not only are my plans for a romantic dinner announcement trashed, but my entire honeymoon as well. It's more than obvious that the Tax Man is in no mood for a life changing conversation, busy as he is trying to get a refund for the remaining days we won't be present and arranging for a flight back to Boston. I decide it's best to wait to tell him about Baby Fitzpatrick until we arrive home. I've waited this long. What's another day?

TOOTHACHE 62

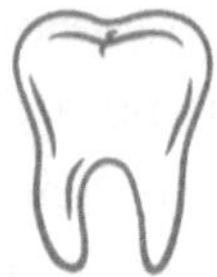

RED EYE REVEAL

AT THIS TIME OF NIGHT, there is only one direct flight from Antigua to Boston, a red-eye that leaves at 11:45 PM island time and arrives in Massachusetts at 3:45 AM Eastern Time. This gives me a few exceptionally tedious hours to kill at the airport with my cranky Declan. No matter how hard I try engaging him in conversation, he is stonily silent. He speaks only enough words to reiterate that the fault in this whole matter rests with him. He refuses to listen to any of my entreaties that I share some of the blame, even when I reveal that perhaps I missed the reviews for The Love Nest Resort that mention they tend to attract folks with alternative lifestyles. His response is to condescendingly pat my hand and yet again apologize for ruining our honeymoon.

After a while, I get tired of talking to myself and head off to explore the few open gift shops. As I browse the array of painted pottery, straw purses, and rum cakes, a rack of tourist T-shirts catches my eye. One of the shirts gives me a bolt-of-lightening idea that is bound to shake my poor Tax Man from his self-imposed penance. I throw it on the counter along with a small gift bag and a pack of tissue paper, then hustle off to the Ladies room to put my plan into action.

The flight to Boston is more crowded than I'd expected, though I can't imagine why anyone in their right mind would select this horrible time to fly when given a choice. I'm thankful to Declan for again booking first class seats for our return flight home. I'm over-tired and appreciate the little bit of extra room as well as the added privacy. It will enable me to carry out my plan a little more easily. I wait until the plane takes off and we are in the air before I pull the gift bag from my carry-on and hand it to Mr. Silent Sam.

"What's this?" he asks, none too cordially.

"It's a little honeymoon gift," I say. "Open it."

Declan makes a sour face and sighs as dramatically as any Broadway actor. He puts the gift bag back in my lap. "Tis vera sweet of ya, Lass, but I am in no mood far trinkets. I don' deserve yar devotion. I have shamed ya, and ma House as well. How can I be expected to be Lord someday when I can so easily be hoodwinked by a dirty *cealgaire* (seducer?)"

"Please stop beating yourself up, Sweetie. You lost your temper. It happens. Even to future Lords." I hand him back the bag. "Now…open your gift."

He gives it right back to me with a scowl. When he's in a mood like this, he looks so much like his nasty Dragon Mama that it's scary. "I'm askin' ya to stop,

Rosie," he growls. " 'Tis best ta just leave me be right now."

At this point I think I've about reached my patient wife limit. I lean over and whisper quietly in his ear, "Declan…Sweetie…if you don't take this gift and open it right now, I swear I won't talk to you for longer than you could ever possibly imagine."

He looks at me, trying to determine how serious I might be. Apparently, I am believable enough, because he takes the bag from my lap and begins rummaging through the tissue, pouting the whole time. He pulls out the tiny, infant-sized T-shirt that reads, "My Parents Went to Antigua and All I Got Is This Lousy T-Shirt." So intent is he on being crabby that the inference goes whoosh…right over his head. "Tis a vera silly gift, Rosie. It's much too small far' me."

I make a face. Sometimes the Tax Man can be a real yutz. "There's more. Keep looking."

He gives another Marlon Brando performance level sigh and pulls out the other tissue wrapped item. Tearing off the paper, he stares at the pregnancy test with unblinking eyes for several seconds before turning to me. "Is this…? Are you…?"

I smile. "Yup! It's official, Tax Man. We're having a baby."

Without warning, Declan unbuckles his seatbelt and crawls over to my side, resting all of himself on my lap and kissing me like a crazed man. We are laughing and hugging and crying until the flight attendant comes over and scolds us. "I'm sorry, Sir. But the Captain still has the seatbelt light engaged. You'll have to return to your seat."

My husband shows her the pregnancy test. "Look… we're gonna have a wee *bairn!*"

The flight attendant smiles. "Congratulations, Sir. That's wonderful news. Unfortunately, you still have to sit in your own seat until the Captain has turned off the seat-belt light."

Declan does as he's asked, though he turns around in his seat and leans over the aisle engaging all the passengers around us with our happy news. Once the seatbelt light is off, my husband is up in a flash, walking the length of the plane's cabin, showing off the pregnancy test to the plane full of the passengers and shaking everyone's hands. He even hands the flight attendant his credit card and offers to buy every adult in the cabin their choice of cocktail in celebration.

As for me, I stay put in my seat, my hands circling my belly, the biggest smile decorating my face. I close my eyes and rest my head on the seat, all the while thanking the Universe…and the IRS…for giving me my beloved Tax Man and our newest little deduction.

Find out what happens to Rosie and Declan in
Baby Tooth And Tangled Roots

More from Serenade Publishing

Brigadier Station Series

By Sarah Williams:

The Brothers of Brigadier Station

The Sky over Brigadier Station

The Legacies of Brigadier Station

Christmas at Brigadier Station (An Outback Christmas Novella)

The Outback Governess (A Sweet Outback Novella)

Heart of the Hinterland Series

By Sarah Williams:

The Dairy Farmer's Daughter

Their Perfect Blend

Beyond the Barre

Primrose Series

By Tanya Renee

Prairie Sky

Prairie Nights

Prairie Fire

Prairie Hearts

The Spring of Love Series

By Virginia Taylor

Forever Delighted

Forever Amused

Forever Heartfelt

A New Page

By Aimee MacRae

It Happened in Paris

By Michelle Beesley

Mim and Wiggy's Grand Adventure

By Jay McKenzie

Winner Winner Chicken Dinner

By Sarah Jackson

For more information visit:

www.serenadepublishing.com

About the Author

Victoria Rocus is a retired educator, accomplished miniaturist, and full-time author living near the home of country music, Nashville, Tennessee, USA. When she's not writing new adventures for her imaginary friends, catering beach parties for mermaids, or finding homes for orphaned dragons, she's building and rehabbing one-of-a-kind dollhouses and accessories, just like her favorite character, Dr. Rosie Parker. Many of her multiple miniature buildings are 1/12 scale replicas of settings from her unique fantasy stories.

Victoria started her writing career as a weekly blogger while still teaching middle school language arts. Now retired from the educational field, she's been able to make writing a full-time adventure, penning several fantasy and romance stories she hopes readers will enjoy with both a sigh and a smile.

Find out more at: victoriarocusauthor.com

instagram.com/victoriarocusauthor
tiktok.com/@victoriarocusauthor

ACKNOWLEDGMENTS

"No man is an island and no book reaches a reader's hands by the author alone." I realize that this isn't how the quote goes, but to my mind, and in my case, it probably should. I have so many people to thank for making this dream a reality. I'll begin with Sarah Williams and the dedicated staff at Serenade Publishing, for their expertise with all the work that goes into making a manuscript draft a completed book…the talented editors, formatters and cover artists, to mention a few.

I am forever grateful to my regular Beta team; Carol Peden Fuller, Donna Gentile-Ruth, Michele S. Kaspar, Daniel Caddigan, and Kaia Vinney, along with fellow authors, Arla Jones and K.C. Nord. You guys never let me down. Hug, hug. Kiss, kiss. A special shout out to Marcia J. Wurmbrand Crabtree and Shannon Green for your unwavering support throughout this crazy ride. My heart is full.

To my family; my husband Victor, and our sons, Steven and Michael, as well as our lovely daughter-in-law, Allison. Thanks for keeping me off the ledge while still keeping the dream alive. A special nod for coming to those signing events and your willingness to act the fool for the sake of my marketing plans. The "tooth" looks good on ya' all.

Finally, I need to thank my loyal readers who continued to follow my beloved Rosie and Declan into book two of the series. These characters mean the world to me, and to know that you are loving them too warms my heart. Hugs to all of you. I hope you keep hangin' on for the ride. There's more to come…